Praise for John Blumenthal

"Frequently hilarious and unexpectedly touching . . . Blumenthal creates smart, funny characters."—*Publishers Weekly*

"Blumenthal has a jaundiced eye and a wonderfully ironic style." —*L.A. Daily News*

"Blumenthal's hilariously descriptive language is a delight. Wonderful."—*The Washington Review*

"Recommended reading."—*Book Magazine*

also by John Blumenthal

What's Wrong with Dorfman? A Novel

*Hollywood High: The History of America's
Most Famous Public School*

The Official Hollywood Handbook

Love's Reckless Rash (coauthor)

The Case of the Hardboiled Dicks

The Tinseltown Murders

john blumenthal

Millard Fillmore,
mon amour

St. Martin's Griffin ⚑ New York

www.stmartins.com

Library of Congress Cataloging-in-Publication Data

Blumenthal, John.
   Millard Fillmore, mon amour : a novel / by John Blumenthal.
     p. cm.
   ISBN 0-312-32368-9
   EAN 978-0312-32368-4
    1. Fillmore, Millard, 1800–1874—Influence—Fiction.   2. Biography
as a literary form—Fiction.   3. Psychotherapist and patient—Fiction.
4. Parent and adult child—Fiction.   5. Mothers and sons—Fiction.
6. Divorced men—Fiction.   7. Biographers—Fiction.   8. Neurotics—
Fiction.   I. Title.
   PS3552.L8485M55   2004
   813'.54—dc22   2004009858

First Edition: September 2004

10 9 8 7 6 5 4 3 2 1

for Bernadette, with gratitude

Boy meets girl. So what?

—BERTOLT BRECHT

Part
one

Chapter 1: Call me a curmudgeon, but

if you ask my opinion, the whole concept of romantic love is unmitigated hogwash. Having given the subject more than a few years of sober contemplation and a modicum of empirical study in the field, I have come to the coldly logical conclusion that romantic love is nothing more than a monstrous flimflam perpetrated on the gullible masses by a cabal of soulless profiteers. It's a fairy tale, you see, the concoction of misty-eyed poets, mawkish songwriters, drippy romance novelists, and those despicable entrepreneurs who earn their livelihoods in the jewelry, floral and greeting card trades.

Love makes the world go round? Oh really? Not according to Galileo. All you need is love? Ha! Try a summer in Death Valley with no food, no shelter and no water, and let's see how long you and your lover survive on love alone. Love conquers all? No, sorry, well-equipped armies with smart bombs and night-vision goggles do that.

What utter horse manure!

Today's insidious purveyors of romantic love would also have us believe that *l'amour* is noble in its pure selflessness. Oh please. Call me a cynic, but as far as I'm concerned, romantic love is really nothing more than modern man's unimaginative method of disguising an absurdly obvious ulterior motive, one that is simply caused by chemical reactions in the brain involving serotonin, dopamine and a host of other irrepressible neurotransmitters.

Frankly, the way I see it, the human race has simply romanticized a basic physiological process into something lofty and exalted. Why? Who knows? Perhaps because we humans are a little embarrassed about the odd, bestial contortions that these nasty hormones and their chemical cohorts compel us to perform. All that huffing and puffing, all that uncivilized grunting and moaning, all that orgasm faking, all those bodily fluids flying hither and thither. I suppose the urge for ordinary sexual congress was simply too undignified for the superior human species, so some arrogant but resourceful Neanderthal with a flower garden invented the concept of romantic love and it became, through the ages, a very profitable venture, particularly when one considers the price of a dozen roses and a small box of Godiva chocolates.

Then there's the equally inane concept of the existence of "one true love" for every personage on earth, another poetic pipe dream. Some years ago, in a moment of uncharacteristic sentimentality, my father told me that I would recognize my one true love the very moment I laid eyes upon her. I was a mere boy of seventeen at the time, and had not yet developed my current skepticism about the very existence of romantic love.

"But how will I know?" I asked him.

"You'll just know," he said. "Trust me. I'm your father."

"So Mom was your one true love?"

We both glanced over at my mother, who was, at that particular moment, slouched on a plastic-covered sofa, perusing the latest issue of *Gastrointestinal Digest*, the only magazine to which she subscribed. They had been married, at that time, for about twenty years. In those days, my mother drew her eyebrows on with a special brown pencil and they were seldom symmetrical, making her look—at least to my young eyes—a bit like someone from the cast of *Pagliacci*. I love my mother dearly, but it was impossible for me to imagine this supposed epiphany of rapture that had once occurred between them.

My father just shrugged, got up and went to bed.

One true love! Ha! Another pile of horse manure!

But don't take my word for it. Consider, if you will, *Canis familiaris*, a species I have observed in depth, owing to the fact that I happen to own a dachshund. Do dogs have one true love? I strongly doubt it. Do they even feel romantic love (as the poets would define it) for one another beyond the occasional investigative posterior sniffing and a few moments of introductory frolic? Do they send each other Hallmark cards on Valentine's Day? Do they eat dinner by candlelight? Do they share similar values and beliefs? Of course not. Yet it is widely believed that the trusty canine, while unable to demonstrate any semblance of pure romantic love for his own species, somehow manages to feel some considerable degree of affection for his master. How is that possible? I doubt they even find us humans attractive, what with our obnoxious tendency to repeat the word "sit" every time we see them, and our total lack of interest in chasing squirrels or retrieving recently deceased ducks. Obviously, the possibility of interspecies romance between dogs and humans is happily remote, leaving only some form of pure, platonic love on the part of the canine. What nonsense! We might just as well say our furniture loves us. In some ways, I'm closer to my Sealy Posturepedic mattress than I am to Isabella, my beloved dachshund, a perfectly lovely mobile sausage of a dog. She occasionally urinates on my Berber carpet; my Posturepedic doesn't. She requires daily maintenance; it requires nothing but an annual rotation. Like humans, canines have their own ulterior motives for displaying affection. The fact is, dogs have learned over time that by exhibiting certain blatantly obsequious behaviors, which the average dog-owning dunderhead stupidly misinterprets as love, they can obtain the one thing they want the most out of life. Not love. *Food.* Canines, to put it simply, have mutated themselves into con artists in search of an easy handout. How else does a wild-eyed mongrel genetically related to wolves evolve into a domestic Milquetoast of a creature that will sit and roll over on command? Kibble might be boring but it's better than prowling the jungle for carrion. The next time your dog turns those big lovable brown eyes on you, ask yourself this: Does the slobbering mutt really, truly love me, or does he just want a hunk of that medium-rare T-bone I'm gnawing on?

No pun intended, but does the name Pavlov ring a bell?

As for Homo sapiens, the bogus concept of love appears to manifest itself in several distinct phases:

First and foremost, there is initial sexual attraction, which, as I mentioned earlier, is largely the effect of visual and olfactory stimuli resulting in a simple chemical response in the human body.

Then comes infatuation, which is really nothing more than the novelty of being with someone new, also involving a rise in hormonal activity. I've been infatuated with new refrigerators, especially the ones that make their own crushed ice, yet I have never "fallen in love" with any of them (although there was a pea green Whirlpool that I once actually embraced in a brief moment of insanity at college).

Next, after sowing some wild oats as nature mandated to proliferate the species, we grow accustomed to the comforts of being in the presence of one person with similar tastes and values, not to mention the guarantee of regular sex, so we give in to laziness and marry that person. Or we marry for money or status or any number of selfish reasons. Then perhaps we do our duty to mankind and produce progeny. Perhaps the chemicals betray us and we fall out of love and divorce each other. Or we stay together for the sake of the children or because we fear loneliness or simply to avoid the utter financial disembowelment of the divorce court.

And ultimately, nobody I know wants to die alone in some

ghastly nursing home surrounded by indifferent strangers in white coats arguing over the meaning of the words "do not resuscitate." Perish the thought, no pun intended.

But is that love? Ha! Sorry. Doesn't exist. Never did, never will.

Chapter 2: Once a year—usually in early

autumn, when the specter of death and decay hangs palpably in the air and the weather is either too cold or too hot, too arid or too humid, and you don't know whether to wear a wool overcoat or just a thin sweater, not to mention the inevitable controversy over galoshes, should a sudden, unexpected rain shower or monsoon erupt—once a year, my psychiatrist, Dr. Alphonso K. Wang, throws an informal barbecue for all of his patients at the local picnic grounds in Van Nuys, California. He is the only psychiatrist I have ever employed who does this. Why he does it nobody really knows for sure since the very idea of social intercourse frightens half of his patients to near distraction, but Dr. Wang is a jovial, gregarious, well-meaning shrink, a third-generation American of Chinese-Italian lineage, with a taste for colorful ties, gourmet cooking and vintage convertibles, and I think he honestly believes that consuming artery-clogging, colon-cancer-causing charred hamburgers off flimsy, toxic plastic plates and sitting on unidentified flora that may or may not actually be poison ivy, cactus or something worse, while shooing away ants, spiders, ticks and mosquitoes, is a genuine form of human pleasure. Or perhaps he just feels that some of us will derive sustenance from observing others who are even more mentally disturbed than we are, although this end can be just as easily achieved simply by watching the evening news on television every night or by reading the daily newspapers. Or perhaps he just likes to party.

(Of course, in keeping with federal privacy laws and the strictures of doctor/patient confidentiality, all patients attending the barbecue are instructed by Dr. Wang to identify themselves using only their first name and no more than the first initial of their last. Naturally, attendance is purely voluntary.)

It's quite a bizarre menagerie, though. Most of the patients who suffer from paranoia rarely show up because they think Wang has some sinister ulterior motive or that he only invited them because he invited everybody else first and felt obligated to invite them, but secretly wants to dismember them and hide their remains in the park under some leaves and twigs. The majority of the obsessive-compulsives can never seem to decide what to wear, or they lose count of the numerals on all the license plates they pass on the way to the park and have to start over. The patients with multiple personality disorder can come to the park and stay home at the same time. The group therapy members, advised by Wang always to express their true inner feelings to one another, cannot stop arguing among themselves from the moment they arrive. And the one agoraphobe, Milton P.—for whom Dr. Wang actually makes house calls, having no other choice—never shows up even though the good doctor has tried everything from bribery to blindfolds to hypnosis to pry him from his dark, gloomy home, all to no avail. One year Milton almost made it, but it took him all of two hours to muster sufficient courage to get from his apartment threshold to the top of the stairwell—a distance of about ten feet—and according to my calculations, at that rate he would have arrived at the park by early spring, which, come to think of it, would actually have been a much better season in which to have a picnic, what with the weather being more agreeable and the specter of death and decay not hanging quite so palpably in the air.

But most of Dr. Wang's patients are, like me, basically normal but a trifle neurotic or somewhat disturbed or ostensibly normal by way of heavy doses of medication. Some simply have temporary marital or family problems that require professional arbitration. Some suffer from too much or too little self-esteem. Some are children who despise their parents for any number of reasons. As Hollywood is just over the hill, Wang also has his share of paranoid failed screenwriters, paranoid successful screenwriters, over-the-hill ingenues wracked with guilt, child stars wracked with guilt, depressed plumbers who once dreamt of being the next Fellini, and depressed directors who once dreamt of being the next Fellini, to cite just a few.

As for me, I'm just your basic, garden-variety neurotic, a bundle of various minor obsessions and insecurities, none of them, thankfully, too disabling. I am fully ambulatory, I leave my place of residence on a regular basis, my socks usually match, I work in a trade that does not involve putting square pegs in round holes all day, I am not too highly medicated, beyond the occasional Xanax, and I don't much care if I step on a crack in the sidewalk, regardless of the distress it might cause my mother's vertebrae. Why do I have these eccentricities? Who knows? Some, no doubt, came directly from my parents. Others I may have inherited from a long-dead ancestor, a caveman perhaps, who liked to keep his rocks in nice, neat rows and was irrationally terrified of mastodons.

However, among certain other petty problems, I suffer from a slight obsession with death, a distinct tendency toward verbosity (as you may have already noted) and a soupçon of compulsive cleanliness, not to mention a tendency toward obsessive punctuality. My most serious problem, however, is nervous anxiety, particularly when encountering attractive members of the opposite sex, and my agitation tends to manifest itself through an annoying habit of spouting spoonerisms and reciting words and proper names backward. I had been making some real progress with the anxiety problem, some genuine positive strides, all of which were summarily dashed when my first marriage came crashing down around me. Dr. Wang believes much of this nervous anxiety may have originated from my mother, who, for obscure reasons, began a career as an agoraphobe when my father retired from the pharmaceutical business five years ago, although over the preceding years, she had been making a steady progression from homebody to recluse. But Wang also concedes that it is partially the fault of my father, for it was he and he alone who straddled me with the name Plato. My mother wanted to name me after my great-grandfather Adolph—a moniker that carries with it its own obvious set of unique problems—but after a coin toss my father prevailed. As it happened, my father was a big fan of the ancient Greeks and I suppose I should be grateful that my given name isn't Herodotus or Aristophanes or Sophocles. Plato is bad enough, believe me. Plato G. Fussell, to be exact. What a name! What a curse! What a punch line!

How so? you ask. Let me take you back to my first day of kindergarten. My family had just moved from Manhattan to Van Nuys, California, in late August 1972 and as a result I had not had enough time to make friends in my age group prior to the beginning of the school year, not that time would have really made much difference. So while the other children formed gaggles in the playground on that first day of school in September, I stood alone feigning preoccupation with a broken sandbox toy. Then a bell rang and we were instructed to line up single file. As soon as we were all gathered in the classroom, the teacher, Mrs. Slowicki—a nervous, fluttering wisp of a woman in harlequin glasses and black orthopedic shoes—asked all of us to sit in a semicircle on the floor and identify ourselves starting with the kid on the far right. The very idea caused my hands to tremble and my young heart to palpitate, for I knew how this would go. The other kids were all delighted to give voice to their names. Of course they were! They had normal, everyday names like Bobby and Timmy and Sally and Megan. There were Richies and Nancys and Buzzys and Billys and Lucys. This being the great melting pot of America, there was even a Rajiv, a Pedro and a Laslo.

And then it was my turn. All eyes turned to me, including those of a heartbreakingly cute blonde in pigtails sitting two feet away, who had just identified herself as Daisy Crane. She actually smiled at me, but I was too nervous, too preoccupied to smile back so instead I just turned crimson. I cleared my throat. I shut my eyes. I looked at the letters of the alphabet taped over the blackboard. I glanced at the drab black-and-white portrait of an unsmiling Richard Nixon hanging by the door. I remember to this day how my face burned as I heard the clock hands tick. My stomach grumbled. I cleared my throat again. And again.

"Speak up, young man," Mrs. Slowicki coaxed playfully. "We won't bite you, will we, children?"

"No, Mrs. Slowicki," the rest of the class droned.

"There you have it," she said. "Now please tell us all your name."

"Fussell," I said.

Mrs. Slowicki looked at her attendance card until she found my name. "Your *first name* isn't Fussell, now is it?"

"No."

"Well, you can't expect us to call you Fussell, can you?" she asked as a few of the kids tittered.

"Why not?"

"Because, as I said, Fussell is not your first name."

"So?"

"Don't be contrary with me, young man," she said, a distinct touch of ire in her voice. "Just tell us all what your first name is and let's be done with it. This instant."

Great, I thought. Two minutes into kindergarten and I've already alienated the teacher. Suddenly I was covered in sweat, but I managed to mumble something deliberately unintelligible.

"Speak up, Mr. Fussell. We can't hear you, can we, class?"

"No, Mrs. Slowicki," they chimed.

I contemplated making a dash for the door, but I would have had to leap over several kids to make it and even if I managed to get through the door without inadvertently kicking somebody in the face, then what? The bathroom? I couldn't stay in the bathroom for the entire school year. I could have run out the school's front door, gotten to the highway and hitchhiked to New York City or Chicago. Or I could—

But now, growing impatient, Mrs. Slowicki cleared her throat and tapped her shoe. Finally, having no choice, I winced, closed my eyes and let the horrid word escape.

"Plato."

"I don't think any of us heard that, Mr. Fussell. Would you be so kind as to repeat—"

"PLATO!" I screamed. "MY NAME IS PLATO!"

It hung in the air for a second or two. The predictable moment of uncomprehending silence was quickly followed by a few tentative giggles, then the predictable outbreak of raucous, derisive laughter. The kids—Pedro, Rajiv, Laslo and all the others—were in hysterics.

"His name is . . . Play-Doh!" one of them screamed. "Hey, Play-Doh!"

"I bet his sister's name is Silly Putty!" shrieked another.

"And his father's Mr. Potato Head!"

More laughter. Even Laslo and Rajiv had tears of merriment in their eyes as they pointed at me, their whole bodies shaking with laughter. I was crushed, forlorn, desolate. I could not even bring myself to look at the delectable Daisy Crane, but assumed she too was in hysterics. Why, I thought, couldn't my father have been a great fan of baseball players or football heroes, like other American fathers? Then my name would be Yogi or Bronco or Hank. Who cared about the damn Greeks? Mortified, I looked to Mrs. Slowicki for help but she had a hand poised over her mouth. Hiding what? A smile? A laugh? Certainly not a belch. I was horrified. Even the teacher was laughing at me! This whole episode, I imagined, would probably make for a rip-roaring anecdote in the teachers' lounge after school. Or worse, in the cafeteria during lunch break. By recess everybody in the school would know my peculiar first name. My first day of school and already I was an outcast, a pariah, a misfit, a laughingstock.

To this day, I can still see myself surrounded by an ocean of hysterical five-year-olds—all of them convulsed with laughter—and wanting nothing more than to melt away into the cracks in the floor.

Chapter 3: "Here's what I want you to

do," Dr. Wang began, just prior to his latest annual patient outing at the park. He was sitting, as always, behind his desk while I occupied a Barcelona chair in front of him.

"Should I take notes?" I asked.

"No."

"Okay," I said. "What do you want me to do?"

"At the next picnic, I want you to force yourself to make contact with a member of the opposite sex."

"Define 'contact,'" I said.

"Initiate a conversation."

"About what?"

"Anything at all. The weather, current affairs, Chaucer."

"I don't know anything about Recuahc."

"Are you feeling nervous now?" Wang asked.

"Why?"

"Because you're doing the wordplay compulsion again."

"In point of fact, I am a little anxious," I admitted. "The prospect of approaching a namow by quoting Recuahc . . ."

"Fine. Not Chaucer then. Another subject."

"Death?"

"I think something a little more upbeat might be better."

"Death is a fascinating, multilayered subject."

"Perhaps," Dr. Wang said. "But not if you're trying to make a good first impression on a strange woman."

"A strange woman? Why would I want to initiate a conversation with a woman who is strange? I have enough problems."

"I meant a woman you don't know. A stranger."

"Is it wise to speak to strangers?"

"In this type of situation, I would say yes, unless you wish to meet women you already know."

"I really don't know any women," I confessed.

"That's the WHOLE POINT, Fussell!" he said. "Now may we please get back to the subject at hand?"

"Which was?"

"A topic for your opening gambit," Wang replied a trifle wearily. "Something pleasant and casual, something that might get a good response?"

"Death is where all other subjects inevitably end up, you know," I said. "It's very mysterious, death."

"Be that as it may . . ."

"It's an experience we all share," I added.

"So is taking a dump, but most people don't find the subject that appetizing."

"Oh? You haven't met my mother."

Dr. Wang forced a smile, then sighed. He was getting annoyed, I could tell. We'd been down this path many times before. Even when I did come up with a useful subject of conversation with which to approach a female, my anxiety prevented me from delivering it properly when the time came. The disaster of my marriage had killed off all remnants of my tenuous ability at social interaction with attractive members of the opposite sex. Nevertheless, Wang was determined to cure me of my anxiety. He considered me a challenge. So far, he had failed miserably.

"Be that as it may," he said patiently, "I would strongly advise another topic as an opener."

"Wind velocities? Forgotten American Presidents? Disease? Plagues? Pestilences? Something along those lines, perhaps?"

"Wind velocities?"

"It's a fascinating subject."

"Given the choice," Wang said, "I'd take it over plagues and pestilences."

"Yes?"

"But only if you can keep it upbeat and cheerful."

"And not too windy," I jested. "Lest I be compared to a windbag, puns not intended."

"Your puns are always intended," Wang observed.

I confess this stumped me. What can you say about wind velocities that is cheerful and upbeat? Nobody I know much likes hurricanes and tornadoes, which, unfortunately, are the only areas on the subject of wind velocity that are at all interesting. And you'd be hard-pressed to find anything remotely upbeat and cheerful about the bubonic plague, although the symptoms of typhoid fever can be quite captivating when explained in graphic detail. And I knew from experience that Wang was strongly against the subject of Forgotten American Presidents, fearing that it would inevitably degenerate into an endless lecture on the moral fiber of my favorite Forgotten American President, Millard Fillmore.

I glanced at the alarm clock on the side table and saw that I had twenty minutes left in the session. Beside the timepiece was a little embroidered sign that read, *Don't worry. Even the Earth is bipolar.* Wang was tapping a pencil on his desk, waiting for me to make a decision. Decisiveness, unfortunately, was not one of my strong suits either. I had never been able to make the decision to be decisive.

"Perhaps I'll brush up on my Chaucer," I said forlornly, although I was unable to imagine how an opening line involving Chaucer would help me woo anyone.

Nevertheless, being an obsessive, I stewed obsessively over this opening line business for the next four days. Even if I managed to create the perfect introductory flourish—which was doubtful—would I be able to curb my incapacitating anxiety long enough to deliver it? That was the real question. Would I stutter? Would I blush? Would nervousness cause my knees to weaken? Would I faint? Fall over like a dead tree? Break out in hives and scratch like a chimpanzee? Would I back down sheepishly in embarrassment—run off into the trees, hide behind a bush, throw a jacket over my face?

None of the above. Most likely, I would simply be overcome with the usual bout of uncontrollable anxiety, and deliver a speech composed of pure mumbo jumbo.

Of course, it was not solely my peculiar first name that had made me a shy, anxiety-ridden, compulsive, death-obsessed, neurotic bundle of insecurities, though it got me off to an excellent start. Growing up as an only child in a household as neurotic as mine probably didn't help much either. My outward appearance as a young lad probably had a profound effect as well, although Dr. Wang always cautioned me not to attribute specific causes to any particular neurosis, and is much in favor of the genetic explanation. Nonetheless, for much of my youth, I was a short, gangly, pigeon-toed kid with crooked teeth, severe myopia and a pair of thick eyebrows that met at the bridge of my nose and resembled two mating caterpillars whenever I became agitated. By my teenage years, I wore black-framed glasses and a wire mesh fence of orthodontic braces in which certain foods like spinach and lettuce would invariably get caught, making me look like a toothless medieval ghoul directly after meals. I was not athletic, nor particularly personable. I was, in fact, clumsy at sports, awkward at social functions and an occasional stutterer. And to make matters even more difficult, I generally sported absurd, ill-fitting clothes because in those days, my mother (who had not yet become an agoraphobe) would drive to the clothing factory outlets by herself and purchase my entire wardrobe for me at a wholesale department store called Fineman's Off-the-Rack, where everything was eternally on sale. Unfortunately, my parents, having lived through the Great Depression, were incredible misers, so in order to save even more money my mother bought everything two or three sizes too big. "Don't worry, Plato, you'll grow into them," she used to say. Yes, but in the meantime, I was forced to wear corduroy pants that fastened just under my chin. I was sporting wool sweaters that could comfortably house an evangelical revival meeting. I was going to school in shoes that looked like they were originally owned by a circus clown. Even my underwear was too big and I was constantly reaching furtively into my trousers to pull up my boxer shorts. By the time I actually grew into them, most of these clothes were too worn out to wear, so my mother trotted back to Fineman's to buy me yet another ill-fitting wardrobe.

As a result of all these tragic factors, I was immediately bestowed with the honorary nickname "Superdork" by the cool kids (of which Daisy Crane was a charter member), and my teenage love life gave new meaning to the word "wallflower"—I was a wall *sequoia*. I had deep roots. The wall was all mine.

"You're doing a great job holding up the building there, Play-Doh," the kids used to cackle at school dances. "Keep up the good work."

Not that I attended too many school social functions, other than the one or two for which attendance was mandatory, or the ones my mother ordered me to go to in order to improve my non-existent social skills. She would dress me up in my oversize clothing—usually gray wool pants that ballooned around my legs and a blue blazer whose cuffs were five inches longer than my arms—pat me on the head and send me on my way to an evening of utter humiliation, in which I would stand alone in the darkest corner, feigning interest in a potted plant.

(Unfortunately, my father was rarely home in those days as his profession kept him on the road for long periods of time, but even if I had appealed to him regarding the clothing dilemma, I strongly doubt he would have contradicted my mother on the subject, for he remembered the Depression even more vividly than she. The fact is my mother bought most of *his* clothes at Fineman's Off-the-Rack as well, but since he was no longer growing, his attire generally fit.)

Although my grades were always excellent and I managed to win a few science fairs, high school was pure torture for me. I had no male friends—except for a few of the other superdorks—and girls generally giggled when I walked by or ignored me completely. The only one who did not giggle at me was the lovely but unapproachable Daisy Crane, who had come in second in one of the science fairs and also maintained a straight-A average. (Her father, a local minister, was apparently strict about grades, or so I had heard through the grapevine.) I liked to think that Daisy respected me in some offbeat way, but this was probably just pure self-delusion. In truth, she existed on such a lofty social plane that in order to giggle at someone as pathetic as I, she would have had to descend to my lowly level. I doubt she had a clue that I even existed.

But she did actually speak to me once. It was in American history class, toward the end of the period, March 6, freshman year. It took me completely by surprise when she turned around at her desk and asked to borrow an eraser. I was so addled by this sudden attention, the only sound that emanated from my mouth was a stream of inane gibberish. Before she could ask for clarification, the bell rang and I leapt out of my seat and escaped into the anonymity of the crowded hallway.

By the close of my senior year, however, things had begun to gradually improve in regards to my appearance. The braces had been removed during my junior year, yielding a perfect set of sparkling white teeth. That summer, I underwent what my mother termed a "sudden growth spurt" and added six inches to my height. This caused me to eat more and I gained enough weight to put some fat on my skinny, formless frame. As my face filled out, my eyebrows began to separate at the center, and I began to develop a prominent chin. When I turned seventeen, I changed my hairstyle from the long-lasting crew cut my mother favored to a more stylish length. By the time I started college in 1985, I was taller than both my parents and had the beginnings of a manly five o'clock shadow. My voice had become a sonorous baritone. I was never athletic—I can't abide the odor of sweating and there's always the chance of getting a heart attack from overexertion, not to mention broken bones, head injuries and torn muscles—but somehow, my body turned into a semimuscular unit that surprised even me, no doubt the result of four years of physical education at high school. At eighteen, in spite of my mother's protests, I started purchasing my own garments at the local mall, so suddenly my clothes actually fit properly. In other words, by my freshman year in college I was—and I say this with all modesty—quite a handsome young fellow. I even dated sporadically in college, desperately attempting to overcome what was then only a slight tendency toward timidity, but none of my dates was able to appreciate or overlook my eccentricities, or live up to my neurotically stringent standards of personal hygiene. I was considered an oddball and, as the word spread over the small campus, the old, familiar giggles started up again. I may have been attractive, but underneath the facade, I was still Plato G. Fussell, Superdork.

Later, after college, I stopped using my first name and went by my middle name, George, although most people just called me Fussell. Yet psychologically, in spite of my good looks and my considerable erudition, I remained an insecure, gangly kid inside and probably always would. Then, following the dissolution of my first marriage, which had stung me to the very core of my being, I'd become something of a social hermit as well. By that time, 1995, I had already been a patient of Dr. Wang's for several years and the good doctor was worried that I'd end up like Milton P. The last thing he needed was another agoraphobe on his patient roster. He was not that wild about making house calls.

Chapter 4: As is my habit, I arrived precisely on time at Dr. Wang's picnic, only to find that I was not the first one there. The good doctor was already on the premises himself, cheerfully unloading food and drink from the trunk and passenger seat of his sleek yellow Porsche with the assistance of two or three of his patients. Several of the obsessive-compulsives—some of whom were busy counting leaves, knocking on wood or licking park benches—came early, of course, as did two of the paranoids who feared severe repercussions if they were late. Predictably, Milton P. was not in attendance. I muttered a few cursory greetings to the group at large, most of whom ignored me. After trading a few moments of small talk with Dr. Wang, I grabbed a paper plate and a few plastic utensils, took some victuals and searched for a place to sit that would not involve placing my hindquarters on anything that might be a hiding place for insects, ticks, spiders, snakes or sharp rusty nails, although I had recently had a tetanus shot.

Not wanting to be identified as one of Dr. Wang's lunatic brood, I took my plate of charred food and my Styrofoam cup of thin, watery iced tea and deposited them and myself at a wooden picnic table several hundred yards away from Wang and the others, just behind a gigantic oak tree. After creating a barrier between the wooden picnic bench and my posterior with my raincoat, I watched a squirrel pry loose the crown of an acorn. Then I took in the sight of a hummingbird fluttering noisily above a nearby rosebush. I saw a ladybug climb a blade of grass. This was enough to amuse me for a few moments, though I am generally wary of nature, particularly in the wild. I usually prefer zoos or animal shows on public television to the real thing, as there is less chance of contracting rabies, avian flu, malaria or some other horrible animal-bred disease.

Having decided beforehand that I was much too bashful and anxiety-ridden to attempt a conversational gambit or in any way endeavor to make the acquaintance of a strange woman as proposed by Dr. Wang, I brought along some typed notes for the latest chapter of a book I was in the midst of writing—the definitive biography of our thirteenth president, Millard Fillmore. I had been a passionate Fillmore aficionado for many years and was, at this time, arguably the world's leading authority on this great but largely forgotten and grossly misunderstood statesman. I had been working tirelessly on the book for nine years, ever since I had made and invested my financial fortune and thus had no reason to continue toiling in my former field ever again or in any other tiresome field, for that matter. The Fillmore biography was a labor of love, if you will, and I was almost half finished with volume one (*The Early, Early Years*) of a proposed ten-volume set, although I had in my possession copious notes, as well as photocopies of letters and documents pertaining to Fillmore's entire life span.

I was in the midst of correcting a few minor typographical errors, mostly involving semicolons, which I have a habit of overusing, when suddenly I was struck on the side of the head, just a few centimeters above the right ear, by what appeared to be a small unidentified flying object. An ordinary plastic Frisbee in a light shade of purple, as it turned out.

At first, I assumed the thrower of this errant missile was a child and I was fully prepared to verbally wring the perpetrator's neck, as I am not particularly fond of small children. But the culprit turned out to be a somewhat plain woman of about thirty, although this was only a guess on my part, as her face was partially hidden behind wide sunglasses and a Dodgers cap. She materialized in front of me seconds later, slightly out of breath, accompanied by a brown drooling hound of dubious lineage, also somewhat out of breath.

"Good grief!" I said. "You could have decapitated me!"

"With a plastic Frisbee? Are you drunk?"

"I most certainly am not," I said.

But she was looking suspiciously at the contents of my plastic cup. "What's that then? Looks like scotch or bourbon to me."

"How many people in the civilized world drink scotch or bourbon with a straw and a slice of lemon?" I asked her.

"How should I know?"

"For your information, it happens to be iced tea, although the ice appears to have melted. And what difference does it make if *I* am drunk, which I'm not! *You* threw the Frisbee."

"Yes, well, you certainly have an excellent point there," she conceded, softening. "Are you all right? Are you in any pain?"

"No, I am not all right, in point of fact. I seem to have something of a dent."

"A dent?"

"See for yourself."

I directed her attention to the point of my skull that had received the brunt of the Frisbee's impact. But before bending to examine it, she removed her baseball cap and sunglasses, only to reveal that my original assessment of her as plain was woefully inaccurate. She had jet black hair that fell to her shoulders with high bangs cut straight across her forehead. Her complexion was pale. Her eyes, which had been hidden by the shades, were a deep brown, her cheekbones were high and almost Nordic. She was, in a word, stunning, and I suddenly felt the usual wave of anxiety sweep through my body.

"It's a dent, all right," she said, bending to look at it and probing it gently with her index finger. "But how do I know it wasn't there before?"

"I'm not a mar, cadam," I said nervously.

"What?"

"I said, 'I'm not a car, madam.'"

"I can see that," she said. "And I'm not a madam either. For your information, I happen to be a mademoiselle."

"A pousand thardons, mademoiselle," I said glibly.

"Excuse me?"

"A thousand pardons," I repeated. It was then that I began to feel some moisture on my left foot.

"My God!" I shrieked. "Your mongrel is drooling right on my new argyle socks!"

"Nobody wears argyle socks. Not in this century."

"Yes, well, I do," I said, as the dogged mutt (no pun intended) continued to release saliva. "I happen to prefer patterned socks to the single-color variety."

"Fascinating."

"Yes, well, will you kindly shoo this oversalivating lamina away!"

"This what?"

"This animal!" I said. "Remove him!"

"Back off, Ferdinand!" she said sharply. Obediently, the mongrel moved away and drooled on the lawn several feet to the left of my shoe, from which I was wiping away its saliva with a paper napkin. Once I had finished, I put the napkin aside and commenced to sterilize my fingers with several alcohol wipes, which I always carry on my person for such emergencies. There's no telling what sinister bacteria are housed in the saliva of a canine. After all, their tongues can reach practically every orifice of their bodies.

"He's not a mongrel," she said. "You'll hurt his feelings."

He was clearly a mongrel, but I did not choose to belabor the point, lest it upset her unnecessarily.

"This is quite a coincidence," I declared, marveling at my ability to verbalize an entire sentence without resorting to gibberish.

"Oh?" she said. "And why is that?"

"My dachshund is named Allebasi." *Curses*, I was doing it again.

"And that's a coincidence because . . . ?"

"I meant to say Isabella," I explained. "My dog's name is Isabella."

She wrinkled her delightful brow for a second, then caught the drift.

"Ferdinand and Isabella," she recited. "Fifteenth-century Spanish monarchs. Hosted the Spanish Inquisition. Gave Columbus the money for his trip. Are you a fan?"

"Of Columbus, Ferdinand, Isabella or the Spanish Inquisition?" I asked. (There, I'd done it again, a complete sentence!)

"Isabella."

"Not really. My aunt's name was Isabella."

"You named a dachshund after your aunt?"

"No, I just like the name."

"I see," she remarked, though her look betrayed some confusion.

An awkward moment passed. Most of my connections with attractive women involve a majority of long, awkward moments, interspersed with short, inane conversational moments. Nonetheless, I was amazed at how well things seemed to be going between us. I was actually having a dialogue with an attractive female of the species! How odd. But the conversation had stopped. To fill the silence, I feigned a short coughing fit. But the silence prevailed. I felt myself beginning to panic. Could I get up and run away? Hide behind a tree? No, I had to see this through to the end. Desperate to continue the conversation, I harkened back to what had originally brought us together.

"Um . . ." I stammered.

"Yes?"

"What if there are subsequent complications?" I ventured, gently caressing the dented area of my skull, which was sore and actually beginning to swell slightly. "A concussion? Headaches? Migraines? Eventually a train bumor? Or possibly even an aneurysm?"

"Your health insurance should cover most of it," she said. "You do have health insurance, I hope?"

"Of course," I said. "But I have a very high deductible."

"Really? So do I."

"It's the only way to go."

"I couldn't agree more."

"A considerable savings, but you're covered for catastrophic illness."

"Precisely."

"Which is unlikely to happen to people in our age group anyway."

"Exactly!"

"So why pay an elderly person's premiums?"

"I couldn't agree more."

I was delighted that we seemed to have so much in common, so delighted that I actually felt my heart stop palpitating and my hands cease trembling. I removed my sunglasses and looked at her face in the light of day. She was really quite striking and I felt the first stirrings of infatuation, which was probably nothing more than a mild burst of epinephrine in one of my cranial lobes. It then occurred to me—a bit late, I admit—that perhaps there had been some hidden meaning behind her insistence that she was not a madam, but a mademoiselle. After all, I am not a bad-looking fellow.

But there was no obvious flirtation from her end. "May I borrow this?" she asked, indicating my pencil.

"Only if you don't plan to use it as a weapon," said I, quite mirthfully, I thought, an attempt at lightening the tension. Unfortunately, it received no response other than a slightly condescending smirk. Nonetheless, I was somewhat amazed at how easy it was for me to engage in actual fluent conversation with this woman. Usually, I am utterly hopeless.

She grabbed the pencil and tore off a piece of blank notepaper from my pad and I watched her as she began to scrawl something. As she bent down, I got a noseful of the most divine lavender-scented perfume. I also noticed that she was wearing galoshes.

"Um . . ." I stammered again.

"Yes?"

"Expecting rain?" I asked, indicating her feet.

"Better safe than sorry," she said.

"I couldn't agree more."

"You can't really trust the weather forecast."

"That's for sure!" I said. "They never seem to get it right."

"It's amazing meteorologists actually get paid!"

"Yes, it is!" I was hoping to continue this stimulating discourse regarding the galoshes and the chance of inclement weather, when she handed me back my pencil.

"Here's my name and cell phone number," she said, giving me the paper. "If you have any medical expenses, I'll be glad to reimburse you. Within reason, of course."

"Most generous of you," I noted. "I appreciate your thoughtfulness."

"It's the least I can do," she said, looking up into my eyes, which are light blue, similar in hue to those of the Weimaraner canine breed.

I glanced at the piece of paper.

"Ylime Ekydnroht," I said.

"What?"

"What?"

"You said my name backward," she observed.

"You know your name backward?"

"Sure. Doesn't everybody?"

"I don't know."

"Why did you say it that way?" she asked.

"Um . . ."

"Yes?"

"It's a little embarrassing, actually," I confessed.

"Not as embarrassing as hitting a total stranger in the head with a Frisbee," she replied. "Come on. I won't make fun of you. I promise."

"It's something I do when I get nervous," I said. "Word games and such."

"Do I make you nervous?"

"Frankly, yes."

"Sorry," she said. "I don't mean to."

"I know, it's not your fault," I blubbered. "It generally happens whenever I'm in the presence of . . ."

"Yes?"

". . . that is, whenever I'm around . . ."

"Around?"

I closed my eyes. "Beautiful nemow," I blurted out.

"Oh," she mused. "Thank you. I accept the compliment."

"It's a compulsion of sorts," I continued.

"I see."

"Do you find it annoying?" I asked. "Saying people's names backward?"

"Not particularly."

"Mine is Otalp."

"Your first name is Plato?"

I cringed, expecting the inevitable guffaw, but amazingly none came, not even a titter.

"I dated an Aristotle once," she reflected. "But he was Greek. You don't look Greek to me."

"I'm not. For some reason, my father liked the name."

Now she was staring at me again, so intensely that I felt compelled to avert my eyes. I nervously cleared my throat five or six times, scratched my head, itched my thigh, twiddled my thumbs. . . .

"Did anybody ever tell you you're really quite adorable?" she asked.

"My aunt Velma did once, but I think I was twelve at the time," I replied. "She had glaucoma, so I'm not sure how much of me she actually saw."

She smiled, quite radiantly, and nodded. Once again, I struggled desperately to think of something upbeat and cheerful to say, something about Chaucer, perhaps, something to make the conversation continue.

"Do you like Chaucer?" I asked.

"Not particularly."

"Nor do I."

Ah ha! Another thing we had in common!

"I really must go," she said. "I have to take a shower."

"Shake a tower?" I said.

"What?"

"Sorry. Another bad compulsive habit of mine. A spoonerism. You take the—"

"First letter or letters of each word and reverse them. I know what a spoonerism is, thank you. I went to college too."

"I'm sorry," I said. "I didn't mean to offend you."

"No offense taken."

"It's just that most people have no idea what a spoonerism is."

"I'm not most people."

I had no idea what to say to that, so like a dolt, I said nothing. I cleared my throat several hundred times again. She glanced at her watch.

"Yes, well. I must be off," she said. "Ta-ta."

Then, before I could beseech her to stay, she grabbed her Frisbee, gave me a little wave and ran off, her oafish canine trailing at her heels, dog drool flying every which way. Halfway across the park grounds, she suddenly stopped and threw the Frisbee high into the air, and much to my astonishment, Ferdinand ran, leapt up and caught it in his teeth a second before it landed. I never knew untrained mutts could jump that high. In awe, I watched until they disappeared behind a clump of maple trees. I was suddenly giddy—I had conversed successfully with a strange woman who was not only familiar with spoonerisms (a somewhat lost and forgotten art) but shared with me an interest in insurance premiums and the necessity of being prepared for inclement weather at all times.

"I met quite a fascinating young woman," I told Wang at my next therapy appointment two days later.

"Marvelous! At the picnic?"

"Sort of."

"A patient?"

"Good grief, no!"

"Do you have something against my female patients?" he asked, bristling slightly.

"I can't say," I reflected. "I've never actually spoken to one."

"Some of them are really quite fascinating," Wang said. "And well educated too."

"I'm sure they are."

"One of them is a professor of classical literature at a local university."

"Is that a fact?"

"Another is a high-level corporate executive with a Fortune 500 company."

"Really?"

"Another is a very well-known sitcom writer."

"Is that so?"

"Most are just like you, intelligent but a little neurotic, perhaps a little compulsive, nothing more. No need to be afraid of any of them."

Then he leaned forward at his desk and gave me a little wink. "So tell me, Fussell," he said. "How did you manage it?"

"Manage what?"

"Manage to meet this fascinating young woman you were telling me about before we digressed?"

"Oddly enough, I wasn't particularly shy or anxiety-ridden around her," I said. "I mean, I felt the old anxiety at the outset, but I was not utterly paralyzed by it."

"Excellent!" Wang exclaimed proudly. "Tell me, how did you approach her?"

"The Chaucer gambit worked beautifully," I lied. "It was really quite amazing."

Happily, Dr. Wang clapped his hands together. "Bravo!" he said.

Chapter 5: I suppose you might say I was smitten, assuming such a condition exists. Try as I might, I could not get the image of the lovely, charming and thoroughly enchanting Emily Thorndyke out of my head. Romantic scenarios of a wide variety and in vivid detail kept popping into my brain at the oddest of times, many of them, I confess, of an erotic nature. I knew this to be merely a hormonal secretion in my neocortex, followed by a series of impulses to and from my genitalia, nothing more, but unfortunately the knowledge that it was all just chemistry did not help to make my growing obsession with her any less compelling. Those lovely deep brown eyes, that beautiful white skin, that delicious smell of lavender, those marvelous galoshes! I was thoroughly intoxicated! At night, as I lay in bed unable to make myself go to sleep, I went over and over the events that had transpired between us on that marvelous day at the park. The evidence would suggest that she was desirous of making some sort of romantic affiliation with me. For one thing, she had obviously gone out of her way to make it clear that she was not a married woman when she corrected my "madam" faux pas. On the other hand, that might just have been an innocent, reflexive reaction on her part. I could not be certain. But she had also made a point of offering me—a perfect stranger—her name and cell phone number. Was she truly concerned that subsequent complications of my cranial injury might incur substantial medical charges or did she want me to call her for dinner? How could I be sure? I certainly did not want to make a complete ninny of myself by misinterpreting these ambiguous signals. Yet, she *had* called me "adorable," had she not? I also felt we had made a real psychic connection in several other areas—the coincidence regarding our dogs' names struck me as pure kismet and her knowledge of spoonerisms was a delight.

In short, I was thoroughly obsessed.

Predictably, Dr. Wang suggested I phone her immediately and set up a rendezvous before she completely forgot who I was.

"Are you saying I'm forgettable?" I inquired, with a touch of distress in my voice. "I may be a lot of things, Dr. Wang, but forgettable is not one of them."

"You sound upset," Wang observed.

"Do I?"

"May I speculate?" he asked.

"Be my guest," I replied. "You're the doctor."

Wang took a deep breath, gathered his thoughts.

"Perhaps you're afraid of being forgotten in a larger sense," he began. "Perhaps you're afraid that you will die a forgotten man. Perhaps that partly explains your obsession with death. Perhaps that is why you're so wrapped up in writing your biography of America's most forgotten president, Millard Fillmore. Perhaps you identify with him in some subtle way. Perhaps you feel sorry for him?"

"Nonsense!" I cried a bit loudly. "The biography was your idea!"

"True," he conceded. "But you were already somewhat obsessed by the subject."

"That's correct," I admitted. "But your thesis is absurd!"

"Do I detect a little anger in your tone?"

"Certainly not."

"Do I?"

"No," I repeated. "But do you in fact think I am forgettable?"

"Of course not, Fussell, but if you dillydally around for six months, as is your habit, and then suddenly call her, there's a good chance she will have forgotten your short meeting in the park, even if you haven't."

"I see," I conceded. "Point taken."

"Go ahead, Fussell, call her, what can you lose? You can even use my phone if you like. Go ahead. I dare you!"

"Not now," I said. "I have to build up my courage first, perform a few compulsive rituals for good luck and so forth."

"The worst thing that can happen is you ask her out and she says no, thank you."

"What can I lose?" I repeated. "My self-esteem, for one thing."

"You don't have any self-esteem," he said, checking his notes. "You told me so yourself nine weeks ago."

"Right. So I did."

"Have you somehow picked up some self-esteem in the last nine weeks?"

"I don't think so."

"So what's stopping you?"

"After all these years of therapy you still have to ask?"

"Fussell, you're rich, you're handsome, you're what they call an eligible bachelor," Wang said. "Half the single women in the Valley would probably love to meet you."

"I'm also obsessive, anxiety-ridden and a terrible dancer."

"All men are terrible dancers," Wang remarked.

"What about obsessive and anxiety-ridden?"

"Minor neuroses," Wang said.

"Yes, but I also compulsively say names backwards, I spray Lysol on everything in my house twice a day, it takes me a month to decide which tie to wear for a particular occasion, I wear rain gear on sunny days, I—"

"She wore galoshes, you told me," Wang recalled. "Besides, didn't you tell me you didn't feel the usual anxiety in her presence?"

"Yes. That's true."

"Who knows, Fussell?" Wang said, with a wink. "Perhaps this particular woman is your soul mate. This could be your one chance for true happiness."

"Rubbish," I said, although I realized Dr. Wang had said this partly in jest, for he knew very well that I did not accept the concept of soul mates, a ridiculous notion dreamed up by the very same people who would have us believe there was such a thing as romantic love. Need I point out that it is utter nonsense to think that there is only one person, out of all the billions of people on the earth, who is the one and only person meant for you? What are the odds of actually meeting this person? A hundred million to one? A billion to one? What if your one and only soul mate lives in a remote village in Kazakhstan and you live in Bumpass, Virginia? Not likely that you would ever cross paths. Did people actually believe that God spent all of his time arranging for certain people to meet each other? What idiocy! But this was not an argument I cared to wage again, having already done so many times before in therapy. It had become something of a broken record and even I was bored with it as a topic of discussion.

As it happened, my therapy time was up anyway, so I took my leave of Dr. Wang, wishing him a good day.

But I was still uncertain about my next step. Wang's advice was genuine and I knew he meant well, but his outlook was invariably optimistic. I desperately needed another opinion, so I decided to consult my one and only dear friend, Teppelman.

Teppelman was a dealer in autographs and historical documents, which he sold primarily to collectors, but occasionally to libraries and university archives. He maintained a small gallery in West Hollywood—a wonderful musty old place stacked with old first editions and endless file cabinets—where he bought and sold letters and documents written and signed by U.S. presidents and first ladies, deceased world leaders, authors, artists, astronauts and the like, as well as vintage Hollywood material, consisting mainly of inscribed glamour photographs from the 1920s and 1930s. But his specialty was the correspondence of presidents and first ladies. On a number of occasions, he had been hired to verify the authenticity of disputed signatures and had made something of a name for himself recently by declaring that a certain love letter purportedly written by Herbert Hoover to Zasu Pitts was indeed a fraud. I had befriended Teppelman some years ago while in search of correspondence written by Millard Fillmore. Teppelman had supplied me with several letters of interesting historical content, which he had purchased from an estate sale in Buffalo, New York, where Fillmore had spent some time practicing law. Over the years we had become good friends.

Teppelman was a diminutive, ferretlike fellow with a gray walrus mustache, rosy cheeks and a head of untamed white hair that obeyed the commands of no comb or brush. Dandruff fell from his scalp like snow flurries and there were scaly patches of eczema all over his forehead. Although he was married to a woman I had never met, Teppelman was not especially outgoing, and rarely interacted with others outside his professional field. I believe I was his only friend.

"I'm not a handwriting analyst, Fussell," he said modestly. "Sure, I can tell a forgery well enough, but I don't pretend to know anything about psychology as it appears in handwriting."

"Give it your best shot anyway," I said, handing him the paper on which Emily had written her name and cell phone number.

Teppelman studied the paper for a moment, then scratched his head, releasing a small blizzard.

"Her writing of the lowercase letter *i* bears a slight resemblance to the letter *i* in Kate Smith's signature," he said finally. "Is she a large woman?"

"Au contraire," I said. "She's quite slender."

"Perhaps she sings?"

"I wouldn't know."

He studied the signature again. "She has a slightly flattened lowercase *l* with a loop at the top, not unlike that of Benjamin Disraeli."

"I doubt if she aspires to be a deceased prime minister of England," I said, quite humorously.

"No, but perhaps she writes romance novels. Disraeli was a prolific author in that genre. Not many people know that."

"Hmmm," I mused. "Possible, I suppose."

"He was also extremely charming and members of the opposite sex apparently found him quite attractive."

"Yes!" I exclaimed. "She is certainly charming and attractive. Please go on."

Teppelman was on a roll now. "Her capital E is a bit high, not unlike the capital letter E in Dwight Eisenhower's signature. Does she have a foreign policy?"

"Not that I know of."

"That was an attempt at humor, Fussell," he explained.

"Ah yes," I said. "Ha ha, ho ho. Very funny indeed, Teppelman. Did you know, by the bye, that Eisenhower spelled backwards is Rewohnesie?"

"Never gave it much thought," he said.

"Most people wouldn't," I conceded. "Sounds like an African country a bit, doesn't it?"

"No, not really." Teppelman sighed and handed back the piece of paper.

"She wore galoshes," I added.

"Oh yes? Was it raining?"

"No."

"Was rain forecast?"

"No."

"Flash flood?"

"No."

"How very odd."

"I found it endearing," I said.

"Knowing you, I'm not surprised."

"What should I do, Teppelman?" I cried, forlorn. "Should I ask her out on a date? What if she agrees? Where should we go? What should I say if I get her voice mail? What should I say if I don't get her voice mail? I tell you, Teppelman, I'm at my wit's end."

Teppelman shrugged. "Come now, Fussell," he remarked. "Do I strike you as the kind of person people come to for romantic advice?"

Chapter 6: After a bit of minor edema,

my Frisbee-induced skull injury all but disappeared. Though I experienced no headaches or subsequent pain, no double vision or grotesque facial tics, no paralysis or tingling in the extremities, no memory loss or befuddlement (other than my normal, everyday befuddlement), I managed to convince my neurologist that further tests were indicated, if only to assuage my irrational fear that a malignant tumor, aneurysm or blood clot was presently germinating unnoticed in the warm gray mush of my brain and would cause me to drop dead at the most inopportune time. I was no stranger to the MRI machine; this would be my fifth time in the long white tube. Claustrophobia not being one of my many ailments, I found the experience strangely relaxing.

Although the results were negative, I decided to have a CAT scan just to be safe, but those results were negative as well. Since I had already met my sizable deductible, the insurance company paid 80 percent of the $2,000 cost, leaving me to pay the remaining $400, certainly not a particularly large amount of money for someone of my means, but enough of an expense to justify a phone call to the alluring Emily.

Not that I hadn't already considered the idea, as Wang had suggested, of simply calling her for a date. In fact, I had agonized over it for days prior to my medical tests but I was, as usual, paralyzed with anxiety. How could I just come out and bluntly ask her out to dinner or a movie? That was not why she had given me her cell phone number. She had given it to me in case there were uncovered medical expenses. I felt I needed this concrete reason to phone her so that I would be able to feel out the situation and not make a total fool of myself.

I sat by my phone for two nights, rehearsing opening lines, but nothing I concocted sounded even remotely charming. I even bounced a few attempts off Isabella but she did not so much as wag her tail, not a good sign. That's how pathetic I was, testing dialogue on a canine.

The same difficult questions kept tormenting me: What if Emily didn't remember me? How would I reintroduce myself? How could I tell her she owed me $400 without sounding petty? After all, I certainly didn't need the $400, for my fortune was in the millions. I thought perhaps a somewhat humorous, self-deprecating approach might work, but could think of nothing amusing. What if I opened with a wisecrack and she didn't catch it? What if I got her voice mail? What sort of message would I leave then? What if I stuttered or lapsed into word games, as was my unfortunate tendency? Or what if I mentioned the $400 and she decided to send me a check in the mail? Then what? I'd probably never see her again.

I'm not a believer in destiny, but what transpired next almost made me an advocate. A week of dillydallying in front of the telephone had passed and I was just about to enter the lobby elevator to Dr. Wang's floor for my Tuesday appointment, when who should I see already inside the same elevator but Emily herself! She was wearing a very becoming black business suit and carrying an umbrella. There was a streak of white zinc oxide down the length of her nose, which, although prudent, made her look a bit like someone who had just returned from an Apache rain dance.

We saw each other immediately and our eyes locked as people milled in and out of the elevator. She smiled. I smiled back. We were both frozen in our places, her place being inside the elevator, my place being outside.

"Hello there," she said pleasantly.

"Olleh," I repeated, my heart suddenly aflutter. "How, um, very ecin to—"

And then suddenly the elevator doors whooshed closed, separating us. I quickly unfroze and banged on the elevator doors to no avail. The elevator was going up (as there was no other direction from the lobby) and it was a ten-story building. What could I do? I couldn't let this opportunity slip away. I looked frantically around the lobby area and found the entrance to the stairwell. I tore the door open and began climbing the stairs two at a time.

I had made it to the fourth stairwell when I suddenly realized that the original destination of Emily's elevator must have been the lobby, as it had been a down elevator. I smacked my forehead in disgust at my own incredible stupidity, did an abrupt about-face, and flew back down the stairs. When I got to the bottom, I ripped the door open, practically pulling it off its hinges, and stepped into the lobby again. I was out of breath, my legs ached and I felt a slight dampness under my armpits. I looked about me; then I raced to the elevator bank. Which elevator had she been in, right or left? I'd forgotten. The left elevator was descending. I paced like a madman as it slowly made its way down. Finally, there was a light thud and the elevator doors opened.

But she was not inside. Crestfallen, and exhausted from my dash up and down the stairs, I leaned against the wall to rest. I felt sweat begin to moisten several parts of my body. I abhor sweating.

It was then that I had an ingenious idea.

Although I realize that some scientists claim that cell phones can cause brain tumors, I carry one on my person for emergencies and thus use it rarely, careful to hold the phone at least three inches from my head to minimize the risk. As I stood panting in the lobby of Wang's building, praying silently that my recent exertions would not result in a myocardial infarction or a stroke, I decided that this present situation qualified as an emergency so I pulled out my wallet and plucked out the shred of paper with her phone number on it. My hands shaking, I dialed the digits and held my breath. If she was somewhere in the building I would be able to reach her, assuming she was carrying her cell phone. Somehow, all my fears and anxieties about speaking to her had miraculously evaporated. Perhaps it was that look we had exchanged in the elevator. Perhaps it was instinct. Perhaps desperation.

After three rings, she clicked on. I would be late for my appointment with Dr. Wang, but so what? The good doctor and I had been going around in circles for the last few weeks anyway and I was getting motion sickness.

"Um . . ."

"Hello?"

"Hello there," said I. "This is Otalp Llessuf, the human Trisbee farget." *Damn*, I was suddenly nervous again.

"Oh yes, hello," she said. "I'm so glad you called."

This was clearly a positive omen. Not only had she ignored my nervous gibberish, she was glad I called. Ha! I felt a rush of adrenaline shoot into my spleen. My face flushed with warmth. All chemical reactions. Of course my opening line had been a stroke of genius, if I do say so myself. "Plato Fussell, human Frisbee target." This was truly a gem! And it was totally unrehearsed—somehow it had just popped out of my mouth. If only I hadn't completely messed up the words. But it didn't matter; she clearly understood me.

"How's your dent?" she asked.

"Buch metter."

"No complications? No tumors or blood clots? No aneurysms?"

"Not yet."

"I'm glad to hear it."

"But there's always the possibility one will develop." (At last, a normal sentence.)

"Yes."

"I might not know for years."

"True."

"I could just dop dread," I said.

"Yes, well, we'll just have to keep our fingers crossed that you don't," she said playfully.

A moment of silence passed. Oh God, now what? I pulled a monogrammed handkerchief out of my breast pocket and wiped my sweating brow. The cloth was soaked through in two seconds and I deposited it in a nearby trash barrel. I faked a coughing fit and searched my brain for something to fill the growing void of silence.

It was she who continued the dialogue. "When I saw you from the elevator I'm afraid I was temporarily immobilized," she said. "I can't explain it."

"Me too," I responded. "Strangest thing."

"Do you believe in kismet?" she asked.

"No."

"Nor do I."

"The very idea that there is an omniscient, omnipotent deity of some sort who treeps kack of every single move made by every pingle serson on earth is beyond ludicrous." (Damn it!)

"I couldn't agree more," she said. "God must have better things to do. Bunch of claptrap."

"Poetic jumbo mumbo," I said.

Frankly, I was pleased with how smoothly this was going. Sure, I was nervous, my hand was even shaking a trifle, not every word was coming out correctly, but the conversation was moving along well. For some reason I felt fairly comfortable talking to this woman. Somehow, I felt as if we were old friends.

"So, um, what brings you to Number Ten Vineland Avenue, if I may ask?" I said, proud of myself for rescuing the conversation from another deadly hiatus.

"I have an office in the building."

"Oh? What sort of business?"

"I'm an interior designer."

"Hivate promes? Offices?" *Damnation!*

"No," she said. "Actually I mostly do funeral parlors and the occasional city morgue. Those are my specialties."

"Is that so," I said enthusiastically, as this was yet another interest we shared—death. "I never knew those places were actually . . . designed by someone." (Another completely coherent sentence—*hallelujah!*)

"Oh yes," she said. "It's not easy doing design work when all you have to work with is basic black. And you have to be careful about what kinds of pictures you hang on the walls."

"Yes, I suppose you do," I said.

"Paintings of circus clowns, for example, don't usually work in that sort of environment."

"Quite right," I said. "Do you enjoy it?"

"It pays the bills," she responded. "Sometimes the odors are a little hard to endure."

"I can imagine."

"All that embalming fluid. Rotting corpses. Dead people staring vacantly at the ceiling. Am I making you nauseous?"

"On the contrary," I said. "I'm something of a borgue muff myself."

"A morgue buff?" she said. "Is there a club?"

"No, it's just a hobby," I told her. "Minor death obsession. My own mostly."

"I see."

"Do you find that odd?"

"Not really."

"Most people do," I admitted. "By the way, I was . . ."

"Yes?"

"Um . . ."

"Yes?"

"I was just thinking . . ."

"Of?"

"Perhaps we could . . . um, meet for . . . [gulp] coffee?"

"Where?"

"I don't know," I fumbled. "At a shoffee cop."

"I'm not keen on coffee shops," she said. "You're never sure if the food preparers wash their hands thoroughly after visiting the lavatory. Even when there are signs."

"True."

"You wouldn't want to get hepatitis."

"No."

"Or meningitis."

"No."

"Or typhoid fever."

"Certainly not."

"Then there's the possibility of getting salmonella from under-cooked meat, not that I even eat meat."

"Some places actually use raw eggs in their Caesar dralad sessing," I pointed out. "Can you believe that? Raw eggs!"

"Some places still serve steak tartare!"

"Incredible."

"Then there's sushi."

"Oh God, yes!"

"So where shall we meet?" she asked.

There was a momentary pause as we both contemplated the difficulty of deciding on a place to rendezvous. Frankly, I was at a loss. I rarely ate out, preferring the safety of my own well-scrubbed kitchen. At home, there was no one around to contaminate my food.

"Perhaps we could make our own coffee and meet in the park," she suggested.

"Actually," I said, "I don't drink coffee. It gives me anxiety and raises my blood pressure. The caffeine. I get very agitated."

"But it was you who suggested coffee."

"I suppose I should have given it more thought."

"Well, you can bring tea then."

"I have the same problem with tea."

"But you were drinking tea when we met."

"I never actually drank it," I said. "I only took it to be polite."

"Well, just bring whatever it is you drink."

"Okay."

"When shall we meet?"

"When?"

"When."

"Um, I don't know."

"How about Saturday around noon at the park?"

"Pich whark?"

"The park where we met."

"That's fine," I said. "Where will we sit?"

"I don't know. How about one of the picnic tables?"

"What if they're all taken?"

"The ground?"

"I'm not wild about gritting on the sound," I said.

"Bring a blanket."

"Yes. I'll bling a branket," I said. "Good idea!"

"I'll bring bug spray. Just in case."

"Excellent."

"And sunscreen. I use the 300 SPF."

"Okay."

"Then it's a date."

"I guess so."

"Good."

"What if it rains?" I asked. "Or what if there's an earthquake?"

"You have my cell phone number."

"Ah yes, of course."

"If it's anything over a 4.0 on the Richter scale, we should probably call it off."

"Of course," I agreed.

"Wouldn't make any sense."

"By the way, where exactly are you at the moment?" I asked.

"About three yards behind you, to your left."

I swiveled. There she was, an angel bathed in a ray of sunlight, standing in front of a newspaper kiosk, holding her cell phone about three inches away from her head.

Chapter 7: You would have actually had

to meet my mother and father in the flesh to believe that my subsequent descriptions of them are not flagrant fabrications. My mother in particular offers irrefutable proof that neuroses are genetically transmitted. Gladys Fussell, née Russo, was a veritable amalgam of minor neuroses during my youth, but following my father's retirement some five years ago, she turned bitter, obsessive and cynical to boot and, much to my father's chagrin, stopped leaving their apartment for any reason other than medical checkups and appointments with her hairdresser.

My father had had a triple-bypass operation several years ago, but he was still energetic and, since my mother was mostly housebound, it was he who was left to perform all the routine errands. Before his retirement, he had been a salesman of pharmaceuticals for years, a profession I suspect he tolerated mainly because it got him out of the apartment and away from my mother for long periods of time. Who could blame him? He was something of a Milquetoast, my father, but an amiable Milquetoast, and I often wondered how he managed to make a living selling anything, for he did not possess the outgoing, glad-handing, toadying personality one might expect from a successful salesman. He never struck me as aggressive or in any way adept at flattery. He was, if anything, fairly self-effacing. Whenever he was home, he liked to sit quietly in his corner chair in the den, while perusing the expensive yachting magazine he subscribed to, though he neither possessed the means nor the temperament to even contemplate buying an oceangoing vessel more flamboyant than a used dinghy, let alone a yacht. Although I was very fond of my father, he always struck me as one of those countless American men who, fitting Thoreau's description, led a life of quiet desperation.

Naturally, I was completely wrong.

On the night following my second impromptu meeting with Emily, I was scheduled to have dinner with my parents and, as always, I brought my mother a little gift, a box of fresh, organically grown candied prunes that I had picked up at my local produce market. I had paid a few dollars extra to have the box professionally gift-wrapped in an attractive floral pattern, in spite of the wrapper's looks of derisive disbelief. What kind of world is this when a man can't even get a simple box of fresh candied prunes gift-wrapped for his mother without encountering attitude? I considered complaining to the manager, but being terrified of confrontation, merely smiled and took my package. Nevertheless, I was confident my mother would enjoy my thoughtfulness, as she was somewhat obsessed with the performance of her bowels or rather, the lack thereof. I've never known for certain whether this obsession was real or imaginary, but she could wax rhapsodic on the subject for hours at a time, and had bent the ears of more than a few doctors and pharmacists, as well as my poor father and me, concerning her adventures on the toilet.

"Hi, Dad," I said as my father answered the door. We shook hands and hugged.

"You're looking undernourished, Plato," my father said. "Are you eating enough herring?"

"What?"

"Herring? Are you eating enough herring?"

"I don't care for herring," I said.

"That's news to me."

"You're late, Plato," my mother snapped as I set foot in the apartment. She was holding a stopwatch, one that I myself had bought her several Christmases ago, as a joke. I had no idea she would turn it into a compulsion, but I suppose I should have known better.

"Thirty-two seconds," she said.

"What?"

"Thirty-two seconds late," she said.

"He's not late, Gladys," my father said. "Leave the poor boy alone. He's right on time, according to my watch."

"I tell you he's late."

"He's close enough. Dinner's not even ready. What's the fuss?"

"He's not on time, Victor."

"I beg to differ, Mother," said I. To prove my point, I picked up the nearest phone, dialed a number from memory and held the receiver to my ear. After a few seconds I put the phone down, trying to keep any hint of smugness out of my expression.

"According to Greenwich Mean Time, the number of which I just called, when I crossed the threshold of your doorway I was exactly four seconds early," I said.

"Ha!" my father said. "There you have it! What've you got to say about that, Gladys?"

"Early isn't on time," my mother said. "Early is early."

My father rolled his eyes, but as usual, refrained from any further confrontation with my mother. Not that he was afraid of her—he just preferred not to argue about it. My mother could bicker tediously over nothing for hours on end and my father just didn't have the patience. Nor did I.

Rather than belabor the issue, I apologized for being early and handed her the gift. She shook the box gently.

"It's not another box of urine specimen jars?"

"No."

"I've run out of urine specimen jars."

"Well, Christmas is coming up."

She held the box to her ear. "Is that ticking I hear? It's probably an explosive device," she said. "You can't wait for me to die, can you, Plato? So you can inherit all my money."

"What money would that be, Mother?" I asked.

"If your father wasn't such a cheapskate, we could have made a fortune by now," she said. "In stocks."

"*I'm* a cheapskate?" my father said, slightly incredulous. "That's rich. No pun intended."

"That's right, you spent every cent on yourself, drinking, carousing and gambling on the road when you were a salesman, while Plato and I practically starved to death at home in this hovel," she said.

My father was a teetotaler, never did anything that could be even remotely construed as "carousing" and the only time he gambled was when he bet me a nickel the Dodgers would win the pennant in 1979. My father just shook his head wearily. My mother finally opened her present, which took about twenty minutes, as she likes to save used wrapping paper, not to mention tinfoil, string, rubber bands and those address stickers contained in charitable requests.

"Prunes!" she said with mock enthusiasm. "Just what I needed. More prunes!"

"Not just prunes," I said. "Organically grown candied prunes."

"Such a big spender. Like father like son."

You can't win with my mother. The fact that I had offered on numerous occasions to buy them a three-bedroom house in Ventura near the beach had evidently made no impression.

"I thought they might be good for your bowels," I said. "Did you, uh, make today?"

"Yes, I did. Not much, just a little one, but it's a start."

"Yes. Congratulations."

"Thank you."

Perhaps I should have warned you—this was a ritual with my mother. If I did not inquire about her bowel movements at least once a week, she would fall into a funk and claim that I did not truly care about her. I wanted to be a good son, so I inquired.

"Dark brown."

"Glad to hear it," I said.

Dinner was the usual spiceless, tasteless, overboiled piece of mystery meat (I guessed chicken), which my mother cooked every other day because it was easy on their dentures. The rest of the time they ate runny soft-boiled eggs with applesauce or noodle soup with pickles. The Fussell household had never been much of an epicurean showplace. Food to my mother was something that primarily housed bacteria. Everything was boiled for hours until every living cell was exterminated. Sometimes the food tasted so horrible I often suspected that she sprayed it with disinfectant just to be sure. Instructions on how to perform the Heimlich maneuver could be found in every nook of the kitchen. Ipecac was always handy. After taking something out of the refrigerator, it had to pass her smell test. The refrigerator itself was always kept on high so that produce and cold cuts all had an appetizing layer of frost on them. And in the freezer, you needed an ice pick to separate the food from the rest of the iceberg. Once a year, my father put on a parka and a ski hat and defrosted it with a small pickax.

We ate in silence. I watched my mother slice her food into tiny pieces and arrange and rearrange them into neat little patterns on her plate. She drank only water that had been put through a special five-step process to remove impurities. Several air purifiers hummed in the background. I wondered what it was about this odd woman that had attracted my father enough to marry her. I had seen their wedding pictures and she had been somewhat attractive—slender, shapely and blonde—in her twenties. How had they decided that they loved each other?

Feeling bold and reckless, and desperately in need of some wisdom on the subject of love, I asked them precisely that question, phrased a little more delicately.

"Strudel," my mother said, after giving it no more than a second or two of thought.

"Strudel?"

"Your father and I both loved exactly the same kind of strudel," she added, looking at my father, who nodded.

"What kind was that?"

"Boysenberry," my father recalled.

"I didn't know they even made a boysenberry strudel," I said.

"Yes, boysenberry. Fresh boysenberry," my mother said. "Now I can't even eat boysenberries—the seeds get caught in my dentures."

"They sell seedless now," my father said.

"They do not."

"Of course they do! At the supermarket!"

"What supermarket?"

"The one on Magnolia Boulevard."

"You married over similar tastes in strudel?" I asked before the seedless boysenberry argument could gather too much steam and derail the conversation.

"That's how we met, Plato," my mother explained. "There was one boysenberry left in the bakery and we both wanted it. So we sat down and shared it and we got to talking about things."

"What things?"

"Things," she repeated. "Music, sports, current events . . ."

"What do you know about sports?" I asked my mother.

"I faked it."

"What else?" I inquired. "How did you know you were in love?"

"There was a certain attraction. . . ."

"Sex?" I asked.

"Is that so hard to believe?" my father clucked. I looked at both of them. Yes frankly, it was hard to believe. Impossible to believe. Just picturing it in my mind was making me nauseous.

"It was 1962," my mother said. "There was no sex."

"That comes as news to me," my father objected, winking at me. "What your mother means is that people just didn't talk about it much. It wasn't the kind of topic you discussed openly."

"Why not?"

"In those days it was a private matter," my father said. "Today it's all you see on television. You can't watch the evening news without seeing sex. Doesn't matter what the news item is, somehow they always stick it in, no pun intended. And have you seen MTV lately?"

"You watch MTV?" I asked.

"Sure," my father admitted. "Doesn't everybody?"

"I don't," I said. My father shrugged sheepishly—the man was full of surprises.

"Is it so hard for you to believe your parents had a sex life?" my mother asked.

"Frankly, yes."

"You're living proof," my father pointed out. True, I thought, though it occurred to me that I was living proof that they had had sex *once*.

"And may we please change the subject?" my mother begged. "I'm getting hives. I'm itching all over. Look at this."

She extended her wrist, but I saw no rash or anything resembling hives.

"So it was just sex," I said.

"Of course not," my mother retorted. "It took a while, but we managed to fall in love with each other eventually."

"How did you know you were in love?" I asked. "How could you be sure? What did it feel like?"

"We knew," my father explained. "There was a certain chemistry."

"Chemistry?"

"Yeah," my father said. "You can't explain it."

"Of course you can," I said. "It has to do with hormones."

"At first maybe," my father agreed. "But then . . ."

"Then?"

"I don't know," he said with a shrug. "You develop an appreciation for the other person."

"An appreciation?" I asked. "That's not very romantic."

"After a certain point, the romance fades away," my father continued. "You develop a deep . . . fondness."

"A deep fondness?" I asked. "What does that mean?"

"You explain it, Gladys," my father said.

"Who can explain it?" she replied. "Nobody can explain love."

"Why not?" I persisted.

"You just can't," my father said. "It's like electricity. You know what it does, but you don't really know what it is."

"You mean if it looks like a duck and sounds like a duck, it must be a duck?"

"Yeah, something like that."

"Your father was quite the dashing fellow in his day," my mother said quite tenderly. "In those days he wore his hair in a pompadour, he was slim and muscular and he had a thin little pencil mustache. He broke more than a few hearts, I can tell you."

"Your mother was no slouch in the looks department either," my father added, placing his hand on hers. "She had long wavy blonde hair. She resembled Joan Crawford." He moved his hands in an hourglass shape and winked. My mother blushed.

"Why all the questions, Plato?" my mother inquired suspiciously. "Have you met someone?"

"Will we be grandparents soon?" my father asked, winking again. He had winked at me so many times that evening I wondered whether he was developing a facial tic.

Naturally, I found it somewhat premature to answer their questions in the affirmative, particularly since Emily and I had not even gone on our first date yet.

"Just idle curiosity," I said.

Chapter 8: Except for the fact that it took me two days to decide what to wear, my first official date with Emily Thorndyke went extremely well. The weather forecast for that Saturday was partly cloudy with a chance of light drizzle and temperatures in the mid-sixties. If you are a pessimist like me, you know that a forecast like that probably means there will be a small monsoon, followed by flash floods and tornado warnings. I must have called the National Weather Forecast twenty times (their number is on my speed dial), and after the nineteenth, they became annoyed and connected me to a meteorologist, to whom I spoke for half an hour. Although, as a result, I can give you detailed dissertations on isobars, cold fronts and global warming, I was unable to pin the weatherman down to an actual forecast for the day of our date.

If it did not rain and I wore full rain gear—galoshes, rain hat, rain slicker and rain pants—I would look like an utter nitwit. If I wore my regular street clothes and it did rain, I could catch a cold and possibly die of pneumonia. It was a difficult choice and one that I lost a fair amount of sleep worrying about in the nights preceding our rendezvous. Losing sleep produced unattractive circles under my eyes, so I was compelled to wear a pair of sunglasses, which, if it rained, would make me appear even more ridiculous. After a three-hour anxiety attack, I finally decided to wear regular clothes, but packed an umbrella and full rain gear in a small suitcase with wheels, just in case.

In order to keep a lively conversation going, I wrote down a number of interesting subjects on my hand, and read three books on basic interior design, which I borrowed from the local library. Frankly, I found the subject somewhat less than fascinating, so I also read a short biography of Frank Lloyd Wright, just in case she wanted to take the dialogue to a slightly higher plane. Nevertheless, my knowledge of drapery fabric, upholstery, carpet pile, interior wall paints, window treatments and the pros and cons of indirect lighting increased a thousandfold.

Much to my delight, Emily had apparently had similar worries regarding the weather for when I found her at the park, she was in the process of erecting a large beach umbrella over one of the vacant picnic tables. As the sun was most assuredly not out, I assumed she was doing this to protect us from the rain, should it appear. And if the sun did eventually show itself, the umbrella would protect us from it's carcinoma-producing UVA rays as well. The moment I arrived she told me to close my mouth and proceeded to spray the exposed skin of my face, neck, arms and hands with 300 SPF sunscreen, noting quite correctly that UVA rays are still present on overcast days, and that these are the kinds of days on which most people get seriously sunburned without realizing it until it is too late. Just in case the 300 SPF sunscreen was somehow defective, there was a large tube of sunburn salve in her enormous bag. After wiping the sunscreen off my sunglasses, I thanked her profusely. This was a woman after my own heart! We were clearly birds of a feather, linked by the common bond of similar neuroses, and I think this had a pronounced dulling effect on my usual anxiety in the company of beautiful women. I was, amazingly enough, downright loquacious in her presence!

We spoke for hours, sipping our respective drinks and gnawing on organic, pesticide-free carrot sticks. Much to my relief, she was not seeing anyone romantically. She was a marvelous raconteur, and regaled me with tales of her neurotic family and her miserable high school years. She was from the Midwest, a small town in Iowa, had studied art history at the University of Indiana and had two older brothers, Frank and Udo. Her father, a vegetarian and sometime manic-depressive, had been a high school history teacher; her mother, normal except for an irrational fear of vacuum cleaners, had worked for the phone company. Emily herself had been something of a loner at school, she admitted. In those days, she wrote dark, depressing poetry on the lavender pages of a locked diary, dressed primarily in black and played the oboe in the high school band, where she'd suffered through a four-year unrequited crush on a member of the tuba section named Arthur Pruett. Coincidentally, her favorite classical music piece was the same as mine—Mozart's "Requiem Mass." I mostly listened, although I did manage to say a few words about my biography of Millard Fillmore. She seemed enthralled by the subject (for some bizarre reason, most people aren't) and asked me some very intelligent questions. The more we spoke, the more confident I became. This fascinating woman had an absolute knack for making me comfortable in her presence. It was really quite exciting.

But did she have more than just a friendly interest in our affiliation?

"So what do you think?" I asked after a time, since frankly, the suspense was killing me. "Do you think we're—"

"Yes?"

"That is, are you . . ."

"Spit it out, Plato."

"No, it's too soon," I fumbled. "I'm seing billy." *Oops, nerves again.*

"You're seeing Billy? Billy who? Are you telling me you're gay?"

"No, no, no," I assured her. "I meant to say I'm being silly."

"Oh."

"Um, as I was saying before . . . do you . . ."

"Please," she beseeched me. "Tell me what's on your mind."

"What I'm trying to say, and I don't mean to be too forward or aggressive or suggestive or premature or anything of that sort. What I mean to say is . . . do you think we're . . ."

"Yes?"

I shut my eyes and spoke. "Compatible?" I said. "Do you think we're compatible?"

"So far so good," she said.

"Really?" I was overjoyed.

"Really."

"We seem to have a great deal in common."

"Yes, we do."

I was feeling bolder by the minute. "So does this mean that you'll go on another etad with me?" I asked.

"Yes," she said. "Absolutely."

By now, I was practically swooning with excitement. "Really?"

"Really."

"There are a few things you should know about me first," I said.

"You didn't kill somebody, did you?"

"Who me? Ha ha, ho ho. Of course not."

"Spent some time in jail?"

"No," I said. "Nothing of that nature."

"What then?" she asked.

"I must warn you," I began, "I'm not a terribly romantic fellow. I'm somewhat inept in that area."

"I'm okay with that," Emily said.

"I don't much care for candles because of the potential fire hazard," I ventured.

"Not a problem."

"I probably won't ever coo sweet nothings in your ear," I said. "I don't know how to coo."

"I can live without cooing."

"I probably won't fling you browers," I continued. "I have allergies."

"Doesn't matter. I get tons of flowers free. From the funeral homes, after the memorial services."

"On the positive side," I said, "I like to think I'm a pice nerson. I'm honest and loyal, generous and compassionate, reliable . . ."

"I can tell."

"You can?"

"Female intuition."

"And you?" I asked. "No prison record, I presume?"

"Of course not," she said. "Unless you count those sixteen counts of grand larceny I was convicted of two years ago."

"What!" I exclaimed.

"A little joke, Fussell," she said. "I've never even gotten so much as a parking ticket."

Toward dusk, we stopped talking for a while and sat silently beside each other on a clean splinterless park bench, watching the sunset. Her thigh rubbed against mine a few times and I felt a slight hormonal surge. Gradually, inch by inch, I began to snake my arm around her shoulders.

"Would you like to kiss me?" she asked, before the snake had made it past the nape of her neck.

"Um . . . yes," I said. "Very much."

"And I would like to kiss you too . . ."

I leaned my face closer to hers in anticipation, puckered my lips and closed my eyes.

"But," she said, backing away, "don't you think it would be prudent if, before exchanging bodily fluids, we both had the opportunity to see each other's medical records?"

"Good idea," I said.

"I mean, we don't really know each other that well, do we? I might have a cold sore brewing on my lip. Or HIV. Or hepatitis. Or herpes. Or God knows what else. If you were to catch anything, I wouldn't want that on my conscience."

"Toint paken," I said. "Very considerate of you."

"Or you might have something contagious yourself."

"I doubt it. My health record is pretty spotless," I assured her. "I had chickenpox in third grade, measles in the fifth grade and a mild case of dysentery after a trip to Biloxi, Mississippi, for my grandmother's funeral in 1978. Of course, it might have been a case of irritable bowel syndrome and thus not contagious. I never received a definitive diagnosis, and the doctors down South are a bit on the primitive side. If you ever go to Mississippi, my advice is don't drink the water. Then in 1982 I had a slight case of—"

"And I believe you," she said. "You appear to be the picture of health. But I'd still feel safer if I saw a doctor's signature. An ordinary board-certified internist will do. No specialists necessary."

"Understandable," said I. "My former wife and I often took a dose or two of tetracycline prior to having intercourse."

"So you've been married before?"

"Yes," I admitted. "An unfortunate mistake. I was young and diputs." (Any mention of my ex-wife caused anxiety.)

Just then, a flash of lightning split the sky, followed by an explosion of thunder and suddenly it was pouring. Emily reached into her large pocketbook and pulled out a full set of collapsible rain gear.

And I suppose you could say I was falling in love, that is, if you believe in such nonsense.

Chapter 9: By the time I saw Dr. Wang again, Emily and I had had three more delightful dates, two more at the park, and another at our local water filtration plant, where we were given a tour. As a result, I may never drink water again, any kind of water, not even distilled or so-called "mountain spring." After working up the nerve to ask the tour guide a number of probing questions—to the slight annoyance of the other three members of the tour, an elderly couple and their grandson—I was not entirely convinced that the filtration process the guide boasted of was quite as efficient or foolproof as he claimed it to be. And the people who worked there did not strike me as being terribly conscientious. God knows what would happen if one of them made even a minor blunder. When you get right down to it, the fact is we are drinking slightly refined toilet water, and one misthrown switch could result in the most unpleasant drinking experience imaginable.

As for our medical records, they were taking some time to process—Emily's doctor was on vacation in the Bahamas for several weeks—so the most intimate physical contact we had allowed ourselves thus far involved holding hands and the occasional impromptu game of footsie, which she often initiated. The flow of testosterone in my brain and genitalia would soon go berserk if it took much longer for us to consummate the relationship.

Meanwhile, Emily and I were becoming more intimate on a platonic level, revealing to each other our deepest insights and feelings. Remarkably, I found myself waxing rhapsodic on any number of subjects without resorting to the usual scrambled verbiage. Moreover, I found myself thinking of her all the time and she admitted that she too was consumed with thoughts of me on a fairly regular basis.

Naturally, Dr. Wang was utterly delighted when I told him the details of my new relationship following our third date. It was a sign, he said, that I was finally climbing out of my shell.

"I'm very proud of you, Fussell," he said. "You've made some real progress, a veritable breakthrough. How do you feel about all this?"

"Good," I said. "I feel good. But of course, something could go wrong. Something usually does. One has to stay alert."

"Now, now," Wang counseled. "Let's try to stay as optimistic as we can, shall we?"

"I've never been an optimist," I said. "Why start now?"

"It's healthier, for one thing."

"Oh?" I said. "Bad things happen to optimists. Bad things happen to pessimists too, but they expect it."

"Nevertheless," Wang said after writing something down in his black notebook, "you must resist your pessimism and call her again at your earliest convenience."

"Yes, of course."

"Clearly she likes you a great deal and wishes to continue the relationship."

"Do you think so?"

"From what you've told me, most definitely."

"How can you be so sure?"

"Call it shrink's intuition," he explained. "It's a sixth sense of sorts."

"I wonder if she'll still like me if I tell her about Aunt Sophie."

"I'd leave that part of your biography out for the time being if I were you," Dr. Wang suggested. "Might be a little too much for her to take this early in the relationship."

Did I happen to mention that my aunt Sophie is serving a fifty-year sentence at San Quentin penitentiary for manslaughter? Aunt Sophie is my mother's sister and one day about eight years ago, while strolling down the Embarcadero in San Francisco, she went temporarily insane and murdered someone in cold blood. As there were about one hundred witnesses at the scene, she was found guilty of manslaughter and sentenced to fifty years in prison. The next time I saw her, she was wearing a bright orange jumpsuit, leg irons and handcuffs and she had taken up smoking. I had always liked Aunt Sophie and was truly sorry that she was stuck with such a monotonously garish wardrobe.

"Some things are better left unsaid," Wang advised. "At least at the outset of a relationship."

"You're right, of course," I said. "Mum's the word. Though there were extenuating circumstances."

"True."

"Perhaps you should send her flowers," Dr. Wang suggested.

"Aunt Sophie?"

"No, your new girlfriend."

"Why?"

"It's a romantic gesture."

"I know," I said. "Why do you suppose that is?"

"Nobody really knows."

"I'm not much of a romantic," I said. "Plus I'm allergic."

"Have them delivered."

"What kind of flowers?"

"Roses? Daffodils?"

"How many?"

"I'll leave that up to you, Fussell. Most women love to receive flowers. Flowers mean you're serious. A dozen roses or a colorful mixed bouquet would suffice. It would be a nice gesture at this stage, I think."

"But she gets a variety of flowers from her work," I said.

"Not the same as getting them from a lover," Wang pointed out. "Trust me on this, Fussell."

"Okay," I said. "Flowers it is. A dozen roses or a mixed bouquet."

"Have you told her about Obit dot com yet?"

"No."

"I'd wait awhile on breaking that news as well," Wang suggested "Remember what happened the last time."

"Right," I said. "But I don't think she's that kind of a woman. Her motives seem to be entirely sincere."

"You never can tell with women," Wang postulated. "Women are a complete and utter mystery. Just when you think you—"

Then a very odd thing happened. Dr. Wang began to sob. At first, I thought he was retching or gagging, but it soon became clear that he was overcome with tears. He hid his face in shame and pulled a handkerchief out of his pocket. I was completely nonplussed. This had never happened before.

"Was it something I said?" I asked. "Aunt Sophie? Granted it's a sad story but—"

"No, no, no, of course not, Fussell," he sobbed. "It's just the . . ."

"What?" I asked.

"It's nothing."

"Nothing? Good grief, man, you're openly weeping."

"You're a patient," Wang said, dabbing his eyes with the corner of the hanky. "I don't want to trouble you with my personal problems. It might alter our professional doctor-patient relationship."

"Nonsense. You can confide in me. We've known each other for years."

Wang cleared his throat a few times, blew his nose and tucked the handkerchief back in his pocket.

"I seem to be going through a divorce is all," he said. "It's taking its toll on my psyche."

"You're divorcing your wife?" I asked, a bit incredulous, although I had never met his wife.

"Actually she's divorcing me," Wang said. "She calls it a trial separation but I'm afraid it's all over for us. She's already moved out of the house into some studio apartment somewhere."

"But why?"

"She says I'm too analytical. She says I'm always looking for deeper meaning in everything she does and says."

"Are you?"

"Of course! I'm a psychoanalyst."

"But I thought you two were happily married."

"So did I," Wang said. "Everything was going well, then two weeks ago she asked me for a divorce and left. Out of the blue. Just like that."

"I'm sorry," I said. "Would you like a hug?"

"Yes. That would be nice."

We both rose and I hugged him. He smelled slightly of sauerkraut.

"Thank you, Fussell," he said, forcing a smile. "You're very kind."

"Don't mention it."

I released him from my embrace and went back to the Barcelona chair. Tears still streaked down his cheeks, so I handed him the box of Kleenex on the table beside me. The Kleenex were meant for the patients. In my experience, the doctor rarely wept.

"I should have known better than to marry a patient," Wang moaned. "I could kick myself. It's a cardinal rule of psychiatry. But I couldn't resist her. She charmed me, she disarmed me completely. I'm only human, Fussell."

"I know," I said consolingly. "How does all this make you feel, Doctor?"

"Angry."

"Just angry?"

"Angry and helpless."

"Angry at whom?"

"Me, her, the world . . ." he said.

"Have you been repressing this anger?"

"To a certain degree, yes," Wang admitted.

"Why?"

"I really don't know."

"Perhaps we should explore that," I said.

"You think?"

"Let it out," I said. "Have a catharsis. You'll feel a lot better. Really. Go ahead."

"I just had a catharsis and I don't feel any better at all."

"So have another one. I'm not going anywhere. I could stay all afternoon. We could have catharses until dinnertime."

"I'd have to charge you, though," Wang pointed out.

"Why?"

Wang shrugged and then began sobbing again. It lasted about thirty seconds. Finally, he pulled himself together and took a deep breath.

"Better?"

"Yes, actually."

"Good."

"You're pretty good at this, Fussell," he said. "Maybe you should be the psychiatrist."

"If mocking me will make you feel better . . ."

"I wasn't mocking you, Fussell, I was—"

Then Wang began to weep again and this time he reached across his desk. There was a photograph in a silver standing frame, facing him. He took it in his hands and stared at it for a moment, then clasped it to his chest and let forth with another gushing sob.

Finally, he placed it back on the desk, facedown. I assumed it was a photo of his soon-to-be-ex wife, but as far as I knew it could just as well have been a photograph of an orangutan, although why he would keep a picture of an orangutan on his desk is anybody's guess.

"I think you need to channel those emotions," I said.

"Oh God, not that old line," he replied, rolling his eyes.

"Why not?" I asked. "It's a reliable old standby."

"I don't even use that line anymore," he said. "It's totally passé."

"Really?"

"Common knowledge in psychiatric circles. The whole chan-neling thing is generally considered to be old hat."

"Oh. Sorry."

"I'm surprised you hadn't noticed," Wang said. "I haven't used the term in ages. Are you paying attention?"

"You do have a lot of pent-up anger," I noted. "If insulting me will help you release it, by all means be my guest."

"I'm sorry, Fussell. I shouldn't be taking this out on you. Where's my professional etiquette?"

"You're only human, Doc," I said.

Naturally, I was genuinely saddened by Wang's marital difficul-ties, but there was little I could do other than offer him my deepest sympathies. On the way home from his office, I stopped at a Hall-mark store and, after reading through several hundred cards, I chose one that seemed appropriate ("Cheer up, this too shall pass"), purchased a stamp and mailed it to his office.

That night, I was once again scheduled to have dinner with my parents. This time, rather than suffer through the overcooked, un-derspiced gruel my mother invariably prepared, I bought several cartons of take-out food from a very reputable and exceedingly sanitary Chinese restaurant in my neighborhood (some time ago, the owner had allowed me to conduct a thorough inspection of his kitchen and bathroom facilities).

Predictably, my mother, after accusing me of being late, sniffed the contents of each carton, and then announced they were not suitable for ingestion.

"You want me to contract dysentery?" she asked.

"Of course not," I said.

"A little case of dysentery might be just the thing to loosen up those stubborn old bowels of yours," my father suggested facetiously.

"Not funny, Victor," my mother replied, glaring at him.

My father ignored her. "Hand over the Mongolian beef," he said to me. "I'm starving."

And so my father and I began to eat Mongolian beef, kung pao chicken and egg rolls while my mother sat stiffly across from us at the kitchen table, munching listlessly on a dry piece of zwieback and glowering at both of us. To fill the silence, I told them all about Emily and the details of our various dates.

"Sounds very promising," my father said. "See, I told you there would be someone out there for you, Plato."

"This time maybe you'll even invite us to the wedding," my mother said. "For a wedding I might even leave the apartment."

"A bit premature," I cautioned. "But if we do get married, I'm sure it will be a proper wedding, not like the last time."

"So when do we get to meet this delightful young lady?" my father asked, shoveling a spoonful of white rice into his mouth.

This was a tricky question. My relationship with Emily would have to progress to fairly solid ground before I would dare to expose her to my mother and her odd scatological complaints and bizarre cooking rituals.

Fortunately, I never got a chance to answer the question. My mother picked up one of the take-out cartons and looked inside, moving the food around with an unused chopstick.

"Smells pretty good," she said.

"Go ahead, Mother," I urged her. "Help yourself. It's delicious."

"Live dangerously," my father added.

She hesitated, tempted but not entirely convinced.

"Maybe if I nuked it in the microwave for an hour or so it would be safe to eat," she said tentatively.

"After an hour in the microwave," my father observed, "you could either eat it or make a pair of shoes out of it."

She smirked. "My husband, the comedian."

Chapter 10: By now, you're probably

wondering how an odd duck like me happened to amass a small fortune before the age of thirty. If nothing else, it's a testament to the blind equality of the American Dream. Even stammering social dolts like yours truly can achieve it with a little creativity, a modicum of effort and some fortuitous timing. I was, in other words, at the right place at the right time with the right notion.

I'm afraid it's your archetypal Horatio Alger story. Poor boy gets brilliant idea and makes big bucks (although I was never actually destitute as a youth). A bit of a snore really. After getting a master's degree from the university, where my utterly useless but highly captivating major was Death Studies (a major that was created at my request), I answered a classified ad and managed to get a job writing obituaries for a large urban newspaper. No doubt the editor who interviewed me was not only impressed by my credentials—I had written several incisive collegiate term papers on the subject of cadaver decomposition—but by my somewhat grave demeanor as well, no pun intended. Obituary writing frequently involved conversing on the phone with grieving family members of the dearly departed and my characteristic low-key monotone was perfect for the task. I had, as my editor pointed out on numerous occasions, the personality of a mortician with a terminal disease. I took this as a compliment, though it may not have been intended as such. Of course, my obsession with death made the job endlessly fascinating. Due to my position, I was privy to all the gruesome details of each and every death in the area. Deaths by fire, car accidents, suicides, overdoses, complications from surgery, decapitations, impalements, cancer, heart disease, leukemia, murder, AIDS, stabbings, aneurysms, drownings, gunshot wounds, leaps from tall buildings, plane crashes, motorcycle accidents, the occasional gangland execution, lethal injections at the local penitentiary . . . every day there was at least one new, bizarre death. Perhaps the oddest was the case in which a noted local author, while innocently tending to her flower garden, was struck on the head by the contents of a passing airplane's lavatory receptacle. She was DOA at St. Joseph's in Burbank and it took more than a little journalistic probing on my part to get the real story behind this unusual death, which the family had decided to call "an unfortunate accident involving an airplane."

It occurred to me after about a week on the job that there is a precise formula for writing obituaries, a template, if you will. Name the deceased, briefly say what he or she was known for, mention how he or she succumbed and where. Then include a paragraph or two about his or her accomplishments, list the survivors and give funeral information, which usually specifies date and time of memorial services and where to send donations in lieu of flowers. A no-brainer, as they say. A chimpanzee could learn how to do it in no time.

My newspaper was one of the larger, more urbane metropolitan dailies and only ran obits on people who had achieved something significant during their lifetimes. Movie stars, authors of renown, sports figures, artists, politicians, local philanthropists and so forth. Since writing the obituaries only took me an hour or so each day, I had a great deal of free time on my hands, so my boss assigned me the task of writing "anticipatory obits," as they are called in the newspaper trade. These were obituaries of famous elderly people who had not yet died but had, as they say, one foot in the grave. Given my obsessive-compulsive nature, I was quite a whiz at this, churning out ten to twenty of them in a single day, and occasionally even writing some of them at home during my free time. At first, I thought this vast output would eventually make me look good to my editor, a wizened old hack named Silverman.

"Write me an obit on so and so," Silverman would say at three o'clock and, having already written and stored the obit (minus a few minor details), I would miraculously hand him the copy by 3:05.

Unfortunately, Silverman was something of a sourpuss and didn't really care how long it took me to write the obits, as long as I handed them in before the paper was put to bed. It was also unfortunate that obituaries did not carry bylines, so there was little hope of promotion at the paper, not that I had much ambition regarding the newspaper business. I found journalism tedious. Nevertheless, I continued to write them on my own time just for the pure fun of it. I even wrote my own obituary. It went something like this:

> Plato G. Fussell of Sherman Oaks, California, a renowned scholar, jurist, Nobelist, sportsman and movie star, died Tuesday, June 4, 2070, at Riverside Medical Center. The cause of death was terminal boredom and a long-time desire to see what it was like "on the other side." He was 102 years old.
>
> Fussell was the son of Victor Fussell, a pharmaceutical salesman, and Gladys Fussell née Russo. He was also the nephew of Sophie Russo, whose trial for murder in 1996 captured the imagination of the public.
>
> He was born on June 10, 1967.

Fussell began his career by writing obituaries of some of the world's leading personages. He later went on to become Chief Justice of the Supreme Court and starred in several hit motion pictures, followed by a stellar career as a pitcher for the Los Angeles Dodgers. He received Nobel Prizes in Peace (2009), Literature (2015) and Physics (2026).

Fussell was married three times. His wives included Julia Roberts, Princess Stephanie of Monaco, and Madonna. Fussell was also noted for his unparalleled good looks and charm.

He is survived by no one worth noting. Memorial contributions may be made to the Plato G. Fussell International Scholarship Fund.

Like I said, a no-brainer. But as the imaginary achievements of my own somewhat overblown obituary plainly indicated, I was all of twenty-six years old and hadn't accomplished very much in life.

Then I had what turned out to be a highly lucrative idea that capitalized on the brand-new Internet craze. I would write short, pithy biographies of famous people who, although not terribly old, were likely to die prematurely. People like rock stars with serious drug habits or criminals on death row or inept boxers or near-sighted ski jumpers or alcoholic authors who smoked three packs a day, that sort of thing. I'd construct a database and put the information along with my obituary template on a Web site called Obit dot com. Newspapers around the world could subscribe for an outrageously exorbitant annual fee and get instant obituaries seconds after these death-prone celebrities had met their Maker, thus completely eliminating the need for obit writers. I had nothing to lose. The whole enterprise cost me exactly $2,500, which I borrowed from my father, and most of that was spent designing the Web site and obtaining a mailing list. When it came time to pay him back a year later, I presented him with a check for $10,000.

It was an immediate triumph. Within weeks, I had over two thousand subscribers and the list was growing rapidly. No one wanted to be left out. No one wanted the competition to get there first. People were dying to sign up, no pun intended. Money flowed in and my bank account grew so fast I had to employ a business manager, a stockbroker and a Beverly Hills accountant. That summer, I hired a few college kids at minimum wage to complete and update the database and I raked in the profits without having to lift a finger. In 1994, I was interviewed by *Fortune* magazine. Later that year, I sold the business to an Australian media conglomerate for $16,000,000.

Suddenly I was rich. Rich, handsome and available.

Though my sudden wealth relieved me of all financial anxieties, it left me with quite a lot of free time—twenty-four hours a day, to be exact. Except for my parents, I had no immediate family—no wife to support, no children to raise. I disliked all sports, as I found them to be dangerous, not to mention an utter waste of time. Win, lose, tie, who cares? Nor did I much care for world travel. I have never quite understood what motivates people to leave behind the relative comfort and safety of a spacious home in a country where it is safe to drink tap water and where most people speak English, to travel for hours on end in overcrowded jets to places where one can not drink the water, where people do not speak English and where one's temporary abode for the duration is a tiny, uncomfortable hotel room with a lumpy mattress and insufficient pillows. What, I ask you, is the pleasure in that?

So, having no family, no hobbies and no travel plans, what was I to do with my time? It was then that I decided (with a little prodding from Dr. Wang) to dedicate the remainder of my life to the task of writing a ten-volume biography of America's most forgotten president.

My fascination with Millard Fillmore goes back to my childhood. My father originally came from Locke Township, New York, Fillmore's birthplace. It was here that Fillmore attended school, where he bought his first book (an English dictionary) and where he decided to become a lawyer. Many biographers have portrayed Fillmore as a weak, indecisive political animal who compromised too often on controversial issues of the day, including the spread of slavery; others applaud him for keeping the nation out of civil war. In my opinion, Fillmore, although far from flawless, was a man of strong character and tenacious spirit, a political pragmatist and, judging from his letters, a fairly affable fellow as well. Not the life of the party, not the sort of fellow who gets drunk and waltzes around with a lamp shade on his head, but a solid citizen, an honest man, a pillar of his community. Strikingly handsome as a young man, he did not smoke, imbibe alcoholic beverages or gamble, and turned down an honorary degree from Oxford because he thought himself unworthy. During his term in Congress, he introduced a bill making imprisonment for debt illegal.

I could go into detail about how he sent Admiral Perry to Japan in 1852, thus opening up the Orient to American trade, how he made the ill-advised decision to run for President again in 1856 as the nominee of a deplorable nativist political group called the Know-Nothing Party and was resoundingly defeated, how he supported Lincoln in 1860 but voted for McClellan in 1864, how he died at the age of seventy-four, bequeathing a large sum of money to a local orphanage . . .

But I won't.

Years ago, when I was but a lad, my father took our family on a trip back to his hometown. There, we retraced Fillmore's footsteps. Somehow, this experience had a profound effect upon me and I found myself becoming fascinated by this peculiar man who had risen to the presidency, only to become, over the course of time, largely forgotten by the public as well as the annals of history. Granted, I was young and impressionable then, but over the years my interest in Fillmore slowly grew, and in 1995 I set pen to paper. I would rescue poor Fillmore from historical anonymity! Millard Fillmore would live again in the hearts and minds of Americans!

Like most people of that era, Fillmore was a prolific writer of letters, long, poetic missives on any number of subjects from dairy farming to weather patterns to theological arguments. One year, I spent an entire summer in Buffalo, New York (where Fillmore once lived and practiced law), going through his correspondence, which was housed in the Buffalo and Erie County Historical Society.

What fascinated me the most was the four-year period Fillmore spent between wives, shortly after leaving the White House. His first wife, Abigail Powers, passed away in 1853, following a bout of pneumonia and it was not until 1858 that Fillmore married his second wife, Caroline Carmichael McIntosh, an Albany widow. He was fifty-eight at the time. For some reason there is a distinct paucity of personal correspondence between 1854 and 1856, and the few missives that do exist are somewhat desolate in tone. Apparently, Fillmore was thrown into a sort of mild depression after Abigail passed away and traveled abroad for some time. He became something of a lonely eccentric at this stage in his life, although his political career remained active. I admit his letters spoke to me. I felt a certain kinship with the man. Teppelman had been on the lookout for more letters to and from Fillmore during that particular time period, but had not managed to turn up very much of true significance.

Nine years later, I was deeply involved in *Volume One: The Early, Early Years*, the book that covers his ancestors, his mother's pregnancy and historical events that transpired during Fillmore's time in the womb (eight months, two weeks and nine days). After so many years of research concerning all aspects of Fillmoredania, I felt I knew Millard Fillmore as if he were a close family relation.

Chapter 11: On our fifth date, Emily

and I spent a charming afternoon and early evening exploring the huge pharmaceutical department of my local Sav-On, which is not only open twenty-four hours, seven days a week including Christmas and Thanksgiving, but also claims to have the largest assortment of over-the-counter drugs and pharmaceutical products in all of Southern California. Fifteen complete aisles of every medication under the sun is really quite an impressive inventory. We began in the section entitled "Digestion" and worked our merry way through the endless aisles past "Oral Hygiene," "Feminine Hygiene," "Expectorants," "Foot Medications," and "Bandages" and eventually ended up in "Colds and Allergies."

After a short break for dinner, we returned to Sav-On to play an amusing game we had just invented called Stump the Pharmacist, in which we both asked the druggist on duty a number of difficult questions regarding the products on his shelves. For example, would the Colgate whitener also loosen plaque, thus preventing or delaying the onset of periodontal disease? Which version of

Tylenol was most effective—the extra-strength gel caps or the extra-strength tablets? How large a dose did you have to take with alcohol to have an adverse reaction and die? How much foot powder could a person inhale before feeling ill? Was Beano the most effective product for flatulence? Did he prefer Tums to Maalox for indigestion and if so, why? Was Midol superior to Advil? Would a whole bottle of Dimetapp make an adult tipsy? And the capper—one that I thought of myself—why did ingesting Pepto-Bismol turn one's stool black?

His answer: "Are you people gonna buy something here or what?"

He had no idea. I had stumped the pharmacist!

Shortly after that, we were asked to leave the premises by two beefy, shiny-headed, unsmiling gentlemen in makeshift, ill-fitting brown security guard outfits who escorted us out the front entrance.

Just before dark, Emily pulled her lustrous black hair back, donned a pair of sunglasses and a cap and bravely ventured back inside to purchase my prize—a Fleet enema—from the same pharmacist, who, fortunately, did not seem to recognize her.

On our sixth date (once again at the park), I belatedly (and somewhat reluctantly) followed Dr. Wang's recommendation and brought Emily a mixed bouquet of cut flowers—daffodils, roses, mums and geraniums—which I purchased at the corner florist. Of course, I ingested several allergy pills prior to this adventure to prevent the inevitable deluge of mucus and phlegm that would no doubt overtake me the moment I walked into a flower store. I hurriedly made my decision and vanished from the shop before succumbing to a sneezing fit. All of which did not matter, for the flowers turned out to be a huge mistake. Although Emily was deeply touched, or at least she seemed to be, she too suffered from allergies and we both spent most of the date sneezing, wheezing, itching and attending to our watering eyes, until I finally grabbed the offending bouquet and tossed it into a garbage barrel some fifty yards from where we sat.

"My hero," Emily crooned when I returned. Then she turned

her head and sneezed five or six times in a row, thus eliminating any real prospects of physical contact on this particular occasion.

Fortunately, I had with me a vial of Visine, a small bottle of Benadryl and several unused nasal inhalers, but these did little to eliminate the problem. Phlegm and mucus, it appears, are not conducive to romance. You may quote me on that.

After the mucus was under control, Emily made a confession that took me quite by surprise.

"I think I'm in love, Fussell," she said suddenly.

I was crestfallen. Did this mean she was seeing someone else? Why hadn't she told me this before?

"With whom, not that it's any of my business," I said, trying to disguise my disappointment. "Someone from work, perhaps?"

"I think I'm falling in love with *you*, you silly goose," she said, sneezing into her tissue.

"With *me*?" I blubbered, with surprise in my tone. My fallen crest was suddenly on the rise, if that's even possible. "Me? Plato G. Fussell?"

"Yes."

"How do you know?"

"No idea," she mused. "Sparks fly whenever I'm with you."

"Sparks?"

"The earth moves when you touch me," she added. "I really can't describe it."

"Actually, the earth is constantly in a state of motion, even if it does not appear so," I pointed out.

"A figure of speech, Fussell," she said, sneezing wildly. "I just feel like I'm . . . falling in love with you."

"Ditto," said I romantically. "And gesundheit."

"Really?" she cried, taking my hand and squeezing it, not the most sanitary of gestures considering she had just sneezed into a tissue she had held in that very hand. I refrained from pointing this out because I did not wish to spoil the moment.

"You really think you're falling in love with me too, Fussell?" she asked.

"Well . . ." I began, subtly removing my hand from her grasp and wondering where the nearest antiseptic towelette might be found. "I suppose it all depends on your definition of love. Let's just say that when I see you, when I touch you, even when I think about you, which I do quite often but in a wholesome way, of course, my physiology reacts with the appropriate dispensation of hormones, in particular testosterone, to name just one, and the other bodily chemicals and neurotransmitters associated with what we commonly know as love."

"Is that a yes or a no?"

"That's a yes!" I cried. "Yes, yes, yes. A thousand times yes!"

Instead of kissing, we both accidentally sneezed in each other's face.

Two days later, I was back in Wang's office telling him about what a fiasco the flowers had been, getting quite a bit of a laugh out of him in fact. We moved on to the subject of love.

"Let me see if I have the terminology correct," I began. "Falling in love is not exactly the same as being in love. Correct?"

"Falling comes before being," Wang said. "You fall first, then you are."

"Are what?"

"You *are* in love."

"After that?"

"After that? I don't know."

"But why does one have to fall first?"

"Nobody knows."

"The fact is, falling is not a particularly pleasant sensation," I pointed out. "People get hurt falling. People can die from falling. Heck, it's a form of suicide when accomplished from a great height on purpose."

"It's a figure of speech," he explained. "Like when you say, 'I'm dying to know.' You're not really *dying* to know, because if you died what good would knowing be?"

"Excellent point," I said. "Thanks for the clarification, although my interest was primarily in the derivation of the term."

At that moment, his cordless emergency line suddenly rang. This had happened several times before and Wang either told the caller he was in the midst of a therapy session and would call back later or, if it was a true emergency—as this one appeared to be—he would beg my pardon, vacate the room and take the cordless phone with him, making sure to close the door behind him, so I would be unable to hear the conversation.

"Hold that thought," he whispered to me, cupping his hand over the receiver. "I'll be back in a second."

"Take your time," I said as he waltzed out of the room. "I'll just sit here and twiddle my thumbs for two hours, or maybe I'll write a novel, perhaps reorganize your file system . . ."

But Wang was no longer paying attention to me—he exited the office and closed the door behind him.

The call took quite some time and I found myself growing restless. I stood up and walked to the picture window, which looked out over the San Fernando Valley and the San Gabriel Mountains, which happened to be a light shade of purple that day. Quite a vista, if you like that sort of thing. Frankly, views never thrilled me that much—snowcapped mountains, landscapes, full moons, seascapes, shooting stars, sunsets—who cares? If you've seen one, you've seen them all. Yawning and more than a little bored, I went over to his floor-to-ceiling bookcase and admired his voluminous collection of books, most of them by the giants of modern psychiatry—Freud, Adler, Jung and others of that ilk—but there were a few novels as well—*Moby-Dick*, *The Sun Also Rises*, *Tender Is the Night*. I had never actually been on this side of Dr. Wang's desk before, and I wasn't sure he would like it very much if he found me there. But there was little chance of that happening—I could make out the sound of his voice still droning consolingly from the other room, though I could not make out any distinct words. The phone call dragged on for quite a while. As a rule, people in need of emergency psychiatric consultation tend to talk a lot. Unfortunately, none of Wang's patients possessed his home phone number and thus had to squeeze everything in during his working hours. Maybe it was a potential suicide. Maybe Wang would be out there for two hours or longer talking some poor soul out of jumping off the Hollywood sign. Or maybe it was Milton P.—the agoraphobe—wondering what to do because he'd run out of toilet paper.

Before returning to my side of the room, I noticed that Dr. Wang had carelessly left his notorious black notebook open on his desk. This was a temptation I could not withstand! To read Wang's confidential notes about me! To see what he really thought of me and my inane problems! To see if he was even paying any attention. Perhaps the book was filled with blank pages or insulting doodles of my face. Perhaps he was secretly writing a screenplay while I bared my soul twice a week. No, I was probably just being paranoid. Wang was the picture of professionalism and always had been. Whether or not he harbored any real affection for me, I didn't know for certain, and even if he did, it would probably have been unprofessional of him to admit it. On the other hand, I felt nothing but sincere gratitude toward him. He was my oracle, my sounding board, my salvation. I was completely and utterly dependent upon him and had been for nearly ten years.

Nonetheless, this did not lessen my curiosity about the contents of his notebook.

Of course, if he caught me, if he strolled back into the room while I browsed casually through his notes, he would probably wring my neck, but it was worth the risk, and I was in a mischievous mood. What the hell? I was just about to lean in closer to have a good look at his handwritten notes when I spotted the picture of his recently estranged wife in the silver standing frame on his desk, the one he had clutched to his chest so dramatically two weeks ago. At first, I did not believe my eyes. My mouth fell open. I blinked. Then I nearly fainted.

Chapter 12: Yes, well, this was, as they

say, a fine kettle of fish.

After all those agonizing years of celibacy, after years of barely being able to *speak* to a female, after years of total deprivation and misery, after all those YEARS OF LIVING HELL, yours truly had to fall in love with his psychiatrist's wife.

Of all the women, in all the towns, in all the world . . .

Just my luck.

On first viewing the photograph, I was completely mystified. Were my eyes deceiving me? Was I seeing hallucinations of Emily's face in this frame on Wang's desk? Granted, she had been in my thoughts every waking hour of my life of late, and granted I had become somewhat obsessed with her, but was the human mind capable of such a bizarre transposition? A few blinks of the eyes and mystified soon turned to shock when it became clear that this was no hallucination, this was indeed a snapshot of Emily Thorndyke, my Emily, in that silver frame and that she was indeed the wife of my psychiatrist. Shock slowly metamorphosed into confusion. How could this be? A thousand thoughts raced through my brain. For one thing, Emily had told me her last name was Thorndyke; Dr. Wang's last name was, obviously, Wang. Had her last name been Wang, I would have thought twice, even though there were probably plenty of Wangs in the area. Had she lied to me? Perhaps. Or maybe, like many professional women, she had maintained her maiden name rather than go through the tiresome bureaucracy of changing stationary, driver's license, credit cards and the like.

Or even more absurd, did she have a twin sister? Were there two identical Emily Thorndykes wandering about the earth?

Not likely.

Soon more became clear to me—for starters, Emily's presence at Wang's recent autumn picnic and our subsequent chance meeting in Wang's office building. It had not even occurred to me at the picnic that she might have been a patient, let alone Wang's wife, because like me, she had been several hundred yards away from the area in which the picnic was actually taking place, and I never even saw her speak to or make contact with Wang. They had not, it seemed, even arrived in the same car, but I had arrived late so maybe they had. Perhaps they were already separated at that point and both Emily and Wang were at the same park on the same day purely by coincidence? I don't recall Wang ever mentioning his wife by name and I never knew Wang had a dog. In all those years of therapy, he had never mentioned that he possessed a pet of any sort and, to the best of my memory, he had not even made the slightest canine-related remark in my presence. In retrospect, this was peculiar, as I had on numerous occasions referred to my dachshund, Isabella.

But there were other anomalies that were more pressing. Had Emily, for example, lied to me about maintaining an office in the same building that housed Wang's office? Had she, in fact, been up to see him on that day we met by chance in the office building?

As you can well imagine, I had a million questions.

None of which I could actually ask, for the moment I sat back down in the Barcelona chair, in something closely resembling a state of mental paralysis. Dr. Wang returned to the office, sat down at the desk, put his cordless phone receiver back on its cradle and apologized profusely for the long intrusion, assuring me that I would not be billed for the missing time in my session, approximately ten minutes.

"Sorry," Wang said. "Just a compulsive who wanted me to tell him how many times he needed to knock on wood."

"Wock on knood?"

"Are you nervous about something, Fussell?"

"Suovren?" I replied. "Um, no, not at all. Why?"

"You're doing the word thing again."

"Sorry," I said, realizing that I would have to be more careful, lest I make him suspicious. "So what did you tell him? The compulsive?"

"About what?"

"Knocking on wood. How many times?"

"Twelve."

"Why twelve?" I asked. "Did Freud recommend twelve?"

"We haggled," Wang said. "He started at eight, I started at sixteen and we met at twelve."

"Ah."

"Now where were we?" he asked, thumbing through his notes.

"Ummm . . ."

Wang looked up. "My God, Fussell," he remarked. "You look like you've just seen a ghost! Your face is white as a death mask. Are you all right?"

"It's nothing," I said with as much composure as I could muster.

Suddenly, I had some difficulty actually looking him directly in the eye. He was no longer just Dr. Wang, Psychiatrist. He was now Dr. Wang, Husband of My Girlfriend. Dr. Wang, Cuckold. Dr. Wang, the Competition. I felt queasy.

"Don't hold back, Fussell," he coaxed. "Whatever it is, you must tell me."

"Well, I . . ."

"Does it have something to do with your new girlfriend . . . I'm sorry, I seem to have forgotten her name."

"Did I ever tell you her name?" I asked, suddenly uneasy.

"Come to think of it, I don't believe you did," Wang said, searching through his notes again. "What is it?"

"What is what?"

"Her name. What is your new girlfriend's name?"

I stammered for a moment, then glanced furtively at the bookcase. "Ahab," I said.

"You're dating a woman named Ahab?" he asked. "That's usually a man's name, isn't it?"

"Her father was related somehow to, um, Herman Melville," I said, making it up quite ineptly as I went along. "Her sister's name is Ishmael." I was on a roll. Would he see through this nonsense?

Apparently not. Wang evidently found the Ishmael business hilarious, for he began to laugh hysterically. He had a high-pitched staccato laugh that was somewhat annoying.

Meanwhile, the same questions kept nagging at me—should I tell Wang the truth right here and now? That I was falling in love with *his wife*? His recently estranged soon-to-be-ex wife? The wife that had caused him to weep uncontrollably in front of me, a patient? The wife that had hurt him so deeply? And if I did tell him everything, what would the repercussions be? Would he shoot me? Hit me on the head with a blunt object? Challenge me to a round of fisticuffs? Perhaps a duel?

No, that was not Wang's style. He would drop me as a patient.

Which was, to me, a fate worse than death. I couldn't possibly function in the real world without Wang. He was my anchor. He knew everything there was to know about me. Well, almost.

I would have to keep lying.

Wang stopped laughing, regained his composure and looked

again at his notes: "We were talking about you and your relationship with . . . Ahab," he continued, still chuckling slightly.

"Were we?"

"Yes. You had been telling me about the flowers and how you both declared your love for one another, or rather, how she had declared her love for you and you had said 'ditto.' Remember?"

"Right."

"Do you think 'ditto' was maybe a little impersonal?"

"Perhaps."

"Any regrets?"

"Not really."

"Can you actually say the words 'I love you'?"

"Of course. I'm not verbally impaired."

"Let me hear you then."

"Why?"

"Because I don't think you can do it."

"Of course I can."

"But I thought you don't believe in love," Wang reminded me. "You've told me that a hundred times."

"That doesn't mean I can't say it," I said.

"Then do it."

"I don't want to."

"Because you can't."

"Oh no?" I said wearily. "I love you. I love you, I love you, I love you. There. Happy now?"

"Well done, Fussell. I'm deeply touched."

"Ha ha, ho ho," I said sarcastically.

"Do you wish to continue in this vein?"

I thought it over for a moment or two. This vein was a dead end. It had clotted shut. In any case, there was something else I desperately needed to tell him, but how? Would he catch on?

"She's married," I said suddenly, just blurting it out with my eyes shut. "My girlfriend is married. I, um . . . just found out."

This threw him for a loop. Wang blinked once or twice, and for a brief moment, I thought perhaps he had made the connection.

"Oh," he said. "Really? That certainly complicates matters a bit, now doesn't it?"

"Actually, she and her husband are separated," I said. "She's filed for divorce. Or he has, I forget which."

"Oh, well then, you're probably on safe ground," Wang concluded.

"I am?"

"Sure. Did their breakup happen prior to your involvement with her?"

"Yes," I said. "I believe so."

"No problem then," Wang assured me. "Smooth sailing. Her problems with her husband are not your concern. You're not responsible at all."

"Are you sure?" I asked, a bit dumbfounded. If he knew the truth, would his opinion have been the same?

"Absolutely."

"So carnal relations would be okay too?"

"Sure. Why not?"

"So I have your blessing then?"

"Why in God's name would you need *my* blessing?"

"It would relieve some of the guilt," I said, suddenly realizing that I was treading on dangerous ground. "Humor me."

"Fine. Live it up, Fussell," he said, oblivious. "You deserve it."

Chapter 13: I left Dr. Wang's office that afternoon in something of a stupor and found myself walking aimlessly down the corridors of his floor, searching in vain for an elevator that was actually located two steps to the right of his office. Once I got my bearings, I stopped at the men's room, splashed some cold water on my face and, with my ever-present bottle of distilled water, swallowed a Xanax.

Somehow, I managed to float into the next down elevator, but forgot to exit at the lobby and went up three floors before realizing my error. Five minutes later, on the way out of Wang's building, I checked the office roster. As it turned out, Emily had not lied to me about her profession or its location. There was indeed a Thorndyke Interiors listed. I assumed that this was the name of her business.

But what was I to say when I next saw her? That I knew she was married? That I knew she was married to my psychiatrist? That I knew she was also a former patient of my psychiatrist? That I knew she was breaking the poor man's heart? Obviously, she had not been entirely straightforward that first day in the park when she told me she was not a "madam" but rather a "mademoiselle." She was, technically speaking, still a missus or, if you will, a ms., for the divorce papers had not yet been officially signed, although she probably had been separated from Wang at the time of our initial meeting.

On the other hand, had she been truthful and told me she was a married woman, I probably would not have pursued her any further. I'm not a home-wrecker. I have no wish to come between a man and his wife. I'm also not keen on being hunted down by enraged vengeful husbands carrying revolvers or recently honed kitchen cutlery (not that Wang struck me as that sort of fellow).

There had also been no wedding ring on Emily's finger when I first encountered her. Perhaps she was on the prowl for romantic attachments and had therefore taken it off. Or, perhaps she had simply removed the ring to avoid losing it during her Frisbee-throwing sport that afternoon.

The question was: Did I want to confront her about any of this?

Being the nonconfrontational type, the answer was simple.

No.

And even if I were the confrontational type and even if I had the guts to challenge her, what guarantee would I have that Emily wouldn't immediately confess everything to Dr. Wang, who would then probably be compelled to drop me as a patient, citing conflict of interest and irrational hatred of a client, among other things?

Naturally, I was also curious about precisely what mental disorder Dr. Wang had been treating Emily for when she had been his patient. Was she really deeply nuts or just irritatingly neurotic like me? Psychopath or phobic? Bipolar or multiple personality disorder? Compulsive or obsessive? Or all of the above?

But before I even had a chance to see Emily again, I found this letter in my mail receptacle when I returned home:

To whom it may concern:

This letter is to certify that my patient, Emily Thorndyke, is in excellent physical health and presently has no contagious or communicable diseases. She recently tested negative for HIV, hepatitis A, hepatitis B, hepatitis C, syphilis, gonorrhea, herpes simplex, herpes complex, conjunctivitis, cholera, typhoid fever, bubonic plague, ebola and the Hanta virus.

Sincerely yours,

Dr. Rajaim K. Gupta, Internal Medicine

Cedars-Sinai Medical Center

We were, it seemed, cleared for takeoff. Hell, I even had her husband's blessing. How painfully ironic.

But what was I to do?

Obviously, I was emotionally torn, to say the least. Could I survive without Emily? Did I truly love her? Did I even know what love was? Did anybody? And, given my anxiety, how long would it be before I could even meet another woman with whom I shared so much? How many beautiful neurotics with allergies, compulsions and impeccable personal hygiene could one meet in one lifetime? How many women walked around in public wearing black business suits and stripes of zinc oxide on their noses? Perhaps I would never meet anyone like Emily ever again. Perhaps I would perish a lonely, forgotten old man. Perhaps I would even die prematurely from melancholy and a depressing lack of companionship.

On the other side of the coin, the possibility of losing Dr. Wang was unthinkable. He was my moral support, my confidant, my very lifeline to society. No one, I was certain, could ever replace him. Besides, I had known Wang for almost ten years, while my acquaintance with Emily Thorndyke was no more than a month old.

After giving the matter many hours of deep thought, after staying up nights and pacing in my apartment, after consulting Isabella, whose only response was to raise a sympathetic paw to my lap, I decided that the most prudent course of action would be for me to simply stop seeing Emily. Sure, I had intense feelings for her, but the state of my sanity (such as it was) depended to a great extent on the ministrations of Dr. Wang. The whole enterprise had become too complicated, and eventually I was certain the truth would come out. But since I lacked the courage to actually notify Emily of my decision over the phone or in person, I took the coward's route and simply refrained from calling her. When she called me and left plaintive or sarcastic messages on my answering machine, I refrained from returning her calls. I knew this was horribly rude and inconsiderate of me, possibly even cruel, but I was completely paralyzed. What if I told her we were through and she wept in anguish? What if she became violent? Suicidal? How would I even word such a dreadful confession without mentioning my knowledge of her relationship with Wang? What sort of lie could I concoct? Prevarication was not one of my strong points.

"Are you crazy?" Dr. Wang asked several days later, when I told him about my decision to end my relationship with Ahab.

"You're asking me? You're supposed to be the doctor."

"A rhetorical question," Wang said. "Your decision to suddenly break up with Ahab strikes me as a bit unhinged."

"Unhinged?" I repeated. "Is that a medical term?"

"Stop beating around the bush, Fussell," he said, a slight tone of exasperation in his voice. "Answer the question."

"My professional diagnosis is yes, I am definitely somewhat crazy," I said. "Otherwise, why in God's name would I be seeing you twice a week?"

"You're not crazy, Fussell," he said. "Not in the usual sense of the term. You simply have some neuroses."

"Some? I'm compulsive, obsessive, paranoid . . ."

"Yes, but look at it this way: How different is a neurotic compulsion from a normal religious ritual? Both involve seemingly random requirements. Both have the same ends—to ward off the indiscriminate wrath of a Superior Being, which may or may not even exist. True?"

"Well . . ."

"How diffcrent," he continued, "is obsession from passion? Was Louis Pasteur obsessive or passionate? Marie Curie? The Wright Brothers? Had Orville and Wilbur not been obsessive, would we have the airplane today?"

"Well . . ."

"And as for paranoia," he went on, "in this age of incurable viruses, random terrorism, identity theft and do-it-yourself wire tapping, you'd have to be crazy *not* to be paranoid."

I didn't know quite what to say. Wang had never presented it to me in quite that light before. Perhaps he had read a new tract or heard a recent revisionist lecture on the subject. It struck me that if he put forth this thesis to all of his patients, he would soon put himself out of business.

"Just a theory, mind you," Wang conceded. "A different perspective, if you will. An attempt to define your problems less drastically."

"Be that as it may," I said. "Crazy or not, I still think it prudent that I break off relations with Ahab."

"Fussell," he said, leaning forward, "This is the first woman you've had any contact with since your wife left you. She's clearly in love with you and you, in your own peculiar way, are clearly in love with her. How can you just drop her like this?"

"As you know, I don't really believe in the concept of love," I said.

"Fine, call it what you will," Wang responded. "There's clearly a certain chemistry between you too. You must continue."

"I can't."

"Tell me why," he said. "You've never withheld personal information from me before."

I couldn't think of anything to say. Should I fabricate something or tell him the truth? No, the truth was obviously out of the question, although it occurred to me then that if I was too mysterious about it, he might put two and two together. Unlikely, but possible.

"She's an atheist," I said finally.

"So?"

"I'm an agnostic."

"So?"

"Our basic philosophies of life are different," I explained, making it up as I went along. "We're religiously incompatible."

"That's it?"

"In a nutshell."

"For that ridiculous reason alone you're breaking up with this lovely woman?" Wang asked.

"Yes."

"Maybe you should convert to atheism," he advised humorously. "Or she could convert to agnosticism."

"You think this is easy?" I said, feigning anger. "It's very difficult."

"Because you're *making* it difficult, Fussell," he cried. "Surely, you know you will miss her terribly. Think about what you're losing here."

"I am," I said. "I long to be with her. I adore her."

This was true. Though I recognized all this as a simple alignment of cells, creating a response in some nook of my neocortex, I missed her terribly. I could not sleep at night—images of Emily appeared in my head whenever I closed my eyes. During the day, when I sat down to work on my Fillmore biography, I could not concentrate for more than ten minutes at a stretch. Half the time I wrote the word "Emily" where the word "Millard" was supposed to be. On the street, every raven-haired woman I saw reminded me of her. I thought about her during every waking hour.

"Then call her, man!" Wang implored. "Make a date. Tell her your concerns regarding your religious incompatibility, however preposterous they may be."

"I can't."

"You must."

"Impossible."

"Sometimes I really don't understand you at all, Fussell," he said, throwing up his hands. "Do you want to be a lonely old bachelor all your life? Do you want to grow old alone? This is your big chance to be happy. The opportunity might not come again so soon. Seize the day, man!"

How interesting, I thought. Wang was making the very same arguments I had made to myself. He was quite persuasive, but then he didn't really know of whom he was talking. Had I revealed everything to him, I wonder what his advice would have been then. Fortunately, the alarm bell rang, signifying that the session was at an end. What a relief! Wang rose and walked me to the door.

"How is your divorce going?" I asked him offhandedly.

"Lousy."

"I'm sorry to hear that."

"Thank you, Fussell," he said. "You're most kind."

No, I thought, I am anything but kind. I am a cad, a fiend, a blackguard, a miserable louse.

"By the way—I believe you said your wife was a former patient."

"Yes."

"What were you treating her for?"

"Why do you ask?"

"Idle curiosity."

"I can't tell you that, Fussell," he said. "That's confidential doctor-patient information."

"Of course," I muttered. "Sorry for asking."

At this juncture, perhaps it would be appropriate to illuminate the exact history of my long association with Dr. Wang, a relationship I credit with, among other things, preserving my mental stability.

In 1994, shortly after selling my obituary database, I suffered something of a mild nervous breakdown. With my business gone, I had no profession, no hobbies, no motivation to get out of bed in the morning, nothing to take up my time, nobody to see but my parents. As a result I became something of a recluse, spending all my time at home reading, sterilizing my flatware or vacuuming my apartment several times a day. As you can well imagine, my various compulsions and eccentricities flourished in this claustrophobic atmosphere. Shortly thereafter, I began to develop certain physical symptoms—insomnia, night sweats, a tremor, fatigue, facial tics, occasional heart palpitations and a distinct loss of appetite. I felt as if I were falling into an abyss and that, if left unchecked, my destiny would be to develop into an agoraphobe, a prospect that frankly terrified me out of my wits.

During my monthly physical examination, Dr. Rothstein, one of my six internists, delicately suggested that I consult a psychiatrist and recommended Dr. Wang. After I put up an unconvincing protest that I was not in need of psychiatric help, Rothstein gave me Wang's phone number anyway and sent me on my way with a prescription for Prozac.

Over the following few weeks I did not appreciably improve in spite of the Prozac, so I gave in and made an appointment with Dr. Wang. At first, I was reluctant to admit to any neurotic problems, but the involuntary eruptions of spoonerisms and backward spelling soon gave me away, not to mention my habit of spraying the arms of his Barcelona chair with Lysol prior to each session.

After the first few months, I actually began to look forward to our weekly meetings because I found it soothing to have someone to converse with other than my parents and Isabella, who, although attentive, rarely responded in any coherent way. Wang was not only my confidant, he was becoming my sole companion and I soon found myself increasing my appointments to two per week.

As I mentioned before, it was Wang himself who convinced me to write a biography of Millard Fillmore. At several of my initial sessions, I had spoken nostalgically of my childhood trip to my father's hometown, and of my longtime interest in this unfortunate, unheralded statesman. Wang, noting that I had nothing with which to occupy my time besides worrying, cleaning and sterilizing, thought that writing a definitive tome on the thirteenth president would be therapeutic for me. He was right. I soon became obsessive about Fillmore and, to this day, I still am. I looked upon the project as no less than a significant contribution to the annals of American history. I would resurrect Fillmore's flagging reputation and, in the process, justify my own existence for posterity. And, as an added but unexpected benefit of my work on Fillmore's biography, I actually made a close friend—Teppelman.

Over time, I grew to trust Wang and eventually gave in to the temptation to tell him all about my odd little problems, many of which he had already discerned from merely watching me in action. Although I grew to comprehend my neuroses more, I was unable for the most part to abandon them completely. Yet, the more aware I became of my symptoms, the more I was able to confront them.

I had been making some steady progress on a number of fronts with Dr. Wang, when our many months of work were completely nullified by the catastrophic demise of my disastrous marriage. After that, it was, as they say, back to square one. The rock of Sisyphus had tumbled down the long, steep mountain and I was not exactly overjoyed at the prospect of pushing it all the way back up. But Dr. Wang was indefatigable. He coaxed and cajoled and nurtured me back to a semblance of mental health, until I was able to once again make romantic contact with a woman. Emily was living proof of my considerable progress.

And now, here I was again, back at the bottom of the mountain.

After three more endless, heartbreaking days of total separation from Emily, I could endure it no longer. In spite of my determination, I just could not prevail over the rising tide of hormonal molecules that was blasting away relentlessly in my gray matter. I was becoming desperate. I had to hear her voice.

Thus, as Emily was about to leave another message on my answering machine, I impulsively snatched up the receiver.

"Where the devil have you been, Fussell?" she demanded, with a detectable trace of impatience in her voice. "I've called you five times."

"Yes, I know. I'm so sorry. Really I am," I said.

"You're not giving me the cold shoulder, are you?"

"No, of course not."

"I've been worried sick about you."

"My apologies," I said. "I've been . . . ill. With the . . . flu."

"Gastric or sinus?"

"Both, actually," I lied. I was getting good at lying. Perhaps I had been a con artist in a former life. Unfortunately, I didn't believe in reincarnation.

"You poor boy. You should have told me. I could have brought you some chicken soup. What were your symptoms?"

"I was primarily tired."

"How do you know it's not narcolepsy?"

"Because I'm not tired anymore," I said.

"It could be latent."

"How do you mean?"

"Like malaria. Comes and goes."

"Do you think I should have it checked out?"

"I certainly would."

I was suddenly terrified that I may actually have something serious, something terminal, perhaps, something truly ghastly until I remembered that I had fabricated the whole story.

"I assume you have a doctor?" she asked.

"Are you kidding? I have twelve doctors, but two of them are podiatrists."

"Well, go see one of them then," she said.

"But my feet are fine."

"See one of the others, I meant."

"For what?"

"Fatigue! You said you were tired, didn't you? If I were you, I'd

start with an endocrinologist and work my way up to gastroen-
terologist."

"Really?"

"Or perhaps you could start with a neurologist."

"Okay."

"Do you have a neurologist?"

"Of course," I said. "Doesn't everybody?"

A few moments later, by pretending there was someone knocking on my door, I actually managed to hang up on Emily without
asking her out on a date. Would I call her again? No, I couldn't.
Somehow, I would have to survive this longing I had for her. Willpower was all it would take. Willpower and stamina. Willpower,
stamina and perhaps some of those mind-numbing little yellow
foot soldiers I kept in my medicine cabinet. I would fight chemicals
with chemicals, that's what I would do! I would change my phone
number as well. Maybe I would even move to another address.
Change my name. Get a job in a hardware store. Grow a beard.
Hell's bells, I had to do something.

Chapter 14: In spite of my profound

appreciation for Wang's feelings and my determination to do the right thing, my resolve to desist from seeing Emily again lasted an awe-inspiring two more days. What fortitude! What strength! I was so groggy from sleepless nights and the effects of the various mind-numbing medications that littered my night table that I could barely dial her number without a magnifying glass. The trembling hands did not help much either, but a Xanax quickly solved that problem. And so I gave in to temptation and called her. We agreed to meet for dinner at a nearby Indian restaurant that served an excellent, extra-spicy saag aloo, then walk back to my house for a cognac, although neither of us actually drank liquor. But then I didn't eat saag aloo either, as I had grown quite fond of the lining of my esophagus.

Later, after taking Emily on a tour of my roomy abode, I made us both a cup of chamomile tea, and we settled down on the sofa. I handed her a small folder of papers.

"What's this?" she asked.

"My redical mecords."

She gave me a slightly lascivious smile. "Guess you've got more in mind for tonight than just a cup of tea," she said, nudging me gently in the ribs.

"Am I being too . . . drawrof?" I asked nervously.

"Not at all," she said. "But let me peruse these first. Just to be safe."

My medical records were easily as impressive as hers, although I didn't *really* believe I was in such perfect health. I had occasional aches and pains in various critical places, which were probably polyps or lesions that had been overlooked by the pathologists and would one day evolve into malignant tumors. And of course, short of an angiogram, there was really no way to tell if my arteries were clogged or not.

There was something I desperately needed to ask her before our sexual congress got under way. As no good segue presented itself, I just blurted it out.

"You don't have a sin twister, do you?"

"Am I making you nervous?"

"Just a little," I admitted. "Do you? Have a twin sister?"

"Why do you ask?"

"Just curious."

"No, I don't have a twin sister. I would have told you. It's just me, Frank and Udo. Is it important?"

"Not really," I said. "Ever been treated by a psychiatrist?"

"Why is that relevant?"

"Kind of an addendum to the physical report," I lied. "Mental stability is important in a relationship."

"Yes," she said. "I was treated by a psychiatrist some years ago."

"For what exactly?"

"Anxiety, obsessive-compulsive behavior, paranoia, nothing terribly serious. How about you?"

"Ditto on all counts," I said. "I'm also incredibly timid, especially around attractive women."

"I couldn't help but notice that," she said playfully. "It's definitely one of your more agreeable charms, Fussell. The handsome shy guy. Very, very sexy."

As for our imminent sexual relations, I admit to having been a trifle hesitant at the prospect. Who wouldn't have been? There was, for one thing, the blatant immorality of sleeping with someone else's wife and the even greater depravity of sleeping with the wife of someone you were not only acquainted with but deeply connected to. But then Wang himself had told me that it was not immoral, which didn't really count because he lacked significant details. Of course, if he ever found out about Emily and me, the fact that he had given me his blessing would be utterly meaningless. Then again, there was the distinct possibility (as voiced by Wang himself) that their marriage would soon be over. After all, they had separated weeks ago and Emily had filed for divorce. Technically, I was in the clear.

Beyond the excellent possibility of overwhelming guilt on my part, there was the factor of plain old sexual panic. Not only was I worried that I would be committing a heinous transgression and that somehow Dr. Wang would find out about us, I was also concerned that, after all those years of celibacy, my sexual apparatus might have forgotten how to perform the task in the proper way. Moreover, after consulting my *Physicians' Desk Reference*, I was distressed to learn that several of the medications I took regularly had side effects involving a lowering of the libido. I could feel my anxiety steadily building. I began to sweat profusely and my salivary glands temporarily stopped producing saliva. I was slightly flustered and my heart was thumping. I moved away from her and wiped my brow with a handkerchief.

"You aren't afraid of having sex with me, are you?" Emily said.

"Afraid? Who me? Nertainly cot," I said nervously.

"I don't bite, but I will if you want me to. Just tell me where."

"I'm afraid I'm fairly conservative," I said. "No biting, no whips, no chains, no cunny follars."

"You *do* believe in taking off your clothes, I hope."

"As long as the heat is on and there are no dold crafts."

"Do you feel any cold drafts now?"

"No."

Since we were at my house, heat regulation was not really an issue as I always kept the thermostat at the correct temperature. The windows were closed, walls filled with multiple layers of insulation, weather stripping in place. Once, during a particularly frigid winter, I wore a wool sweater, wool socks, earmuffs and a pair of tight long johns during intercourse with my first wife. She was not amused.

"I must warn you," I said. "I'm not particularly fond of perspiration."

"So you don't like to move around a lot?"

"If possible," I said. "Nor do I like to physically exert myself too much."

"Don't worry," Emily said. "I promise I won't give you a heart attack. Too much friction down there, and I usually get a heat rash anyway."

"We'll keep some baby powder handy just in case," I suggested.

"Fine," Emily said. "Anything else?"

"The pissionary mosition would be my preference," I said. "Doggy style repulses me. Not that I dislike dogs. On the contrary. I—"

"I can live with the missionary position," Emily interrupted. "Just don't crush me."

"Foreplay?" I asked.

"Ten minutes usually does it for me."

"Moderate or intense?"

"Moderation is my middle name."

"Ditto."

"Thank God," she said. "My ex-husband always insisted on at least forty-five minutes of intense foreplay. Can you imagine? Forty-five minutes! Sex was not meant to be an Olympic decathlon, for God's sakes. By the time we were done with the fore-play I was too exhausted to finish."

"Your ex-husband?" I asked, feigning surprise. "You never told me you'd been married."

"Of course I did," she claimed. I noticed again that no rings adorned her fingers.

"No, I don't think so."

"Well, actually he's my soon-to-be-ex husband," she said. "A shrink. A shrink with a few interesting psychological issues, if you ask me."

"You never told me this before."

"It's not my favorite topic," Emily replied. "Does it matter?"

"Not really," said I. "What kinds of psychological issues, if I may ask?"

"Well, for one thing, he liked to wear my shoes," Emily said. "Mostly high heels but there was one orange pair of flats—"

"You're kidding!" I exclaimed, trying to picture Wang in a pair of lady's shoes. "What else?"

"I really would rather not talk about it," she said. "It's water under the bridge, or water over the dam, I never know which."

"But—"

"Can we please drop it?"

Dying of curiosity, I was extremely reluctant to change the subject, but agreed to desist anyway. There would be plenty of time to learn more, although it occurred to me that it might be counter-productive for a patient to find out too much about his psychiatrist's more personal idiosyncrasies. What if Wang was crazier than I was, only better at hiding it? What if his counseling was actually making me worse? No matter how you sliced it, it was a can of worms (pardon the mixed metaphor).

After that, we checked and double-checked a series of condoms, which Emily had brought along, by blowing them up and filling them with water, just to make sure they were in good working condition, no leakage or weak spots. Both of us took a megadose of tetracycline just in case one of our physicians had made an error. Plus I insisted we each take a long hot shower with a special surgical soap. By coincidence, she had brought her own bottle of the identical brand. In spite of all these precautions, I decided to put on not one but two condoms.

"You don't mind if I leave my socks on?" I inquired.

"As long as the place you leave them on is your feet," she purred.

"Of course. Where else?"

"You'd be amazed."

"I don't think I want to know," I said. "So may I leave them on?"

"By all means. Whatever turns you on."

"I'm not getting cold feet, no pun intended," I joked. "My circulation isn't what it used to be."

"You sound like a newspaper publisher."

It took me a second to get the witticism. "Excellent play on words," I observed. "Very clever indeed."

"Anything else I should know before we start?" she asked.

"I don't like whip cream on my body," I told her. "It could go bad."

"Got it. No whip cream."

"Or chocolate sauce."

"Do you have any whip cream or chocolate sauce in the fridge?"

"No."

"Then it's not a problem."

I realized suddenly that I was being a bit selfish, telling her about my preferences without asking about hers.

"How about you?" I asked. "Any particular likes or dislikes regarding the sex act?"

"I should warn you, I'm a screamer," she confessed. "I hope your walls are thick and well insulated."

"They are."

"Don't be too rough."

"Who, me, rough?"

"Good," she said. "I tend to bruise easily."

And so, against my better judgment, Emily Thorndyke and I had our first sexual escapade. Though I will refrain from going into a blow-by-blow summary of the event (this is, after all, none of your business), it was really quite sublime. Her body was magnificent, her technique superb, her moaning first rate (two octaves at least). She was tender, gentle, unselfish, sensitive and knew many excellent places upon which to smear baby oil. Her sense of rhythm was downright uncanny. I could see why Wang was so upset at losing her. She was a treasure!

Of course, right after we finished, I was immediately wracked with a stupefying sense of guilt.

As for my own performance after all those years of monkhood? I don't mean to be immodest, but I was really quite proficient if you must know. I even managed to get both condoms on in less than thirty seconds. I broke my record for foreplay—nine minutes! And I only slid out of bed twice, which was excusable considering that practically my entire body was covered in baby oil by the time we were halfway through. Of course, once I fell under Emily's spell I was a complete goner. Any nervousness or anxiety I may have had about impotence or dirty socks or halitosis or the state of my stock portfolio or Wang or whatever vanished the moment we began our initial caresses. Thank God for those devilish hormones! I even opened a window after we were done! Drafts be damned!

I couldn't wait to tell Dr. Wang all about it.

Chapter 15: To say the least, this was

becoming an increasingly turbulent period of my life. A year ago, turbulence would have been a missing handkerchief or a fifty-cent overcharge on my dry cleaning bill. But now, my life was in utter chaos—there were still missing handkerchiefs as well as fifty-cent overcharges at the dry cleaner *and* I was sleeping regularly with my psychiatrist's wife.

And the turmoil was about to increase.

Several days after consummating my relationship with Emily, my friend Teppelman called me with incredible news—while absentee-bidding in an estate auction held in San Francisco, he had purchased an extremely mysterious letter that had been sent by a certain "L.M." to Millard Fillmore, dated February, 1854. This was, as you will recall, the period during which Fillmore was romantically unattached to any female and prior to his first romantic encounter with his second wife, Caroline.

I immediately made my way over to Teppelman's dark, untidy store and, with bated breath, took the yellowed, fragile letter in my trembling hands and began to devour the contents. The return address on the envelope was 210 East Fiftieth Street, New York City and it was addressed to Fillmore's home in Buffalo, New York (how this letter had gotten to an estate auction in San Francisco was most curious). The ink was a dark purple hue, a popular shade in those days, according to Teppelman, who also identified the quill as one of a variety commonly used in the northeastern United States at the time. I could hardly believe what I was reading:

> *My Dearest Millard,*
>
> *I can barely express to you the depth of my gratitude for your splendid hospitality of last weekend following my performance. Can you believe that I, renowned for my mastery of theatrical speech, have been struck utterly speechless by you, my dear Millard? Your tenderness, your sensitivity, your strength and moral turpitude leave me breathless! If this is not love I do not know what love is. But I do know what love is and this, I am positive beyond all doubt, is indeed love. Love of an exceedingly high order, love of a celestial kind rarely found on this sodden, pedestrian Earth of ours. I so look forward to our next encounter and hope I am not being too bold when I refer to you, lovingly, as Mon Amour!*
>
> *With all my Love,*
> *Your L.M.*

Needless to say, I almost jumped out of my underwear when I finished reading this extraordinary missive. I had to read it twice more just to make certain my eyes were not deceiving me. This was most mysterious! Most intriguing! I congratulated Teppelman for having found something of such earth-shattering historical significance. As usual, Teppelman was quite impassive and offered to sell the letter to me for a mere $2,000.

"Only two thousand?" I remarked. "I would pay a king's ransom for such a piece of history. Ten times a king's ransom!"

"Really?" Teppelman said. "Is it too late to renegotiate?"

"A deal is a deal, as my father always says," said I.

"How much exactly is a king's ransom?" Teppelman inquired.

"You'd have to ask a king," I said. "And I'm afraid I don't know any personally. But I'll throw in an extra one hundred dollars, what do you say?"

"An extra two hundred would be better."

"Two hundred it is!" said I, writing out a check for the amount. I handed it to him. I was in a magnanimous mood.

"So who's this L.M.?" he asked.

"I haven't the slightest idea," I confessed. "I'll have to look over my notes, perhaps L.M. will appear somewhere."

"I never actually thought of Millard Fillmore as being an especially tempestuous guy," Teppelman said.

"Nor I."

"He always struck me as something of a dullard."

"Yes, I'm afraid most people feel that way," I conceded sadly. "They misunderstand him."

"Was he known to be hot with the ladies?"

"Hot with the ladies?"

"A sex maniac."

"Millard Fillmore? Are you insane? Certainly not."

"He had two wives."

"Yes, but not at the same time!" I exclaimed. "The first one died."

"Under suspicious circumstances?"

"Certainly not!" I said.

"You told me you knew him like he was your own brother."

"Yes," I admitted. "I suppose I did."

"But you don't know who L.M. is."

"No, but I would assume from the letter that she was an actress of some sort," I postulated. "She mentions a performance and refers to herself as 'theatrical.'"

"But you don't even know her name."

"True," I said. "But I can't be expected to know about every single person who crossed his path."

"This sounds like more than a mere path crossing," Teppelman pointed out. He was starting to get my goat.

"Possibly."

"Perhaps you need to reevaluate him."

"I doubt it."

"We all have our little secrets, eh?"

"Yes," I admitted tentatively. "I suppose we do."

After explaining to Emily that I would be incommunicado for a short while due to a breakthrough in my Fillmore research, I spent two whole days leafing through all my Fillmore material—the photocopies of hundreds of his letters, the vast pile of notes I had taken on my last visit to the Fillmore archive in the Buffalo and Erie County Historical Society, Fillmore's own autobiography, and the indexes of the nine or ten Fillmore biographies in my possession, some of them written by local western New York scholars in the late nineteenth century, others by more contemporary scholars. The dust and mustiness of this material conspired to give me a severe sinus infection, and the research itself was, I am distressed to admit, all to no avail. The mysterious "L.M." did not seem to exist in the historical record. Or if she did, I had not found her yet.

Chapter 16: As if this weren't distrac-

tion enough, the next day my mother called from a hospital pay phone with the distressing news that my father had suffered a mild heart attack and was in the intensive care unit at Cedars-Sinai Medical Center. Naturally, I dropped what I was doing and immediately drove to the hospital. On the way, I wondered how a certified agoraphobe like my mother had summoned sufficient courage to actually leave her apartment and ride in the rear compartment of a careening ambulance to the hospital emergency room, and had lived to tell about it. More to the point, how had the paramedics lived to tell about it?

"He's going to be fine," she told me when I found her in the ICU waiting room, slipping on a pair of latex rubber gloves. "It was just a small heart attack, thank God."

"Will he need surgery?" I asked. "Another bypass?"

"I don't think so."

"The prognosis?"

"They said it's too early to tell, but that he'd probably be all right after some rest."

"Can I see him?"

"Not yet."

"How are you holding up, Mother?" I asked.

"Me? I almost had a heart attack myself in that ambulance. Sixty miles an hour in heavy traffic! Can you imagine me in that situation?"

"I admit it's a challenge," I conceded. "Otherwise how are you?"

"Otherwise, I haven't had a bowel movement in two days, but I'm surviving. It's just as well—you know how I hate using public toilets."

"I do."

"Sometimes even constipation has its advantages."

"Yes, I suppose it does."

"Here, put this on," she said, handing me a surgical mask. "This place is crawling with germs. Why they put sick people here I'll never know."

"Maybe I should have an electrocardiogram while I'm here," I mused. "I haven't had one in over a month."

"Couldn't hurt."

"Tell me, Mother," I said, curiosity finally getting the better of me. "How *did* you manage to actually leave the apartment?"

"It was a matter of life and death," she said. "I forced myself. Some whiskey helped."

"You drank whiskey?"

"I took a few quick swigs from the bottle before leaving."

"That's a trifle difficult to picture."

"Not to worry, Plato," she said. "It's legal. I'm old enough."

Just as she finished saying this, a scrawny teenager in blue scrubs and a white lab coat stepped through the automatic doors and approached us. He didn't appear to be much older than eighteen. He was short, had a slight case of acne on his forehead and sported the worst excuse for a mustache I've ever seen, nothing more than a fuzzy light shadow under his nose. I've observed better mustaches on certain elderly Greek women. But perhaps this fellow's mustache wasn't meant to be a mustache; perhaps he just hadn't had a chance to shave lately.

"Hello, I'm Dr. Lefkowitz," he said, his voice cracking. "I—"

"You're who?" my mother asked.

"Dr. Lefkowitz."

"You're a doctor?"

"That's correct."

"I think you missed the school bus, sonny," she said. "When's the real doctor coming?"

"I *am* the real doctor," he stated, slightly annoyed.

"On Halloween maybe," my mother continued. "You're not old enough to buy a pack of cigarettes."

"I don't smoke," Lefkowitz said. "And you shouldn't either."

"I don't."

"I'm glad to hear it."

"Can we see a doctor now, please?" my mother asked.

"Mother, he *is* the doctor," I interceded.

"Thank you very much," Lefkowitz said to me.

"So how old are you, sonny?" she asked.

"It's *Doctor*," he said. "Not sonny."

"How old are you, *Doctor*?" my mother asked, rolling her eyes.

"I'm twenty-two." He sighed. "Look, I know I may appear a little on the young side to be an M.D., but I promise you, I'm fully certified with the American Board of—"

"And you started medical school when?" my mother quipped. "In the womb?"

"Let him speak, Mother," I said, tiring of the repartee.

"If you must know," he said wearily, as if he was tired of telling this story. "I completed my undergraduate work at Yale at seventeen, graduated from Harvard Medical School at nineteen, and finished my internship at twenty-one. I've been practicing for a year."

"My sincere congratulations," I said. "That's most impressive."

"Thank you," he said, bowing his head slightly.

"Does your Mommy still pack you a lunch?" my mother asked.

"Certainly not."

"Do you live at home?"

"I don't see how any of this is relevant," he said.

"Mother, please," I said. "Let the doctor tell us about Dad. That's probably what he's here for."

"It is," Lefkowitz said, opening a chart. "Mr. Fussell is doing just fine. Vital signs are stable. His heart had an irregular beat for a while but we fixed that. He should be coming out of the ICU by early this evening."

"May we see him?" I asked.

"Yes, just as long as you promise not to excite him in any way," he warned, looking directly at my mother.

"I brought him pickles," my mother said. "He loves pickles. Is it okay if he eats a pickle?"

"Sure. A little salty, perhaps, but so what?" Lefkowitz mused. "There's nothing like a nice pickle. A nice pickle always hits the spot."

"That's exactly what my husband always says." She then dug in her purse and held open a plastic ziplock bag reeking of garlic. "Have one," she said to Lefkowitz. "Please."

Lefkowitz daintily pulled one out. "Delicious," he muttered, chomping down on it. "I haven't eaten anything in thirty-six hours."

"You're a growing boy," my mother scolded. "You should eat three meals a day."

"I know. You're right," he said.

"What if you get a low blood sugar attack in the middle of a procedure?" my mother asked. "You could kill someone and get sued for a million bucks. Hypoglycemia is no laughing matter."

"I'll keep that in mind," Lefkowitz said.

"And I also could not help but notice that you did not wash your hands before taking that pickle," my mother continued. "You want to come down with something? This place is crawling with germs!"

"You had time to pack pickles?" I asked my mother once Dr. Lefkowitz had gone on his merry way, chomping on another pickle.

"I had to offer the paramedics something to eat, didn't I?"

In spite of Dr. Lefkowitz's optimistic prognosis, my father did not seem very well at all. His skin was sallow, his eyes were lifeless and his lower lip quivered. There was a black and blue mark on the side of his mouth where the breathing tube had been. He looked like he had lost ten pounds since the last time I saw him. His eye sockets were dark and cavernous. My mother and I both tried to hide our shock from each other.

"You're looking good, Victor," my mother said. "Isn't he looking good, Plato?"

"Like a billion mucks," I added. "Healthy as a horse."

"Well, I feel like shit," my father replied.

"Please don't say that word in my presence, Victor," she said. "You know I find it depressing."

"Sorry, I forgot."

"After forty years of marriage you forgot? After—"

I cleared my throat and put a finger to my lips, reminding my mother that she should not excite him, as Dr. Lefkowitz had advised us.

"That's all right, Victor," she said. "Don't worry about it. You can say anything you want to me. Anything at all. But just today."

"I feel like somebody's sitting on my chest," my father croaked. "Is there somebody sitting on my chest?"

"No, Dad."

"Are you sure?"

"I think I would notice if someone was sitting on your chest," I said.

"Maybe there's a large concrete block on my chest," he continued. "Is there?"

"No, Dad."

"Somebody was sitting on my chest," he insisted. "It's all coming back to me now."

"A paramedic perhaps?" I guessed. "Administering CPR in the ambulance?"

"Was it a woman?" he asked.

"I have no idea," I said. "I wasn't there. But it could have been a woman. They have female paramedics now."

"Was she pretty?" he asked.

"I wasn't actually in the ambulance, Dad."

"It was a man and he wasn't pretty," my mother said. "He looked like the village idiot in a Masterpiece Theatre episode."

"Oh," my father whispered, disappointed.

"Here, have a pickle," my mother offered, extracting the ziplock. "You'll feel a lot better."

"You brought me pickles?" he said, brightening. "There's nothing like a nice pickle. A nice pickle always hits the spot."

My mother nudged me in the ribs, as if to say, regarding the pickles, "I told you so."

And so the three of us sat there, chomping on garlic pickles and chatting aimlessly about nothing in particular to the regular, metronomic beat of the heart monitor, until a burly male orderly came in around dusk and transferred my father into a wheelchair headed for the third-floor cardiology ward, where he would remain under observation for the next few days.

Chapter 17: With my father in the hospital,

it was incumbent upon me to look after my mother and, as a result, both my involvement with Emily and my research regarding Fillmore's mysterious paramour would have to wait. I yearned to see Emily again, I truly pined for her in a most wretched way, but my mother was extremely demanding and I found myself spending most of every day and night responding to her various needs, whims and desires, for which I received absolutely no gratitude. Now I understood for the first time what my father was up against and wondered how he had endured it for so long. For example, my mother never made grocery lists. She would say, "Plato, we're out of milk. I need milk right away," and I would drive to the store and bring home milk. Twenty minutes later she would say, "Plato, we're out of fresh eggs, I need fresh eggs right away. Not the brown ones. The white ones." And off I would go again. If I asked her whether there was anything else she needed before going off to the store for the umpteenth time, she always replied in the negative. And when I returned from these journeys, she greeted me with impatience and invariably said, "What took you so long?"

Emily and I had been scheduled to take a tour of Forest Lawn Memorial Park in Glendale that Thursday following my father's hospitalization, but I reluctantly had to cancel. I had been looking forward to touring the crypts and tombs and observing the headstones, but it would have to wait. Emily was most understanding when I phoned her, although I could tell that she too was disappointed.

"If there's anything I can do to help," she offered, "please let me know."

"Yes, I will," I said. "Thank you for the offer."

"As long as it doesn't involve spiders, ticks or snakes. I'm terrified of spiders, ticks and snakes."

"As am I," I admitted, though I was at a complete loss as to what she could possibly do to help me that would in any way involve spiders, ticks, snakes or any other form of wildlife.

"I'm not crazy about jellyfish either," she added. "Or octopi."

"Nor am I."

"Anything with tentacles terrifies me."

"Even calamari?"

"Oh yes," she cried. "Can't go near the stuff. Squid? Are you kidding? Yuck! Feh!"

"I'll make a mental note."

"Fussell . . ." she said.

"Yes?"

"Are you all right?"

"Just fine," I said. "Thank you for asking."

"I love you."

"Ditto," said I. And we left it at that.

Although I could not leave my mother alone long enough to attend my biweekly therapy sessions, I did manage to find a few moments between chores to speak to Dr. Wang over the telephone. The best time was usually between one o'clock and two o'clock in the afternoon, which was when my mother generally stayed in the bathroom coaxing her intransigent bowels into action, usually an exercise in futility, poor woman. Wang was sorry to hear about my father and offered his best wishes, but the conversation soon moved on to the topic of my first sexual encounter with Emily (Ahab).

"I'm delighted to hear it, Fussell," he said. "How did you overcome your religious problem?"

"God only knows."

"This is real progress," Wang said, ignoring my pun. "Welcome back to the human race."

"I wasn't aware that I'd left it," I countered. "How exactly does one leave the human race? By jet plane? Rocket ship? Dogsled?"

"My guess would be death," Wang said.

"Of course. How imbecilic of me."

"May we go back to the original subject now?" Wang asked. "You were telling me about your first sexual encounter with Ahab."

"Oh yes," I said. "Marvelous as it was, I must confess this whole thing is making me a little nervous."

"Which whole thing is that?" he asked.

"My relationship with Ahab."

"How so?"

"I don't know quite how to say it," I stammered. "She's just . . . too good to be true. She says she loves me. How is that possible?"

"Don't be so hard on yourself, Fussell," he advised. "You're a nice person. Educated, articulate, sensitive. You just have a few . . . eccentricities, that's all, but you're entitled to be loved just like anyone else."

"I just can't help but think that she has some . . . ulterior motive."

"Like your first wife, you mean? Is that it?"

"Well, yes, in a nutshell. I was hurt pretty badly the last time, as you will recall. How do I know I'm not being set up for another fall?"

"Because Ahab doesn't sound like that kind of person. I'm getting a very positive vibe from what you've said about her."

"Really?"

"I almost feel like I know her," he said.

I gulped and made a mental note to keep my descriptions of Emily less vivid. One slip of the tongue and I'd be finished.

"And you haven't told her anything about your fortune, correct?" Wang continued.

"Correct."

"Trust me, Fussell," he counseled. "I really think she loves you for who you are."

"How can you be so sure?"

"I don't know for sure," Wang admitted. "But from what you've told me she sounds absolutely delightful. A real find. Yet, even if I'm wrong, you must take a chance. Life has its risks, Fussell. Nothing is guaranteed. No pain, no gain."

"Yes, I suppose," I muttered.

"Look at me," Wang said. "I'm being hurt to the very core of my being by a woman who I thought loved me deeply, yet I'm not sorry I took the plunge. Not even a little."

"Really?"

"Really."

"How's that going, by the way?" I asked with some apprehension. "Your divorce?"

"Lousy."

"How so?"

"I think she's seeing someone."

I gulped again. "Oh?" I croaked, trying to keep the anxiety out of my voice. "Who is it? The nosrep she's seeing?" (*Oops?*)

"I have no idea."

I did my best to stifle a sigh of relief. "Then why do you think she's seeing someone?" I asked.

"Just a hunch. She seems very . . . happy. Like someone who has just fallen in love."

My heart leapt. "Really?"

"Yes, but that's neither here nor there," Wang said. "My problems shouldn't concern you. Let's talk about you, shall we?"

Frankly, I had nothing left to say, but managed to fill the next ten minutes with idle chatter about my mother and her constant demands and how my father was faring in the hospital.

In retrospect, however, as I went over our conversation, I was not convinced Wang's advice regarding Emily was entirely valid. He had, on a few rare occasions in the past, given me advice that turned out to be less than beneficial. After all, it was he and he alone who had advised me to attend my tenth high school reunion in 1995, where I met, or rather remet, the delectable Daisy Crane. And it was he who had advised me to eventually marry her. As I recall, his arguments in favor of my relationship with Daisy did not differ much from his arguments regarding my affair with Emily. But then Wang was the eternal optimist.

"Take the bull by the horns," he had counseled me back then. "No pain, no gain."

Of course much of it was my own fault as well. I had been whining incessantly for months to Wang about the misery and trauma of my high school years, so when I stupidly mentioned that I had received in the mail an invitation to attend my reunion, Wang urged me to go.

"Don't you see, Fussell?" he had said. "This is your chance for vindication! For closure! The high school dork makes good in the real world! You're handsome, you're rich, you're—"

"Neurotic?" I interrupted.

"So is half the world."

"Not Daisy Crane," I said. "Daisy Crane is perfect."

"Nobody's perfect, Fussell," he proclaimed. "Besides, you haven't seen her in ten years."

"You've never met her," I said defensively. "Daisy Crane is a goddess."

"A goddess?" he said skeptically. "I strongly doubt it."

The fact was, at the time I really did not know much about Daisy Crane's recent life, or what had become of her after high school. The alumni newsletter—a cheap, two-page photocopied bulletin written by the school's journalism class—had made no mention of her career, family life or whereabouts, and her name was not listed in the local phone directory. Her parents still lived in a converted mobile home in a rundown section of Van Nuys near Sherman Way. As far as I knew her father was still minister of one of the less affluent local churches.

"There are no goddesses," Wang remarked. "I'm sure Daisy Crane has her own little problems and foibles too. Nobody is exempt."

And so I took his advice and went to the reunion, but not for the reasons he suggested. I didn't care much about closure or showing off to my former classmates. I went to see Daisy Crane.

Of course I dreaded it for weeks, I suffered insomnia every night, I invented the most idiotic excuses not to go, but I went. When the time came, I showered, combed my hair, shaved, splashed on some Bulgari eau de cologne, cut my toenails, polished my best Italian shoes, put on my snazziest, recently dry-cleaned Armani suit and a $200 silk tie, swallowed a Xanax or two for fortitude, climbed into my obscenely expensive new Mercedes with the ten air bags, driving helmet and computerized tracking features, and drove the three miles from my house to my old alma mater, Van Nuys High School.

Chapter 18: I must have waited in the high school parking lot for twenty minutes before I was able to muster sufficient nerve to enter the gymnasium, where the reunion festivities were being held. A huge banner flapping near the entrance read, *Welcome Class of '85!!* and from the parking lot I could hear off-tempo strains of a mediocre rock band playing "Louie, Louie." The huge privet hedge behind which I had hidden more than once to escape the taunts and jeers of the school's class clowns and bullies was still there but looked as if it had been recently trimmed. I wondered whether the current flock of nerds, dorks and misfits still found it a safe refuge.

Once the Xanax kicked in, I glided up the steps to the entrance, walked under a flag with the school's colors emblazoned upon it, ambled nostalgically down the long locker-walled hallways and entered the huge gymnasium, which smelled exactly as it had ten years ago—primarily of sweat, the sweat of countless basketball games and physical education classes, sweat that had been permanently absorbed by walls, ceiling and floor. I estimated that it would take several thousand gallons of Glade to disguise that odor.

The acoustics of the room were such that voices boomed around me as I took a few tentative steps inside, reminding me of the loud, booming voice of the phys ed instructor, Jack Nixon, who considered me a hopeless wimp of the first order and made no secret of it, deliberately mispronouncing my name play-TOE whenever the opportunity presented itself. Ah, the good old days!

I stood nervously at the entrance and quietly surveyed the area—perhaps a hundred people holding plastic cups filled with a thin, orange-colored punch of some sort stood about talking and laughing, no doubt sharing old memories. I immediately recognized a few of my former classmates, although most had predictably put on some weight or lost a bit of hair or both. There on the right, guzzling punch, was a near-hairless version of Tim D'Ambrossi, the school bully, who had tormented me and so many others throughout those miserable years; Charlotte Rice, the class valedictorian—looking exactly as she had ten years ago, possibly even wearing the same clothing—sat on a low bleacher gesticulating to the salutatorian, Harold Brawer, who, during high school, had been noted primarily for a bad case of halitosis that even the strongest mouthwash could not remedy; Russell Benjamin, the football captain, had put on more than fifty pounds as well as several chins and was done up from head to toe in corduroy; Ernie Coslough, the class clown, was making inane faces for the class photographer, Burt Ferguson. But, to my chagrin, I did not see Daisy Crane anywhere in the room.

I took a deep breath, which, along with the Xanax, succeeded in calming my nerves. The mere fact that I was able to walk into this overcrowded room and not have a first-degree anxiety attack was a testament to Wang's ability as a psychiatrist.

"Excuse me," a nearby voice said. I looked behind me and saw a table manned by two of my former classmates—Jennifer Burley, the former president of the girls' chess club, was squinting up at me through thick glasses, and standing right beside her was Howard Gunin, former concert master of the school orchestra who had once performed "Go Down, Moses" at a school recital with his fly open the whole time, and never lived it down. Today, however, his fly was properly in place. He'd probably been compulsively checking it for the last decade.

Jennifer was clearing her throat to get my attention. I turned and walked toward the tables.

"You have to register here," she huffed officiously. "And get a name tag. It's mandatory."

"It's mandatory?" I repeated. "What's the penalty if I don't? A week of study hall? A meeting with the vice principle? Twenty laps around the football field?"

She was not amused. I quickly recalled that she had displayed no sense of humor in high school either. And despite the thick glasses, she was apparently still half blind. I remembered that she had been somewhat notorious for entering the wrong classrooms because, even with her glasses on, she could seldom read the room numbers. The class clowns had dubbed her "Mrs. Magoo." The same people who made fun of me made fun of her.

"You don't recognize me, do you?" I said.

Jennifer squinted with a bit more intensity, but recognition never registered on her face.

"Are you Class of '85?" Howard asked.

"Yes, indeed," said I.

"Are you sure?"

"Positive," I told him. "Why in God's name would I want to come to a reunion if I wasn't part of the class?"

"Good point," Howard muttered.

"Okay, so who are you?" Jennifer asked impatiently.

"Go ahead, take a wild guess," I said.

She put a finger to her lip and narrowed her eyes. "I know!" she shrieked. "You're Herbie Kretchmer?"

I recoiled as if slapped across the cheek. Herbie Kretchmer had been the class moron. If he was coming to the reunion, he would probably have taken the wrong bus.

"Not even close," I said.

"Herbie has blond hair," Howard snapped. "Are you blind?"

"Not legally," Jennifer said. "But pretty close."

"Leave her alone, Howard," I demanded. "People's physical infirmities are no laughing matter."

Howard made a snorting sound.

"Okay, I give up," Jennifer conceded. "Who the heck are you?"

"Guess again," I said.

This time, she removed her glasses, exhaled on each side of the lenses and wiped them clean on her cashmere sweater before returning them to her face. All of which didn't seem to help.

"I got it," she announced after another short inspection. "You're Richie Yamamoto!"

"He's Asian!" Howard bellowed, slapping his forehead. "Does this guy look Asian to you?"

Jennifer turned to Howard. "Do *you* know who he is, Mr. Wiseguy?"

Howard shrugged. "Not a clue."

"Right," she said. "So give me a frigging break." Then she turned her eyes on me again. "So who are you?"

"Plato G. Fussell at your service," I declared, standing at attention for no particular reason.

"Get outa town!" Jennifer cried.

"Why on earth would I want to do that?" I said. "I live here."

"Play-Doh?" Howard said gleefully. "You're Play-Doh Fussell?"

"The very same," I replied. "Loving son of Mr. Potato Head, proud brother of Silly Putty."

Jennifer now stood up, put her face about four inches away from mine and stared at me.

"Boy, oh boy, have you ever changed," Jennifer observed. "In a good way, I mean to say."

"Yes, well, thank you, Jennifer," said I. "You have too."

"Are you married?" she asked.

"No," I said.

"Single?"

"Yes."

"Gay?"

"No," I said. "May I have my name tag now, please?"

Her face was still close to mine as she studied me in disbelief, until I cleared my throat several times. A few seconds later, she sat back down while Howard perused the neat line of adhesive-backed name tags alphabetically arranged on the table, found mine and gave it to Jennifer, who took the liberty of sticking it to the expensive fabric of my Armani sport jacket pocket. Now I would have to have it dry-cleaned again.

"There you go!" she said brightly. "Now you're official."

"By the way," I said. "Has Ysiad Enarc checked in yet?"

"Who?" Howard asked. "You better spell that one."

"Daisy Crane," I said, intelligibly this time.

Howard looked over the roster. "Nope."

"She didn't RSVP," Jennifer said. "So she's probably not coming."

"We don't have a name tag for her," Howard added. "If you don't RSVP you don't get a name tag. And if you don't get a name tag—"

"*C'est dommage,*" I said, trying to disguise the disappointment in my voice. "I guess I'll be going now. Nice seeing you both. Really. Adiós."

"But—"

Before Jennifer could finish, I had walked off. Then I stopped for a second and turned. Cruel, yes, but I couldn't resist.

"By the way, Howard," I snickered. "Your fly is open."

For some reason this actually made Jennifer laugh and I winked at her, although she probably wasn't able to see it. While Howard fumbled to check his fly, I exited the gymnasium and scurried down the hallway. After all, what point was there in staying if

Daisy Crane was not to be in attendance? I certainly did not need to lord my wealth, good looks and success over the likes of Russell Benjamin (currently a Sheetrock salesman) or Tim D'Ambrossi (currently the high school security guard) or Charlotte Rice (currently a Washington, D.C., corporate lawyer). No, it was Daisy Crane I had come to see and Daisy Crane was absent from class, so to speak. Sad as it was, I concluded at the time that Daisy Crane and Plato G. Fussell would most likely never meet again. She was, I assumed, probably married with two adorable kids and a big suburban house somewhere far, far away, and had no reason to return to our old high school for anything as mind-numbing as a class reunion.

Somewhat deflated, I plodded through the parking lot and found my car. But just as I was about to unlock the door, a vintage blue Volkswagen convertible came tearing out of nowhere and pulled into the next parking spot with such a screech of brakes and rattle of metal that I instinctively stood flat against the side of my Mercedes to avoid being killed or seriously maimed. The tubercular VW coughed up some carburetor phlegm before finally sputtering to a noisy stop.

"Craisy Dane!" I exclaimed with surprise, as I peeled myself off the side of my car. Ah yes, it was Daisy, all right. She had not changed much—perhaps a bit blonder, hair a trifle shorter, a bit more filled out in certain crucial anatomical regions, less stylishly dressed, perhaps, a knockoff Vuitton handbag in her hand, low-cut blouse, stiletto heels—but essentially the same astoundingly heart-stopping beauty she had been when I last laid eyes on her at our high school graduation in June of 1985.

She took off her sunglasses, revealing those marvelous blue eyes and those excellent cheekbones, now accentuated with a less than subtle touch of rouge.

"What did you call me?" she asked.

"Um . . ."

"It sounded like Crazy Dane," she said. "I'm not Danish."

"Ha ha, ho ho," I laughed nervously. "I called you Daisy Crane, of course. That's your name, is it not?"

"And who the hell are you?" she asked, lighting up a cigarette and blowing the first puff of smoke directly in my face. Her breath smelled vaguely of alcohol. Scotch, perhaps.

"Take a sseug."

"A what?"

"A guess. Take a guess."

"I'd rather not."

"Please."

"No."

"Humor me."

"Okay," she said, rolling her eyes. "Dwight D. Eisenhower."

Ah, such wit, such charm, such magic! Suddenly, my heart was pounding, the adrenaline was zipping through my veins, the neurotransmitters were getting 911 calls from my genitalia, phero-mones were invading my olfactory nerves. In other words, I was instantaneously "falling in love" with Daisy Crane all over again.

"Whoever you are, that's a real cool set of wheels," she observed. "Must've cost a nice piece of change."

Then she delicately touched the surface of the car's hood with one of her perfectly manicured fingers (on a hand devoid of a wedding ring, I might add) and looked up at me flirtatiously.

"Okay, I'm stumped," she admitted. "Who are you?"

Nervous as I was, I was enjoying this. "Care to take another guess?"

"Can we please cut to the chase?" She sighed, putting her sunglasses back on. "The quiz show bit is getting a little annoying."

I cleared my throat a few times.

"Plato G. Fussell at your service!" I declared finally, my voice cracking slightly on the word "service." Nerves. But at least I managed to avoid saying my name backward.

She narrowed her eyes suspiciously and gave me the once-over.

"No way, Jose," she said.

Chapter 19: In retrospect, had I not been wearing a $3,000 Armani suit and driving an expensive new Mercedes, had I instead been sporting an old threadbare blue blazer with elbow patches and driving a scuffed old Buick that needed a new muffler, chances are Daisy Crane would have yawned and walked on toward the gym by herself on that sunny day in 1995. Sure, she might have made some comment regarding the improvement of my appearance (assuming she even remembered me) but her interest probably would have stopped there or quickly waned. Of course, the only reason I was wearing a ridiculously expensive Armani suit and driving a top-of-the-line Mercedes was to get her attention. It succeeded beyond my wildest expectations. She did not yawn and walk away, no sir. She coughed a few times, dropped her cigarette, stamped it out with the toe of her high heel shoe, sprayed Binaca in her mouth, walked right up to me so that our chins were almost touching, ripped off her sunglasses again and gave me another once-over.

"Play-Doh?" she said, staring into my eyes. "Play-Doh *Fussell*?"

"Yes indeed."

"Superdork?"

"In the flesh," I said proudly, my heart still banging with anxiety.

"You've changed."

"You think so?"

Right then and there, I probably should have commented on her keen powers of observation and walked away, but what could I do? I was caught up in the heat of the moment. I was, in a word, smitten. My expensively shod feet were glued to the tarmac. This was Daisy Crane, homecoming queen, prom queen, queen of any goddamn thing she wanted to be queen of (with the possible exception of a sovereign nation). And she was actually speaking to me, the class pariah, Superdork, grand potentate of the misfits. Flirting with me even! I felt a rush of warmth fill my body as if I had just downed a large glass of cognac. I had been dreaming of this very moment for years.

"You . . . haven't, um, changed at all, Ysiad," I said with a slight stutter.

"What did you call me?"

"Frog in my throat," I lied. "You're even more . . . beautiful than I remember."

"Am I now?" she said, glancing at the Mercedes.

"Oh yes."

"Is that really your car?"

"It is," I said.

"You didn't steal it?"

"Heavens no!" I exclaimed. "Do I look like a tar chief?"

"What's a tar chief?"

"Nothing."

She blew an errant hair from her face and narrowed her eyes at me for a second, then went back to admiring the Mercedes.

"Is it rented?"

"No."

"Leased?"

"Paid for," I said. "Cash."

Now she was looking at me again, but this time with the brightest smile I'd ever seen and I struggled to suppress my delight. She took my hands in hers (subtly checking for a wedding ring, perhaps?) and dropped them. Then she closed one eye and straightened my tie.

"I'll bet that suit cost a bundle too," she said, fondling the fabric of my lapel. "Did you get that off the rack at Penney's?"

"No, um, actually I got it off the rack at Inamra's," I said.

"Never heard of them."

"I meant to say Armani's."

"Really now?" she cooed, warming up to me even more. "Armani, huh? Must've cost six, seven hundred bucks maybe?"

"More like three thousand."

"No shit?"

"Hey, what's a few shekels?" I asked whimsically.

"Beats me," she replied. "What the hell's a shekel? Or is this another frog-in-your-throat thing?"

I confess I was a bit shocked at her lack of knowledge. After all, she had been an A student in high school, not that the academic level of our high school had been particularly outstanding. The fact is, one could probably go through four years of college and never learn the definition of the word *shekel*.

"A shekel is a unit of currency in Israel," I informed her.

"So what are you saying, you bought it in Israel?"

In retrospect, this is precisely where I should have gotten an inkling that I was dealing with a person of limited swiftness (not to mention suspicious intentions), but those insidious hormones were making me temporarily deaf, dumb and blind. This was the girl I had ached for since the age of five. She could have been parading around in jackboots and an SS uniform and it probably wouldn't have fazed me. What a fool I was! What an idiot! What a sucker!

"Not important, Ysiad," I said.

"What did you call me?"

"Nothing," I said. "Never mind."

"No, really," she said. "Are you insulting me in some foreign language or something?"

"Oh no, not at all," I blabbered. "I would never insult you. Never! It's just a . . . nervous habit. I, um, say people's names backward sometimes."

"Oh," she said. "That's a little odd, isn't it?"

"Yes, I suppose it is."

"But kinda funny too," she observed, her tone brightening. "Let's see, you would be . . . Otalp Llessuf."

"Very good!" I bellowed, impressed at the rapidity with which she had conjured the name in reverse. Perhaps there was some real mental aptitude there after all. This was most encouraging.

"So listen, Otalp," she said. "How about you be my date? To the reunion."

"Me?"

"You."

My throat was suddenly dry. "I'd be delighted," I croaked.

And so Daisy Crane snagged my arm and we walked together down the hallway where ten years ago she and her obnoxious friends had so cruelly ignored me. I also recalled fondly the smell of the inside of my locker, into which I had been locked so many times by the school's unimaginative hoodlums. I recalled the sight of the school flagpole, flying the red and white colors of my oversize underpants from Fineman's. I recalled what it felt like to have one's trousers filled with Redi-Whip, or to have one's face pushed into one's mashed potatoes in the school cafeteria.

"Hold on one second," I said as we approached a hallway bathroom. "Nature calls."

"Take your time," she allowed. "I'll be right here."

I entered the bathroom, which, fortunately, was empty. I took a deep breath or two to calm myself. I went to the sink, looked myself over, checked my teeth, my nose, my hair, smelled my armpits. My hands were trembling slightly, so I threw back another Xanax and breathed deeply a few more times. How, I wondered, would the others react to the sight of Daisy Crane and Plato Fussell walking into the gym arm and arm? Would there be taunts and heckling? Would someone give me a wedgie? Would I be laughed out of the room? There was only one way to find out.

"What did you do in there?" Daisy asked when I finally emerged. "Wallpaper the place?"

Moments later, when Daisy and I strode into the gymnasium together, a hush fell over the room. People stared at us. Conversations stopped. Then hubbub commenced. Evidently, nobody knew who I was and I suspect most of them thought I was Daisy's husband, some Latin movie star or Greek shipping magnate. But as we made the rounds and mingled with our former classmates, we soon became the center of attention. Oddly, I actually enjoyed this, although I didn't speak much. Even Tim D'Ambrossi—who ten years ago had given me so many painful noogies every afternoon in the cafeteria that I thought my skull was going to burst open one day—actually shook my hand without trying to break any bones. There was no laughter, no derision, no mockery.

I was suddenly Plato G. Fussell, Big Man on Campus.

That was the good news.

To make a long, dreary story short, Daisy Crane asked me to marry her in the late fall of 1995, after a whirlwind but sexless courtship that lasted about two months. Like a dithering imbecile, I agreed to become her husband without a prenuptial contract, and forthwith she took me to a jewelry store where I purchased a diamond ring at a cost that exceeded the gross national product of Mozambique. What can I say—a dense miasma had descended over my brain and I was temporarily insane (or rather, more insane than usual). I had wanted Daisy Crane to be my wife since that first day in kindergarten and I suppose I simply was not able to perceive her shortcomings, which were plentiful, and obvious to practically everybody but me. I should have let my father meet her, or even Teppelman, before I rushed off to marry her. Had he known her, Wang would certainly have advised me against it. But I was happy, happier than I had ever been before, and perhaps I didn't want anyone to spoil it all. Besides, Wang had made it clear more than a few times that he was truly delighted by my good fortune.

While we courted, Daisy seemed to find my idiosyncrasies "cute," to use her term, which only made my fondness for her increase. And miraculously, once we had spent some time together, my anxiety seemed to ebb, until it practically disappeared.

Why did I marry her so hastily? I suppose because I was terrified she would change her mind if she got to know me better. I feared that once she had to actually live with my compulsions and insecurities for any length of time, she would beg off, dump me, disappear. I guess I was a trifle low on self-esteem in those days.

We were staying in Reno, Nevada (Daisy enjoyed losing at blackjack), when she proposed marriage to me, and before I even had a chance to really contemplate what I was getting myself into, before Daisy even met my parents or I hers, I found myself agreeing to it.

"You'll probably want a big formal wedding," I said.

"Nah."

"Big church, lots of bridesmaids, huge cake."

"Nah."

"Just close family members?"

"Nah."

"What about your parents?"

"Haven't talked to them in six years."

"Why?"

"We don't get along too well," she said. "My holy roller of a father doesn't approve of me or my lifestyle."

"Why not?"

Daisy snickered. "He wanted me to devote my life to Jesus and teach Sunday School," she said. "Can you picture that?"

Admittedly, I had some difficulty summoning forth an image of Daisy Crane instructing legions of children in the nuances of the New Testament.

"So who's going to give you away?" I asked. "At the wedding."

"Who the hell cares?"

Moments later, I found myself standing with her in front of a local justice of the peace who wore a lopsided toupee, at a makeshift chapel that had once been a Greyhound bus depot, saying the words "I do" to the raucous applause and congratulations of two people I had never seen before in my life—a man in a cowboy hat, snakeskin boots and an oversize turquoise belt buckle and his pregnant wife—who were serving as our witnesses. I never even got their names although I think his was Buck. Apparently, acting as legal witnesses to impromptu Reno weddings was their vocation—their services cost me fifty dollars, plus gratuity.

That night, after a delightful candlelight dinner (I had the veal marsala and, throwing caution to the wind, a half bottle of Pinot Grigio; she had spaghetti and meatballs and four rum and Cokes), we consummated the marriage in a lakeside suite at the most romantic, not to mention most expensive, Tahoe hotel my travel agent could find. (Naturally, I had insisted that Daisy have a full panel of blood tests and a throat culture prior to our marriage and she had agreed without a fuss.) As for our first sexual encounter, Daisy kept a lit cigarette in a night table ashtray and occasionally took a puff during the act. When I politely asked her to put it out during foreplay, her reply was "It helps me focus, sugar." Her constant cigarette smoking (she had seldom indulged in the habit during our courtship) had been only one of a vast array of problems that suddenly arose and eventually poisoned our relationship, not that what we had, in truth, could realistically be categorized as a relationship.

Her true colors revealed themselves only after we had been married. She gambled away vast amounts of money (mine); she sometimes watched daytime television for hours; she drank hard liquor (tequila neat) until she slurred her words and could barely stand up straight enough to walk; she drove too fast (sometimes under the influence, usually in my car); she could seldom speak a single sentence without committing at least five colorful grammatical errors (how she had managed to receive an A in high school English was beyond me). Her culinary tastes were generally limited to hamburgers and chili dogs. Once we were betrothed, she made light of all my obsessions and compulsions and regularly referred to me as being "one egg roll short of a combination platter." She despised Isabella, who growled at the mere sight of her, and was chronically late for all appointments, punctuality being one of my compulsions. Her taste in interior decor was beyond belief, she wore only the most revealing clothes—obscene short shorts, miniscule skirts and flimsy see-through blouses—and she flirted shamelessly with practically every male she encountered, from busboys to airline stewards. Gay men, old men, young boys, rabbis, priests, monks, the Pope—it didn't matter to Daisy, anybody with a penis qualified. She winked at them all.

In short, I had married Frankenstein's monster.

Of course, I was thoroughly disillusioned and utterly devastated by Daisy's transformation. Obviously, my schoolboy image of her had been just that—a schoolboy image, completely inaccurate. Either that or she had changed dramatically since high school. In those bygone days, our social castes were at opposite extremes and, to be honest, I had not really known her very well at all. She was pretty, she was popular and, so it had seemed to me, wholesome, intelligent and good-hearted. I had completely romanticized her. I had conjured a vision of the perfect girl, a veritable Aphrodite. I had created a goddess and placed her on the proverbial pedestal—at least that was Dr. Wang's theory. Later, after things fell apart, Wang speculated that Daisy was on some sort of self-destructive bender that might have been caused by the influence of repressive parents.

"Just a wild guess," he told me. "Having never met her, I cannot say for sure what her problem might be."

"What should I do?" I asked him.

"Perhaps you can influence her to improve her ways," Wang, the optimist, suggested. "Granted, it would be a miracle, but perhaps it's worth a try."

"I'm not sure I have the patience for that," I confessed. "Not to mention the money."

"Give it your best shot," Wang said.

I never got the chance. After three months of the most unbearable cohabitation imaginable, Daisy Crane-Fussell suddenly disappeared one night while I was walking the dog. Vanished. Gone. Right out the front door. With all of her clothes and most of her belongings, not to mention a purse full of credit cards, all of my cash, all my gold tie clasps and cuff links, two of my most expensive Armani suits and a sterling silver tea set, a wedding gift from Dr. Wang. Oh, and she also drove off with the Mercedes, of course. Frankly, by that time, I was in no hurry to find her. I suppose I could have called the police and had them track down the car, but I didn't bother. For all I cared, she could rot. Plus the very notion of having to explain all of this to a member of the local constabulary was a fairly intimidating prospect, fraught with predictable humiliation. I later discovered that she had taken up with an old boyfriend, an unemployed short-order cook named Slick Slocum, who lived in a trailer park somewhere in Arizona and shared Daisy's intellectual interests in liquor, cigarettes and gambling. It was Slick's lawyer—a second cousin from Hoboken, New Jersey, named Big Boy Klein—who sent me the divorce papers. I could barely believe what I was reading. I was being accused of "mental cruelty," and a long, ridiculous inventory of 270 or so examples was attached. Here are a few of the more absurd claims:

1. Brushes teeth eight times a day, flosses *during* meals
2. Regularly talks gibberish
3. Sterilizes bottled drinking water
4. Is in love with someone named Millard Fillmore

5. Requires blood tests before sex
6. Changes his socks and underwear three times per day
7. Reads French poetry to his dachshund
8. Wears a nightcap and earmuffs to bed
9. Overuses Lysol spray and other disinfectants
10. Yodels in shower

And so on and so forth. Such slanderous poppycock! Such incredible nonsense! Such utter tripe! I've never yodeled in the shower. In the bathtub, perhaps, but never in the shower. And is there a law I am unaware of that forbids the wearing of a nightcap to bed? Is boiling your drinking water a felony?

Okay, perhaps it was true that, on occasion, I had pointed a finger at Isabella and said the word *"J'accuse,"* but I never read poetry to her, French or otherwise. Nor was I "in love" with our thirteenth president.

What a pile of cow dung!

Even though it would cost me a small fortune—about eight million dollars and change—to be forever rid of Daisy Crane, I did nothing to contest her idiotic accusations, though I did berate myself for months for failing to insist on an ironclad prenuptial agreement. So taken was I by Daisy's apparent affection for me, not to mention her incomparable good looks, and the prospect of engaging in sexual intercourse with her at some point, that the very notion of a divorce never even dawned on me. How could I have been so incredibly naive?

And to think I had duped myself into believing that I actually cared for this creature! What had possessed me? How could I have made such a colossal blunder? How could a man of my erudition and insight have been such a consummate fool?

Could it have been that thing called love? The many-splendored thing? That monumental pile of rubbish?

Once the divorce papers were signed by both parties, I could not resist the temptation of writing her a sarcastic little note inquiring whether eight million dollars was sufficient lucre to support her and her new lover's wide variety of unsavory habits. I received a curt handwritten postcard from her about four months later.

It read: *Yuck fou, Llessuf.*

Part
two

Chapter 20: After about a week in the cardiology ward, my father was healthy enough to return home. As he had been instructed to remain quietly in bed for another two weeks, and as I did not entirely trust my mother to care for him properly, or to refrain from driving him completely mad, and as I had neither the patience nor the mental fortitude to continue as private manservant to my mother, I enlisted the help of a professional nurse, a rotund Jamaican woman named Rose, to stay with them for the entire day, every day for three weeks, and fulfill all of my mother's needs, commands and requests, no matter how bizarre, impossible or inconsiderate. For this, I paid her handsomely—three hundred dollars a day, cash, under the table. I looked at it as combat pay. She seemed a colossus of patience, good cheer and kindness and did not blink when I explained about my mother's intestinal obsession and bizarre culinary tastes. I was hoping Rose would break all known world records and survive in their household for at least a week. Two would be a miracle. Three would qualify her for sainthood.

Having been deprived of Emily's company for over six days—a virtual eternity—I was desperate to see her again. I had not taken her up on her offer to lend a hand with my father mainly because I did not think she and I had been together long enough for her to endure a get-together with my parents, my mother in particular. This parental meeting would come in good time, perhaps after Emily and I had known each other for a decade or so. At this early stage, I did not want anything to jeopardize our relationship.

First, I called and left a message on Emily's voice mail, saying that I missed her terribly and would greatly like to see her, but received no reply. I called again and left a longer message of a similar ilk, to which I also received no response. This was most strange. Was she avoiding me on purpose? Had she decided I was not good enough for her? Had my sexual prowess left something to be desired? Was she, like Daisy, sick of my neuroses and eccentricities, the very traits that I thought had brought us together? Needless to say, my insecurities on this subject caused my paranoid imagination to run wild.

Or maybe something had happened to her. Had she been hit by a bus? Contracted the Ebola virus? Hepatitis? West Nile fever? Had she left town for some reason? Would she have gone on vacation without telling me? Was her phone out of order? Had she been placed in the FBI's witness protection program? Or was she deliberately not returning my calls because she had met someone else? The world was full of handsome, well-to-do eligible bachelors, many of whom were not compulsive, obsessive, anxiety-ridden or paranoid. It occurred to me then that, although we had dated and shared a bed, I did not really know Emily Thorndyke that well. I did know that she had once been a patient of Wang's. But what had he really treated her for? Perhaps she had not told me the whole story. Perhaps she suffered from multiple personality disorder and was currently walking the streets of the city as a lumberjack named Fritz. Anything was possible.

After calling all the area hospital emergency rooms, to no avail, I phoned the local police department and spoke to the detective in charge of missing persons, but no one of Emily's description had been reported. A trip to her office was also fruitless. The door was locked and the uniformed man at the lobby reception desk informed me he had not seen her in several days.

I was too impatient to wait any longer, so I did the only sensible thing—I called the city morgue. To my relief, no one of Emily's name or description was in residence there.

Perhaps Dr. Wang would have the answer. As it happened, during my next session with him, he was so annoyingly ebullient that he slapped me on the back enough times to produce a small welt.

"I'm delighted your father is so much better," he sang. "And I must admit I've missed you these past days, Fussell."

"I've missed you too," I said.

"Really?"

"Yes."

Then he stood up, came over to where I was sitting and gave me a hefty bear hug that lasted a good ten seconds. He smelled vaguely of cilantro and garlic.

"What's good for the goose," he said, explaining the hug. "So what's on your mind this fine day, Fussell?"

"Oh, not much," I lamented. "I'm feeling a bit depressed and lonely if you must know."

"Of course I must know," he insisted. "I'm your psychiatrist. But more importantly, I like to think of myself as your friend."

"You do?"

"Of course."

"I don't have a lot of friends," I said. "But the ones I do have generally don't charge me ninety dollars an hour to see them. Not even my cheap friends."

For some reason, this perfectly logical argument made him laugh so hard he almost fell backward in his desk chair.

"Tell me all about your depression," he coaxed, once he had regained his stability.

"My girlfriend—"

"Ahab."

"Yes, Ahab. She seems to have left me."

"Oh?"

"Yes."

"What makes you say that?"

"She's not returning my calls. She's not showing up at her office."

"Perhaps something happened to her. An accident . . ."

"I've already inquired at all the hospitals and morgues in the area."

"Of course you have."

Wang made a church steeple of his index fingers and gave this dilemma some thought. "Perhaps she's not calling you back on purpose," he said.

"Why?"

"Perhaps she needs some space."

"Some space?"

"To think."

"Think about what?"

"Who knows? Women sometimes need some time out from a relationship," he explained. "Yours in particular seems to have been quite a whirlwind of a romance. Perhaps she needs a break. To interpret her feelings for you, to listen to her inner voice."

"Yes, that very well may be," I said, "but that does not explain why she hasn't been returning my calls. It's impolite, don't you think?"

"Perhaps she thinks talking to you would be too great a temptation to get right back into the relationship. Perhaps she's merely frightened."

"Of me?"

"No, of making a commitment so early."

"But I never asked her to make a commitment."

"Perhaps she felt you were, even if you thought you weren't."

I sighed heavily. "I don't understand women."

"Welcome to the club."

"But you have female patients, correct? You must understand them to some degree?"

"Let me give you a little piece of wisdom I've picked up after many years of psychotherapy," Wang said.

"I'm all ears."

Wang paused for a few seconds, perhaps trying to find the best way to phrase this imminent morsel of insight.

"The fact is, Fussell," he began, "we don't ever really get to know *anybody* that well. You think you know somebody, a best friend, a spouse, a brother or sister, even a parent, but you really don't. People have secret, inner selves. They wear masks. And they project these different selves to different people. Which of these selves is the real one? Does anyone know? Just because you love someone doesn't necessarily mean you know that person completely. Hell, in my opinion, we don't even know *ourselves* completely when you get right down to it."

"Ridiculous," said I. "I know myself thoroughly."

"Oh? In an extreme moral dilemma do you know exactly how you would react?"

"Of course," I huffed. "Morally."

"Are you one hundred percent sure of that, Fussell?"

"Yes. Of course. I would act morally. No question about it."

"That's how you'd like to *think* you'd react. But should such a dilemma ever arise, you may actually react differently."

I gave this some thought and, to my complete surprise, came to the sudden conclusion that he was right. In my case, it was as obvious as the nose on my face. The sad fact was, I did not really know myself at all. Was I not, as we spoke, in the midst of a severe moral dilemma and was I not acting contrary to the way I would have imagined? Not only was I dating and enjoying sexual union with my psychiatrist's wife, I could not resist pumping him for information about her! How moral was that little scenario? Sure, I felt tremendously guilty about it, but not guilty enough to sever all ties with Emily, which was what I should have done were I a truly ethical human being. If this wasn't a moral dilemma, I don't know what was. Yet here I sat, feigning innocence and asking my lover's spouse for dating tips!

"Perhaps you have a point," I conceded. "But don't you have to know someone completely in order to love them? Not that I necessarily believe in love, beyond the simple chemical process."

"You know them up to a point," Wang postulated. "But you would not believe how many patients I have who have been happily married for twenty, thirty years and one day, seemingly out of the blue, the spouse decides to walk out on the so-called happy marriage."

"Food for thought," I said.

"Hell," Wang said. "For a while I thought that very thing was happening to me."

"Oh?" I asked curiously. "How's the, um . . . divorce going?"

"What divorce?"

"I thought you were divorcing your wife."

"Ancient history," Wang said, clapping his hands together. "We're back together. Reconciled! Isn't that marvelous, Fussell?"

I was speechless. Words that formed in my brain would not exit my mouth. My tongue was suddenly devoid of moisture and I realized I was blinking rapidly. The room appeared to be spinning.

"Oh?" was all I could manage.

"Out of the blue!" Wang cried. "She moved back in with me, tore up the divorce papers!"

"Oh?"

"Apparently her *boyfriend* has been neglecting her. What a moron! What a schmuck!"

I said nothing and stared out his picture window. He was right—I'd been a moron and a schmuck. No, much worse. I'd been a—

"Earth to Fussell," Wang said, waving his hand in front of my face.

"Yes. Boyfriend. Must be. A schmuck," I answered robotically.

"My Emily doesn't like to be lonely," Wang informed me. "She goes a little nuts after about three days on her own. Slight case of paranoia. It wasn't easy, but I talked her into giving the marriage another try."

"Did she tell you anything?"

"About what?"

"About her boyfriend?"

"No," Wang said. "And frankly, I'm not interested. It was just a fling, nothing more."

"She said that?"

"Not in so many words," Wang said. "But that's the obvious implication, isn't it?"

"Yes, I suppose."

Neither of us said anything for a moment, though I believe Wang was expecting some sort of congratulatory word from me. At the moment, my mind was too jumbled to respond politely. How could I have been so stupid, so dense? How could I have neglected her? I was suddenly so filled with self-loathing, I could barely speak.

"I thought you'd be happy for me, Fussell," Wang complained after a few moments of silence had elapsed. I tried to smile.

"I am," I replied. "I'm delirious."

Chapter 21: Delirious was putting it

mildly. I was, as you can well imagine, heartbroken. No, heartbroken doesn't even begin to cover the conflagration of emotion that was causing my fragile sanity to come virtually unglued. (Okay, maybe heartbroken might actually cover it, although what the human cardiac muscle has to do with fondness for someone of the opposite sex, I certainly do not know. If I were indeed "heartbroken," if my auricles and ventricles were actually fractured, I would be suffering angina, extraordinary chest pain and shortness of breath, and any sensible cardiologist would prescribe an immediate echocardiagram or, at least, a cardiolite stress test.)

Be that as it may, there was suddenly a huge vacuum in my life where once there was my beloved Emily. Wang was right—it was a moral dilemma and the right thing, the honorable thing, the ethical thing to do was for me to forget Emily Thorndyke forever and allow her to continue with her marriage. The proper thing was for me to back off, to let her resume her life with Dr. Wang. The correct thing was for us never to see each other again for the rest of our lives.

Unfortunately, that was easier said than done.

I tried, I really did. I kept busy. I spent hours in the local library, searching for evidence of Fillmore's mysterious lady love (if that was what she was), all to no avail. I spent many torturous hours with my parents, helping Rose straighten up their apartment and performing a myriad of unnecessary errands. I played canasta for pennies with my mother and let her cheat. I spent a day with a large spray bottle of alcohol making sure everything in their apartment and the downstairs lobby was absolutely sterile. Sure, this was fun, but not nearly enough to rebuild my shattered cardiac muscle.

I had lunch with Teppelman. I had lunch with my accountant. I had lunch with my accountant's seventy-year-old secretary. I saw a movie. I sat alone in the park. I went grocery shopping. I bought a new wardrobe. I rode on a bicycle. I fell off a bicycle. I went to the emergency room. I had lunch with a nurse and a radiologist in a hospital cafeteria.

But almost everywhere I went, what did I see? I saw lovers walking hand in hand, or caressing, or kissing or whispering sweet nothings into each other's ear (whatever that means). They were doing it in the parks, on the streets, in cars, in restaurants, in elevators, on the bus. No doubt, amorous adventures were taking place in broom closets, hospital emergency rooms and airline lavatories. Every single time I turned on the television, no matter what channel I chose, there were people smooching, embracing or mating. Even the normally staid History Channel, certainly not a place where one would expect to see sex and romance, featured an episode on Antony and Cleopatra that week, which culminated in the two lovers making whoopee on a Nile barge. Just my luck—they were broadcasting a weeklong series of shows called Historical and Fictional Love Affairs, which included Pelléas and Mélisande, Abélard and Heloïse, Daphnis and Chloe, Franklin and Eleanor, Adolf and Eva. And the Public Broadcasting Station that week presented an endless series on copulating animals. It seemed that everywhere I turned, I saw men and women mating, or hyenas fornicating, or duck-billed platypuses going through the fertilization process. There was no escaping it.

Days passed and I still had no word from Emily, not that I held out much hope for any further communiqués from her. Consequently, I was sinking deeper and deeper into an exogenous depression.

"There's plenty of fish in the sea, Plato," my father lectured, after I had informed him about Emily's sudden withdrawal, although I was careful to refrain from identifying Dr. Wang as her husband. He seemed to be recovering steadily, although he still looked pallid and frail, and could barely walk much farther than the kitchen without becoming exhausted. Meanwhile, my mother had apparently decided that Rose was an interloper, and refused to speak to her or otherwise acknowledge her existence. Instead, she stared at the television all day, watching the usual inane fare of soap operas, sitcom reruns and daytime talk shows.

"I know," I said to my father. "But I'm not interested in other women. I want Emily, damn it."

"That's what you think now," he assured me. "Believe me, Plato, it's easier than you think to find a good woman. You just have to give it some time, my boy."

"You once told me yourself that every person has but one true love," I reminded him.

"I said that?" he asked. "When?"

"Years ago. I was a teenager at the time."

"That'll teach you not to believe everything you hear," he instructed me. "You're a young man still, Plato. You'll find someone."

"Am I supposed to believe you now?"

"Yes."

"But I'm nearly thirty-seven years old, Dad."

"A young man still," he said. "I'd give my left arm to be your age again, Plato."

"You married at thirty," I reminded him.

"Which might not have been such a wise thing to do," he said, nodding in the direction of the living room, where my mother sat engrossed in a talk show. "If you catch my drift."

"Actually, I don't."

"Never mind. You'll meet plenty of other girls, Plato," he said. "I assure you."

"But I'm shy. I get flustered, I stammer, my hands tremble, my heart palpitates, I talk gibberish."

"Many people are shy. As for the gibberish . . ."

"Emily is one of a kind."

"There's no such thing," he said. "Men, women, animals, we're all just lonely souls looking for a little companionship. Some of us are just better than others at hiding our loneliness."

"Emily understands me."

"Look, Plato, you're a good-looking guy with a lot of dough. You have a good heart. Somebody will come along sooner or later. I guarantee it. Just be a little patient."

"How?" I asked. "I'm not outgoing enough and beautiful women aren't going to drop by my house for no reason."

Just then, Rose walked in and put a cold drink and a Dixie cup full of pills on my father's nightstand.

"Time to be takin' those pills again, Mr. F," Rose said. We smiled at each other. Then, to my amazement, my father reached out his hand and squeezed her posterior.

"Mr. *Fussell*, you old dog!" she said, wagging her index finger at him as if she were scolding a little boy for stealing a cookie. But there was an unmistakably mischievous smile on her face.

"Dad, I'm . . . I'm *shocked!*" I exclaimed. "Shocked!"

"Relax, Plato. Just because I'm your father doesn't mean I'm not still a man. I can still appreciate a nice curvaceous rear end when I see one. And in case you didn't notice, Rosie here has one hell of a nice fanny."

I had noticed, but the description "curvaceous" would not have been my first choice. Before I could reappraise it, my father reached out again but this time I caught his hand.

"Dad, *really!* Behave yourself! Good grief!"

"It's okay," Rose said. "Long as it keeps that old heart of his beatin.' Right, Mr. Fussell?"

"Right, Rosie," he agreed, placing his hand in his pajama top and raising it up and down, while mouthing the words *tha-thump, tha-thump.*

"Now you be a good boy and swallow those pills."

Obediently, my father threw back his pills and chased them with a glass of water.

"Rosie and I are getting married," he said confidentially.

"You already are married," I pointed out.

"Your mother doesn't care about me anymore," he whined. "She doesn't care if I live or die."

"Of course she does."

"She hasn't been in this room once since I came home from the hospital. I might as well already be dead."

It occurred to me that perhaps my mother resented my hiring Rose to care for my father. I had never formally asked her permission—I thought I was doing her a favor. But I suppose she might have construed this gesture to mean that I thought she could not properly take care of the old man herself. So this sudden estrangement was probably my fault, as I had insisted on hiring Rose. The fact is my mother *was* unable to care for my father properly on her own. Who would do the errands? Left to themselves, they would starve to death.

"Dad," I said sotto voce, "do me a favor? Don't fondle anybody's posterior anymore. You want to get sued?"

"For what?"

"Shhhh. For sexual harassment," I whispered. "Don't you read the papers? You can't do this stuff anymore. It's illegal."

"It's not sexual harassment if the harassee likes it," he said. "And she likes it. Right, Rosie? Tell him."

Rosie shrugged. "Don't really bother me too much," she said. "Beats a kick in the ass."

"After I'm all better, Rosie and I are going to move down to Jamaica and buy ourselves a shrimping boat. Right, Rosie?"

She winked at me. "Sure thing, Mr. Fussell. Anything you say." Then she turned to me: "He's a real character, your father."

"Oh?"

"Don't tell your mother, Plato," my dad whispered. "She might get upset. Mum's the word. Okay?"

Upset was a bit of an understatement. I decided my father's brain was most likely a bit addled from the new pain medications he was taking and that he would soon snap out of it.

"Your secret's safe with me," I said.

The next day, I woke up at three o'clock in the morning with a stunningly brilliant idea. It had somehow come to me in my sleep, perhaps as part of a dream or perhaps as part of a nightmare, I didn't really remember. Such an obvious idea! So crafty. So elegant. Why hadn't I thought of it before? I jumped up, put on a robe and a pair of slippers, turned the heat up to eighty, made myself a cup of hot lemon water, scampered off to my study and plopped down in front of my laptop.

After booting up, I went online and did an Internet search for Thorndyke Interiors. My hands were trembling in anticipation. My stomach churned. After a moment, approximately eight "Thorndyke Interiors" came up on my screen so I scrolled down, reading each one thoroughly. My heart was beating rapidly and my hands began to perspire as I approached the bottom of the list and—Eureka!—there it was! The Web site address for Emily's business. It read: "Specializing in Funeral Homes, Crematoria Lobbies and Morgues: No Job Too Small." Written on the logo— a headstone, of course—there was this slogan: "It may be Death to you, but it's our bread and butter." I scanned the page quickly, then scrolled down. Hopefully, her Web site would contain an up-to-date e-mail address. . . .

It did.

Of course, I felt horribly guilty for what I was about to do. I was, after all, betraying Wang, who had only recently informed me that he considered me not only a patient, but a friend. How could I do this to him? How could I be so cruel, so thoughtless, so blatantly immoral?

I really don't know.

After giving it three or four agonizing hours of thought, I decided to go ahead with my plan, come hell or high water. Sure I was fond of Wang, but wasn't I fonder of Emily? Besides, I had to know what was going on in her mind. Why had she dumped me? What had I done wrong? One can, after all, only learn from one's mistakes.

Of course, I had to be careful not to reveal anything I had learned about Emily from Dr. Wang during my sessions. So it was with painstaking attention to detail and wording that I typed the following e-mail message:

Dearest Emily,

You have broken my heart, my darling, and I don't mean that in the cardiac sense. Where have you gone? I long to see you. I cannot sleep or function anymore. I've lost my appetite and have developed a nasty rash on my left thigh. Moreover, my sinuses are acting up again and my stomach is in something of an uproar!

If it was something I said or something I did that drove you from my bosom, I apologize from the bottom of my lonely heart.

Please, please answer me. Perhaps we can meet somewhere and

*just talk about all of this. I am desperate. Have mercy on me! I
beg you.*

Fondly,
Plato G. Fussell
*PS: Do you still have those plaid socks of mine? If so, kindly
have them dry-cleaned (no starch) and send them back. Thanks.*

I read it over maybe fifty times, changing a word here and
there, until I thought it was perfect, until it really sang. Then, closing my eyes and performing a little good luck ritual—tapping
wood twelve times, fondling a little stuffed rabbit I've had since
childhood, facing north and bowing eleven times, reciting the
pseudoscientific message that appears on a tube of Crest tooth-
paste and performing sixteen push-ups nude in the bathtub—after
doing all that, I hit the Send button.

Then I waited.

Chapter 22: To my surprise, I received an e-mail response from Emily exactly fifty-eight minutes later that same morning. It read as follows:

> Dear Plato,
>   I don't think men actually have bosoms.
>
>   Best wishes, Emily
>   P.S.: Your socks are in the mail.

Okay, so perhaps it wasn't the warmest response imaginable, but it was a beginning, by golly! I had finally managed to crack through the icy barrier of silence and once again converse, albeit in cyberspace, with my Emily. Somehow, my usual pessimism gave way to a spark of hope. Soon more words would be exchanged between us and eventually her passion would be rekindled. It was inevitable! I just knew it!

Moreover, after carefully dissecting every word and punctuation mark of her short epistle, it was abundantly clear that she still cared for me a great deal. After all, had she not replied promptly? She could have easily chosen not to respond at all. Or, she might have waited a few days, a week, perhaps a year. Furthermore, had she not referred to me as "*Dear* Plato"? She could have just said "Plato" or "Mr. Fussell," or "To whom it may concern," or nothing at all. Had she not offered me her "*Best* wishes"? And most of all, did it not require a fair degree of affection for her to have gone to the considerable effort and expense of mailing me back my socks? Washing or dry-cleaning them, folding them, placing them in a large envelope, perhaps wrapping them in tissue, addressing the envelope by hand or computer label and driving all the way to the post office or a mailing station to acquire sufficient postage? Perhaps she was even sending them via Federal Express or United Postal Service, either one a considerable expense. This was, in my opinion, irrefutable proof that she still harbored great affection for me.

Then there was the matter of the heart of her reply, which I referred to as the "bosom correction." Had she not cared for me an iota, had she no desire to see me ever again, why would she have felt the need to correct me on this minor detail? As far as I was concerned, the very statement "I don't think men actually have bosoms" reflected her underlying fondness for me, in that it attempted to save me from making the same blunder again in public (although I do indeed think men *can* have bosoms, when the word "bosom" refers to a man's heart or a man's core and not to the mammary glands, generally not found on the male anatomy, except in certain hermaphrodites). Nonetheless, as a scholar of sorts, I was able to read between the lines and discern Emily's true intentions.

I was, in short, ecstatic.

But I needed an objective opinion and, since consulting Wang was obviously out of the question, I immediately called Teppelman, whose very vocation involved letters, notes and communiqués. After a moment of chitchat, he agreed to see me. I threw on some clothes and drove straight to his place of business with a copy of

Emily's e-mail in my hands. When I arrived, he was unshaven, and his hair looked as if an experiment in static electricity had recently gone awry. It was then that I realized it was only 7:45 A.M.

"Isn't it a little early in the morning for this?" he complained.

"I'm wide awake," I said.

"Bully for you," Teppleman mumbled. "You woke me in the midst of a fascinating dream involving a mermaid and a chafing dish."

"Oh," I said. "Terribly sorry."

"Well, let's have the damned thing, as long as you're here."

It was with shaking hands that I handed Emily's missive over to him. He rubbed the sleep from his eyes, put on a pair of bifocals and read it, muttering something unintelligible to himself. When he was done, he turned the page over.

"That's it?" he asked.

"Splendid, isn't it?" I was barely able to contain my excitement.

"I don't know, Fussell," he said, handing it back. "I wouldn't read too much into it if I were you."

"But it's so clear! So obvious!" I cried. "*Dear* Plato, *Best* wishes . . ."

"Yes, well, people use those very same words when they write letters to the gas company."

"Oh really? You would say 'Best wishes' in a letter to the gas company?"

"I was referring specifically to the 'Dear Plato' part," Teppleman said.

"Aha!"

"But I would write 'Best Wishes' to a client I barely knew. It's like 'Sincerely Yours' or 'Yours Truly.' Authors often sign books with the words 'Best Wishes.' Polite, but totally meaningless."

"What about the bosom correction?" I asked. "What does that tell you about her?"

"It tells me she's a little neurotic. Stickler for detail. Not unlike you, Fussell."

"Yes, yes, yes! Perhaps that's the hidden meaning!" I said. "She wants me to know that we remain birds of a feather."

"A long shot, Fussell. In my humble opinion."

"Then there's the business of the socks," I said excitedly. "She clearly goes out of her way to make sure my socks are promptly returned. You must admit she demonstrates some affection there."

"Or she doesn't want her husband to find a pair of men's socks in her sock drawer," Teppelman opined.

"How do you know she's married?"

"You told me so yourself," he said. "When you called at the ungodly hour of seven o'clock."

"Terribly sorry," I said. "But getting back to the discussion at hand, how do you know she even has a sock drawer?"

"I don't."

"And even if she does have a sock drawer, meaning a drawer devoted solely to the housing of socks, a repository, as it were, dedicated exclusively to sheltering socks, a sock sanctuary of sorts, why would her husband want to stick his nose into the privacy of her sock drawer?" I cried. "For what purpose, exactly?"

"To check her socks, perhaps?"

"To check her socks? Why would he check her socks? What is there about socks that requires checking?"

"How should I know? To make sure all her socks were present and accounted for, I suppose. Or, perhaps more likely, to see if one of his socks had found its way mistakenly into her sock drawer. The sorting of socks can often produce such errors."

I gave this absurd notion a moment of thought before dismissing it as ridiculous.

"So now you're an expert on errant hosiery?" I quipped.

"Is there such a thing?"

"Does your wife check *your* socks?" I inquired.

"Religiously."

"Nonsense."

"She does. I kid you not."

"Good heavens, why?"

"I don't know." Teppelman shrugged. "It's just something she does. A compulsion, perhaps. I'll ask her if you like."

"Please do."

"One question," Teppelman continued. "How is it that she happened to have a pair of your socks in the first place?"

"I tore them slightly at one of our picnics," I replied. "On a burr. She offered to sew them up for me. That was quite sweet, don't you agree?"

Just then, the bell over the door jingled annoyingly and a customer entered the store. By now it was just after eight o'clock, but Teppelman did not usually open his place of business until nine. He looked at me and shrugged, then excused himself, ran a hand through his hair, put on something vaguely resembling a smile and bade the young man welcome. Since Teppelman conducted most of his business through the mail, actual living customers were a rarity. I watched them disappear behind the piles of books, files and papers that cluttered Teppelman's store, then I folded Emily's e-mail and stuffed it in my breast pocket. As it happened, I would never find out why Teppelman's wife checked his sock drawer so religiously, though I suspect he was making it all up just to win the argument.

Obviously, I could not get too deeply into the sock drawer question with Wang because I did not want him to know that Ahab had deserted me and gone back to her husband, lest he extrapolate the truth and suddenly realize we were actually talking about the very same person.

But I did mention that Ahab and I had been corresponding via e-mail.

"Good for you, Fussell," he said enthusiastically. "I like your spirit. Never give up. That's the ticket!"

"You think it's a good sign? That she responded?"

"Absolutely."

"Do you think I should continue to write to her?"

"Indeed. But don't get too pushy."

"How do you mean?"

"Write to her about meaningless nonsense for a while, then slowly broach the subject of getting together for coffee."

"I don't drink coffee."

"Glass of wine?"

"No."

"Beer?"

"Afraid not."

"Well, the actual beverage doesn't really matter, Fussell. Ask to meet her in the park to gather acorns. Take her to a movie, out to dinner, miniature golf. . . ."

"Yes, I see . . ."

"But not right away."

"Not right away."

Wang had a mischievous sparkle in his eye. "You might even play . . . hard to get," he suggested.

"How? I'm not one hundred percent sure she even *wants* me at this point. Teppelman was a bit discouraging on the subject."

"Ach, what does Teppelman know? He doesn't really get out much, does he?"

"No."

"Then take my advice," Wang said. "Play hard to get."

"But she has to want me first, right? Otherwise playing hard to get is somewhat self-defeating."

"Later," Wang counseled. "Not now. When you've reached a certain point with her—then you suddenly play hard to get. Women do it to us all the time, but they hate it when we do it to them."

"How exactly does one do it?" I inquired. "Play hard to get? Is there a manual I could peruse? A guidebook, perhaps?"

"One merely has to act coy, seemingly indifferent, noncommittal."

"I see."

"That's how I got my Emily back," Wang said proudly. "I played hard to get. Oldest trick in the book."

As you can imagine, I was delighted with this new strategy. *Hard to get?* An interesting idea indeed. And if it worked for him, it would surely work for me. After all, we were both doing it to the same woman.

Wang was always so darn *helpful.*

"How's that going, by the way?" I asked. "If you don't mind my asking. I don't wish to pry."

"You mean my insane roller coaster of a marriage?"

"Yes."

"Pretty well, I think," Wang said hesitantly.

"You think?" I repeated, leaning forward. "You're not sure?"

"Well, everything was just fine, then suddenly this morning, for no apparent reason, none that I could discern anyway, she became sort of . . ."

"Yes?"

". . . cold, remote, detached."

"How odd," I reflected attentively. "What was she doing at the time?"

"I don't really remember," Wang said, lost in thought for a moment, letting his mind trace back to the morning, I presumed. "The usual morning stuff. Eating cereal, drinking coffee, reading her e-mail . . ."

"So she has a laptop?"

"Well, she doesn't drag a goddamn desktop into the kitchen," Wang snapped. "What difference does it make?"

I noted that he was becoming a bit testy, so I decided to play it cool and not probe any deeper.

"Sorry," I said. "Stickler for detail."

Of course I knew the answer. She had read my desperate e-mail at the breakfast table and it had had the desired effect. The seed had been planted! Plato G. Fussell was back! I had burrowed my way back under her skin like a pesky crab louse. Dastardly and shameful as it was, rotten, fiendish and guilt-ridden as I felt, I would follow Dr. Wang's advice to the letter. I would continue to e-mail her and then—just when we were on the verge of getting back together again—I would play hard to get. It would be a struggle, it would require more than a little rehearsal, not to mention considerable self-restraint and discipline, but I was certain I could master the arts of coyness and indifference. I could hardly wait to get home and devise my next potent e-mail.

Then something truly horrendous happened.

Chapter 23: "I'm telling you, it was that

so-called nurse you hired. It was all her fault. He did nothing but make goo-goo eyes at her all day long."

"Nonsense."

"You never even consulted me about hiring that woman."

"I'm sorry."

"They giggled all day long like teenagers! It was disgusting!"

"He enjoyed the company."

"And what am I? Am I not company? For forty years we've lived in the same apartment, but somehow *I'm* not company?"

"Of course you are."

"Of course? What does 'of course' mean?"

"It means of course, of course."

"Forty years! Do you have any idea how long that is?"

"Fourteen thousand, six hundred days to be exact, not including leap years. I can break that down into hours if you'd like."

"Spare me."

"It's a lot of hours," I said. "Over three hundred and fifty thousand."

"Who knows what they were doing in that room all day," she continued, ignoring me. "I heard all kinds of suspicious noises."

"What noises?"

"Giggles."

"Besides giggles."

"Grunts."

"Anything else?"

"Groans."

"That was probably Dad trying to take a crap."

"Do *not* say that word in my presence, please."

"Sorry."

We sat silently for a moment. Conversational lulls generally make me nervous, but not when my mother is involved. In her case, they are generally quite a relief. Her next statement stunned me:

"Do you have any idea how long it's been since your father and I last had sexual relations?"

"No, and I'm not sure I really want to know either," I said. "It's really none of my—"

"Ten years!" she interrupted. "Ten years! Can you imagine? I tell you, he had the hots for that nurse."

"I'm sure there was nothing going on. Maybe some innocent flirting, nothing more."

"Since when is flirting ever innocent?" she countered.

"I'm sure there was nothing of a sexual nature happening between them."

"You're sure? How would you know? You came by twice. Maybe three times."

"I was there every single day, Mother, remember?"

"And you did nothing but read the paper."

"I ran errands. I cleaned. I disinfected the lobby!"

"Ach, you Fussell men are all alike. I should've married Chad Finkel when I had the chance."

"Who?"

"Chad Finkel. He was a big golf champion at my high school. Very handsome. The smartest boy I ever met. He went to MIT. And he liked me quite a lot. I never told you about him?"

My father had suffered another myocardial infarction and once again my mother had called me from the hospital having narrowly survived the ambulance trip. Once again she had brought a jar of kosher garlic pickles, but this time had lost them in all the excitement. It was past midnight by the time I arrived at the ICU, and the waiting room was empty of people but cluttered with soda cans, Styrofoam cups and half-eaten sandwiches from earlier in the day.

After finishing her diatribe about Rose, my mother began to weep. Apparently, this heart attack had been much more severe than the last one and, although the doctors had been optimistic, she was doubtful my father would survive it this time.

"What am I going to do if he doesn't make it?" she sputtered. "I can't function on my own, Plato."

"He'll make it," I said optimistically. "He'll come through this."

"He's in a coma," she said. "What if he doesn't wake up? What if he dies? Then what?"

"Dad's tough. He survived a war. He'll survive this too."

I handed her one of my monogrammed handkerchiefs. She inspected it carefully, both sides.

"I want to die, Plato! I want to die!"

"Don't say that, Mother," I took her hand in mine. "You don't really mean that."

"Yes, I do," she said, smelling the handkerchief. "Is this clean?"

"Is what clean?"

"This handkerchief. Is it clean?"

"Yes, of course it is. I don't walk around with dirty handkerchiefs."

"It looks a little dirty to me," she said, holding it up to the light. "You blew your nose in this?"

"Yes, but it's been washed fifty times since then," I maintained. "It's safe, you can use it. Believe me. I use Extra-Strength Clorox. Clorox kills everything."

"Who washed it?"

"My housekeeper."

"How can you be sure she did a good job?"

"Because I'm as neurotic as you are," I said. "I check."

"Do you wipe sweat off with it?"

"I don't sweat."

"You should take them to a dry cleaner. Your father always takes his handkerchiefs to the dry cleaner."

I sighed and stood up. One could argue with my mother for hours and never win. "I'm going to see Dad now," I said. "Will you be all right here by yourself?"

"Sure, go on. If he wakes up, call me."

I nodded and padded quietly down the hallway and into his room. He was lying still, under the covers, his eyes closed, hands folded on his chest as if he were practicing how to lie in a coffin. His breathing was irregular and hoarse, but the blips on the heartbeat monitor were steady. At first I didn't know quite what to do, so I just stood there gaping from a distance of about six feet, as if I were expecting him to ask me in. After a moment, I pulled a plastic chair over to the bed and sat down beside him.

"Hi, Dad," I said pleasantly, as if addressing a small child. "It's me, Plato. Your son. Can you hear me? Blink or move your finger or something if you can hear me, okay?"

I waited. Nothing happened.

"Okay," I said. "Maybe that requires too much strength. Can you produce some flatulence, Dad? Nothing bombastic, mind you, just fart if you can hear me."

Again, I waited but no gaseous emissions were forthcoming. Then I pinched his arm but there was no reaction. I took his white, bony hand in mine, but it felt like picking up a liver-spotted cooking utensil, so I placed it carefully back on his chest, where it seemed to belong. Given my obsession with death, what fascinated me the most at that moment was the notion that my father's soul was teetering in a mysterious place, a junction of sorts that was somewhere between life and death. What was that place like? Was it a nice place? Was it a boring place, was it like the slow-moving line at a grocery store checkout counter? Was he thinking about my mother? Was he thinking about me? Was he even able to think at all? Were scenes from his life playing out before him in bright flashes, the last gasps of the memory cells as they shut down for the duration? Or what?

I was dying to know, no pun intended.

So I sat there for a few minutes and just talked to him. Oddly, it felt like I was addressing furniture, but I continued anyway. I rambled on about Millard Fillmore and Emily and my mother and Dr. Wang and the Dodgers and the various brands of surgical soaps, and anything that popped into my head. When I ran out of things to say, I sang two verses of the *"Marseillaise."* Then I picked up an old newspaper that someone had left on a table and started reading the editorials to him. My father used to love lambasting the editorials. He thought all newspaper editors were idiots. Even when he agreed with them.

Finally, after about twenty minutes, I stood up, kissed my father's forehead and returned the chair to its former station. I was about to turn toward the door when I thought I saw his hand move. I rushed over.

"Dad?"

I took his hand. The heart monitor blip accelerated slightly.

"Dad? Can you speak?"

I felt his hand squeeze mine very slightly. I squeezed it back.

"Dad! Say something!"

Then suddenly his eyes popped open and he stared at the ceiling. "Do not forsake Leopold!" he said.

"What? Who's Leopold?"

But his eyes closed again.

"Dad!"

His hand went limp in mine.

"Dad!"

I shook him gently, to no avail. I slapped the palm of his hand. I lifted an eyelid, but his eyes were blank. He was unconscious again. Out cold.

Then suddenly, the beeping sound stopped, giving way to a sustained minor note, and the heart monitor flatlined. Terrified, I ran into the corridor and yelled for a nurse. At that moment, I saw my mother's face freeze into a pale mask of utter horror as she sat immobilized in the waiting room. An attending physician, an intern and two nurses snapped into action and immediately wheeled a nearby crash cart past me and into the room. I rejoined my mother in the waiting area and placed a consoling arm around her quaking shoulders while the doctors and nurses tried to revive my father. But it soon proved hopeless and after a while, with their heads bowed, they walked out of my father's room and came down the corridor to tell us the grim news.

Chapter 24: I wrote my father's obitu-

ary myself—an experience that brought tears of grief to my eyes—and sent copies to the local papers. For some reason, directly following a death in the family (and this was my first), it suddenly becomes imperative for the survivors to notify people—old friends, close and distant relatives, acquaintances. I called every name in my father's address book—even several whom I suspected were plumbers or handymen—and went through the same litany with all of them ("Hello, I have some sad news to tell you. My father, Victor Fussell, passed away the other day. . . ." For some reason I couldn't bring myself to use the word "died."). Then there are the gloomy tasks of arranging the funeral service, buying the headstone and plot, choosing the exact wording for the headstone ("Loving Husband, Beloved Father"), selecting a casket, ordering the death certificates, closing down the charge cards, safe deposit boxes, bank accounts, my father's subscription to his favorite yachting magazine and so on. Most people are completely unprepared for their own deaths and leave all the details to the poor, distraught survivors. Since I do not plan to have any distraught survivors, I have put all the necessary information on a floppy disk that I carry on my person at all times, just in case I get hit by a truck or an asteroid (although if I get hit by an asteroid, I imagine the floppy disk would probably not survive the explosion, unless it is a very small asteroid).

In addition to being thoroughly grief-stricken over my father's sudden demise, I could not help but wonder who this Leopold was. A boyhood chum? An old pet, a parakeet, perhaps, or a schnauzer? A war buddy? My father had served in the army during the Korean War, but I did not know for sure if he even had any war buddies. He certainly never mentioned anyone to me, and my mother was clueless. In fact, for some reason, my father had never wanted to talk about the war or his experiences as a soldier. But I knew this was not unusual—many veterans refrain from discussing their combat experiences. There is little to be nostalgic about in war, I suppose. In any case, I was unable to find any mention of a person named Leopold in any of his personal papers.

For some reason, the task that touched me most involved the sorting and dispensing of my father's clothing and assorted belongings, which, after long discussion, my mother and I decided to donate to our local rescue mission. I was surprised at what a difficult job it turned out to be, separating ourselves from my father's things. How sad those old shoes looked in his shoe rack. How droopy and forlorn his suit jackets were, hanging in the closet. How dismal an old man's toilet paraphernalia seemed in their disarray around the bathroom sink, as if he had just stepped out of the room and was coming back any moment to shave. As if nothing had happened. It was with great melancholy that I placed most of my father's personal belongings in a number of large Hefty bags, which I left out on the curb for the charity truck to pick up.

Oddly enough, the only problem I encountered was canceling my father's subscription to the yachting magazine. For some reason, the publication's customer service department had never heard of him.

Needless to say, my mother was far too hysterical to do anything constructive except weep and complain, so everything was left entirely to me. Which was something of a blessing because all the busywork took my mind off how deeply I was going to miss my father, how deeply I already missed him. He had always been the anchor of our little family, the most grounded one of the three of us, the least neurotic.

"I suppose you'll be putting me in a nursing home now," my mother said when I had a free moment.

"Why?"

"Because that's where lonely old people like me usually end up. 'Assisted living', they call it."

"I haven't given it any thought whatsoever," I replied. "The idea never even crossed my mind."

"Given the choice, I'd rather stay home."

"Fine."

The fact was, I *had* given it some thought. My mother was in good physical health but, considering her agoraphobia, how could she manage to live alone? Who would do her errands? Who would keep her company? Who would listen to her complaints? And what would happen to her if she fell and broke a hip or accidentally cut herself with a kitchen knife? Or had a stroke?

"They do have some very nice modern retirement communities in the area," I said. "They have activities, cruises and everything."

"How do you know?" she asked. "Have you been doing research? Next you'll be showing me brochures."

"It's entirely up to you," I repeated.

"I probably wouldn't like the toilets."

"I'm sure they have state-of-the-art bathroom facilities."

"I'm going to be so lonely, Plato," she moaned.

"No, you won't," I assured her, taking her hand. "I won't allow it."

"But who will take care of me?"

"I don't know. I'll find someone," I promised. "Don't worry."

"Maybe I could live with you?"

"I don't think that would be a very healthy arrangement for either of us," I said gently. "I'll find someone you'll like, a companion."

"Who?"

"I don't know. A caregiver of some sort."

"A live-in caregiver?"

"Perhaps," I ventured. "If you're comfortable with that."

"A man?"

"Probably a woman," I said. "With some nursing experience, perhaps."

My mother gave this prospect a moment of contemplating, then shook her head.

"I'd prefer a man," she said.

I looked at her with surprise. Was she serious? Wasn't this a little too soon to be thinking of substitutes for my father, if indeed that was what she had in mind? Or did she just prefer the company of men? After all, she had lived with a man—my father—for forty years.

"A younger man," she said coyly. "Someone who maybe can dance."

No old army buddies showed up at the funeral, although my father's plumber, dry cleaner and handyman all came with their wives. Also in attendance was Joe Kenton, a man my father had occasionally played billiards with. Lottie Neter, a distant cousin from San Diego, was there, and Rose was good enough to attend, although she stationed herself as far away from my mother as was humanly possible, a sound idea given my mother's irrational hostility toward her. A few members of my father's old poker club arrived as well. I took my mother's hand in both of mine as Reverend Brock read a passage from the Bible that appeared to have no end.

Then between deep religious sighs, he said a few kind words about my father, a man whom he had never met, although prior to the service I had given him some ideas about what to say. My father had been a kind, considerate, generous man, but as I listened to Reverend Brock talk about him, I felt no emotion whatsoever.

Then in the middle of this speech, I saw something that almost made me leap out of my shoes. No more than fifty feet from the gravesite, a car door suddenly slammed shut and when I glanced behind me to determine the identity of this rude car door slammer, I could not believe my eyes. Was I hallucinating? Did my eyes deceive me? Was it an apparition? Or was this figure climbing out of an old BMW and approaching the gravesite really my Emily, dressed from head toe in black and sporting an oversize pair of sunglasses? Yes, *YES*, it was her! Suddenly I felt my heart beating so rapidly I thought I was going to keel over any minute and fall into my father's empty grave. My emotions were suddenly in utter chaos—I was sincerely melancholy about my father's demise, and at the same time inanely giddy at seeing Emily. All of which led to a profound feeling of guilt. But I couldn't help myself. Somber as the occasion was, the same question kept going through my addled mind: Was her coming here not definitive proof that she still loved me? Had I not been at a funeral I might have actually jumped for joy! Or run around in circles, waving my arms in the air like a lunatic. Apparently, she had read the obituary in the paper and felt compelled to console me in my hour of grief. As she approached I gave her a furtive wave, which, for some reason, she did not return.

But then I noticed the figure behind her, catching up. It was Dr. Wang, also dressed in black.

He returned my wave.

Of course. How could I have forgotten? It was I who had informed Dr. Wang of my father's demise and he had obviously decided to comfort me by appearing at the funeral. I admit I was deeply touched by his thoughtfulness, for he had probably canceled several appointments just to be here with me. What a terrific fellow! Of course, this made me ascend to an even higher level of guilt. I could barely endure it. I turned my eyes away from them and watched as my father's coffin was lowered slowly into the ground. My mother wept and I stroked her hand. In spite of all this, the same question kept dogging me: Had Wang asked Emily to accompany him to the funeral or had this been her own idea? That was the crucial point. I wanted to slap myself for even thinking about it at such a solemn moment.

Then, as the minister read a final prayer and my father's coffin was now deep enough in the grave to be out of sight from where we were standing, I suddenly realized that this was shaping up to be a fairly awkward situation. For one thing, when did Emily find out I was a patient of her husband's? Perhaps at this very moment. For another, Emily and I would have to pretend we did not know each other. This was getting too complicated. My heart, which had stopped palpitating for three minutes, started up again for a totally different reason. Had I brought my Xanax along? I would need to consume at least half the bottle.

"I'm so sorry, Plato," Dr. Wang intoned after the funeral service was over. He took my hand. "I know how much your father meant to you."

"Thank you, Doctor," I said, desperately trying to take my eyes off Emily, who was standing beside him, staring at the ground.

"I'm sad to say it, but we all become orphans eventually," Wang said, not knowing that my mother was also standing at my side. "It's just one of those Life Experiences."

"May I introduce my mother," I said. "Mother, this is Dr. Wang, my psychiatrist." Wang took her hand in his.

"So glad to meet you at last," Wang said.

"Likewise," my mother replied.

"Please accept my sincerest condolences," Wang continued.

My mother scrutinized him suspiciously. "So you're Plato's shrink?"

"That's right."

"What does he say about me?" she demanded. "He blames me for everything, right? It's all my fault, am I right? I wiped his tush for five years and now he's complaining about me, am I right?"

"Five years?" Wang said. I gave my mother a dirty look.

"That's right," my mother maintained. "Five years."

I cringed in total embarrassment and felt my face gradually turn hot. I glanced at Emily. Was that a smile of mirth on her face? Hard to tell since she was still looking down at her shoes.

"Okay, okay, maybe I was a little slow in that department," I sputtered in utter mortification. "Can we change the subject, please?"

"Plato has nothing but the nicest things to say about you, Mrs. Fussell," Wang assured my mother. "Really. I swear it."

I was amazed at how well he lied. No blinking, no stuttering. Almost as smooth as me. I was also grateful that Wang had turned the topic away from my somewhat belated success with potty training.

"Baloney," my mother said.

Wang cleared his throat and turned to me. "Plato, Mrs. Fussell, I'd like to introduce my wife, Emily."

Emily looked up and I saw through her dark glasses that there were tears in her eyes. Were these tears of sadness from the funeral? Or tears of joy at seeing me again after all this time? Or generic tears with no particular meaning at all? Anyway, I thanked her for coming and shook her hand. I must have held it too long for after a few moments she wrenched it out of my grip.

"I'm very pleased to meet you," I said. "Dr. Wang has told me so much about you."

"Oh?"

"Nice things," I was quick to add, feeling a bit clumsy. "Only nice things."

She and Wang both gave me a dirty look.

"If we don't get going, we'll miss the food," my mother said. There was to be a small reception at the funeral home. "It's buffet style. Also I think I have to go to the toilet. At my age a good bowel movement is a big event."

"Allow me," Wang said, graciously offering his elbow. My mother looked at it for half a second, then shrugged and took it.

A few moments after they started walking toward the reception hall Emily and I followed side by side. I offered her my elbow but she pushed her hands into her coat pockets.

"You never told me you were one of my husband's patients," she hissed.

"I know. I'm sorry."

"You're sorry. It's a lie of omission."

"I didn't want to lose you, Emily," I said quietly. "And I didn't know right away. By the time I found out—"

"What does he say about me?"

"Nothing."

"Liar."

"Okay, he wants you back. He loves you. He's lost without you. He's forlorn, devastated. . . . Happy now?"

"What else?"

"Nothing. Inconsequential stuff."

"Sex stuff?"

"Of course not. He's not the patient, Emily. We usually talk about *my* problems, not his."

"Did you tell him about me?" she asked, looking up at me.

"I've told him I have a close female acquaintance who is married," I said. "But I've never mentioned your name, of course. He'd kill me."

"Not his style," she mused. "He'd drop you as a patient."

"I assumed as much," I said.

"What do you call me?"

"Pardon?"

"How do you refer to me?" she asked. "What name do you use? At your sessions."

"Don't laugh," I warned her.

"I won't."

"Ahab," I said.

"Ahab?" she repeated. "He thinks I'm an obsessive-compulsive one-legged character from a Melville novel?"

"It's a long story," I told her. "Does he tell you anything about me?"

"Of course not. He would never do that. Doctor-patient confidentiality. He's very conscientious."

"Do you look at his notes?"

"He keeps them locked in the safe."

Just then we walked past Bob Hoover, the funeral director, and entered the funeral parlor. A small buffet of cold cuts, salads, doughnuts, assorted fruits, coffee and soft drinks awaited us in the main room. Wang was hanging up my mother's coat, nodding at something she had said. Emily was looking around as if she were casing the joint in preparation for a robbery.

"My God," she muttered.

"What?"

"This place desperately needs redecorating," she said. "Those curtains are a travesty. And just look at this carpeting! Pea green carpeting? In a funeral parlor? And I've seen better furniture at yard sales!"

"Emily," I whispered, once Wang and my mother had entered the main parlor. "Can we talk?"

"Plastic flower arrangements? This is an abomination! Who designed this place? Frank Lloyd Wrong?"

"Emily, we need to talk," I said, sotto voce.

"About what?"

"About *what*? About us, of course. I thought you loved me. You said you loved me."

"Keep your voice down, Fussell," she whispered. "I thought you didn't believe in love, Mr. *Ditto*."

"I don't, I do," I said. "Whatever it is, love, affection, extreme fondness or just an ordinary hormonal discharge, the fact is, I can't live without you, Emily. I've been miserable without you. Miser-able! I can't eat, I can't sleep, I can't work. And that's the—"

Something about this declaration of mine must have softened her resolve, because before I was able to finish the sentence, she grabbed me by my necktie and yanked me into the closet, where, behind closed doors and between the racks of coats redolent with the aroma of cologne and mothballs, we kissed madly, passionately, feverishly for a good thirty seconds (an estimate; I was unable to actually time it). Then, just as suddenly, Emily pulled away from me, exited the closet, frantically straightened her clothing and her hair, and rushed off to be by Wang's side. Apparently, no one had seen us.

As the son of the deceased, it was incumbent upon me to min-gle among the few people who had been kind enough to attend my father's funeral. Making small talk with people I hardly knew was never one of my fortes, but somehow I managed. I spoke to the plumber for twenty minutes and learned about the nuances of the ball-cock mechanism on toilets, an item I had always been espe-cially interested in. I booked the handyman for some minor paint-ing and puttying at my house for the following week. Mr. Kenton told me an interesting story about my father's lack of talent at bil-liards, and Lottie Neter complained to me about her arthritis. And I even thanked the Reverend Brock for his eloquent, heartfelt eu-logy, even though it was neither eloquent nor heartfelt. For some reason, in spite of my death fixation, I found the business aspects of death—the eulogies, coffins, headstones, embalming, funer-als—pedestrian, tedious and decidedly uninteresting.

Later in the afternoon, I found Emily sitting alone in a corner, fondling the fabric of one of the curtains and wrinkling her nose in disgust. Ah, my Emily. How gorgeous she was, even when dis-gusted. I wanted to speak to her, I needed to hear her voice, to gaze into her eyes, but before I could even get there, my mother grabbed me by the arm.

"That's a nice-looking, charming young lady," she said, indicating Emily by impolitely pointing directly at her. "That's just the kind of young lady you should marry, Plato."

"Really?" I said. It was most unusual for my mother to speak so highly of anyone. In fact, I was never entirely certain she particularly liked *me*, her own son.

"Why is that, Mother?" I asked.

"Find one like her and you have my blessings."

"I'll see what I can do," I said, gently trying to get out of her iron grip. Her bony, viselike fingers didn't budge.

"A nice young lady like her would never dream of putting her mother-in-law in a nursing home," she said.

"Nor would I, Mother," I assured her, finally pulling loose.

But it was too late. When I looked back at the corner, Emily was no longer there. Frantic, I turned to the front window and saw her get into the driver's seat of her car, as the good doctor held the door open for her. And then they were gone.

Chapter 25: In the midst of all this com-

motion, I received, out of the blue, a telephone call from, of all people, Daisy Crane. I had not heard from the shrew since our horrific divorce eight years ago, for which I was extremely grateful. Frankly, outside of my therapy sessions, I had not given her much thought, nostalgic or otherwise, since the dissolution of our marriage, though I'm not entirely sure the term "marriage" even applies to our short, wretched travesty of a union. I assumed she had either drunk or smoked herself to death by now. Unfortunately, I was mistaken.

Apparently, Daisy had heard about my father's death from an old high school classmate who had read the local paper's obituary, and she was calling to offer me her condolences, a word I was certain she could not spell. Needless to say, given my paranoid tendencies, I was more than a little suspicious of her motives.

"Let me guess," I scoffed. "You've run out of money. You've

managed to spend every last cent of the eight million dollars I gave you and you need more?"

"You're still mad at me, aren't you," she noted perceptively. "You're still holding a grudge."

"You have to ask?"

"I was hoping time would have healed some of those old wounds," she mused in a calm, saintly tone of voice that I found irritating.

"You bilked me out of EIGHT MILLION DOLLARS! You made a fool of me!" I shrieked. "It would take a century!"

"Yes, and you have every reason to be angry," she continued. "I behaved like a complete fool."

" 'Fool' doesn't really cover it," I said.

" 'Idiot'?"

"Not even close."

" 'Asshole'?"

"Getting warmer."

"I know. You're right. I treated you like dirt, Plato," she admitted. "No, worse than dirt. Like scum. No, worse even than scum. I treated you like—"

" 'Scum' will cover it nicely," I said. "I don't have the time nor the inclination to sit here and listen to you struggling to come up with inept synonyms for the word 'scum.' Besides, my father just died. I'm not in a very good mood."

"Yes," she said in a low voice. "I understand."

There was a pause. For a moment I thought the line had gone dead.

"Believe me, Plato, I'm not the same Daisy Crane I was when we were married. I'm not that Daisy Crane at all."

"I get it," I quipped sarcastically. "You've changed your name."

"No, I've changed my very self."

"Slastic purgery?" (Why was I suddenly nervous?)

"What?"

"Never mind."

"You're not getting this, are you?"

"Okay, let me guess—you were reborn, right? You found God. Or Vishnu, or Buddha. Or, more likely in your case, Satan."

"Maybe it was a mistake for me to call."

"Why *did* you call?" I asked.

"To offer you my deepest sympathies," she said. "Truly."

"You could have just as easily sent a card or done nothing at all. Believe me, my feelings would not have been hurt if you had done nothing at all."

"I guess I just wanted an excuse to let you know how I've changed," she said. "And to ask for your forgiveness."

"Okay," I said with a chuckle. "I'm game. How have you changed, Daisy? But make it quick—I have to reorganize my sock drawer."

Daisy took a deep breath, as if she were preparing to give a long oration and did not want to interrupt its flow with breathing.

"For one thing, I have a master's degree in sociology," she said. "I got it three years ago."

"One of those colleges you sign up for on matchbook covers?" I asked flippantly. "Pepe's University of Eastern Nogales?"

"Actually, after two years at junior college I transferred to UCLA, where I got my BA," she said. "I got the master's at Berkeley."

Oh please. I could hardly stifle a guffaw. This was too implausible to have any remote basis in fact. Daisy Crane with a master's degree in sociology from Berkeley, a school with an academic reputation on a par with Harvard or Stanford? The local beauty school would have been more than taxing for her.

"You got accepted at UCLA?" I marveled with distinct skepticism. "How many deans, trustees and provosts did you have to sleep with to accomplish that feat?"

There was a moment of silence and I wondered if perhaps I

was being a trifle too harsh, if perhaps it would be better if I just buried the hatchet. But then I recalled how blithely she had planted that very same hatchet in my heart.

"I suppose I deserved that," she said. "But remember, I was always a pretty good student. I guess I just wasn't as motivated then as I am now. My parents expected so much of me . . . every grade had to be an A or else. After high school, I rebelled, dropped out of the religious college my parents had sent me to and then I guess I just went a little crazy. Too much liquor, too much carousing, too many one-night stands. I admit it, I was a low-class, money-grubbing slut. But that was not really me, Plato. It was a long time before I realized I was hurting myself as much as I was hurting my parents, a long time before I was motivated to do anything worthwhile with my life."

"Not that I'm interested," I maintained, "but how, may I ask, did you acquire this so-called sudden motivation?"

"A tragedy," she said. "A former male friend of mine—maybe you remember—his name was Slick Slocum . . ."

"I vaguely recall the name," I said dully.

"Anyway, he and I had a motorcycle accident shortly after you and I divorced. He died. They practically had to scrape his body off this tree with a putty knife. I came pretty close to kicking the old bucket myself. I was in the hospital for months undergoing physical therapy. The experience changed me."

"I don't believe you," I told her. "This is some kind of scam you're trying to pull. You want me to buy six thousand dollars' worth of Tupperware or something, is that it?"

"No," she claimed. "Not at all. I'm sincere, Plato. I'm not trying to sell you anything. Really. I swear it."

"Jehovah's Witnesses then, right?" I guessed. "For several thousand dollars my soul is guaranteed a nice cozy berth in the most upscale neighborhood in heaven."

"I had a feeling you wouldn't believe me," she said.

"Listen," I crooned wearily. "I'm afraid I have other, more pressing things to do at the moment than listen to this. My socks, for one . . ."

"Right. Of course you do," she said, sounding flustered, as if this were not the way she had expected the conversation to turn out. "I'm sorry I called. I should have known better."

"Besides," I continued, "just because you have a master's degree doesn't necessarily mean you're a pice nerson." *Damn!*

"True," she said. "But I am a nice person. Truly. I try to be."

"I'm just curious," I said, before hanging up. "What ever happened to the eight million dollars I gave you?"

She sighed. "Slick and I lost about eight hundred grand at the crap tables in Las Vegas in under a week," she croaked.

"I guess Slick wasn't terribly slick," I said.

"I put aside about two hundred thousand for my education."

"Yeah, right," I clucked skeptically. "And the rest?"

"After Slick died, I donated the rest to the United Way and various other charities. UNICEF, World Vision, the Red Cross . . ."

"How very generous of you," I said. I didn't believe a word of it. The United Way! Ha! Did she think I was born yesterday? Did she think I was as much a moron now as I was then?

"That first day in kindergarten," she said without a segue, "I was the only one who didn't laugh at you."

"Netragrednik?" I stammered. *Drat!*

"Yes," she said. "That first day in netragrednik."

"I'm not angry about kindergarten," I replied calmly, although I felt the signs of an anxiety attack coming on. "I'm angry about our god-awful excuse for a marriage, in which, as you may recall, I was cheated out of a fortune. Not to mention that horrible list of accusations you threw in my face. And the fact that . . . that . . ."

"Yes?"

"The fact that you, for lack of a better term, broke my heart."

There was a long pause from her end. Had we lost the connection?

"I suppose there's no point in my asking for your forgiveness after all," she concluded.

I paused for effect. "Po noint whatsoever."

Chapter 26: "May he rot in hell," my

mother said, spitting the words at me. "May crows pluck his eyes from his head. May vultures come down from the sky and—"

"Mother, please," I beseeched her. "Not again."

"I gave that man the best years of my life!"

"I know, I know. You've told me ten times."

"Don't be a wisecracker," she said. "Are you defending him?"

"No, of course not," I replied. "What he did was indefensible."

"How could he do this to me, Plato?" she asked. "To us? How? Can you tell me that?"

"No," I said. "I can't. It's quite a conundrum. He was just not that type of person. Or so I thought."

"Forty years we were together!" she exclaimed. "Forty years! I thought I knew this man. You live with somebody for forty years, you wash his dirty underwear for forty years, you listen to him snore and talk in his sleep for forty years, you feel you know him so well, and then he does something like this to me?"

"I know, I know," I droned. "We've been through this already, Mother. Drink your coffee."

"Maybe I should sue him."

"Sue whom?

"Your father, of course, the miserable cockroach."

"I think you'd have a little trouble finding a lawyer willing to sue a dead man," I pointed out. "And not a very rich dead man at that."

"I could get a divorce," she suggested.

"A posthumous divorce? I'm not a lawyer, but I doubt it. How would he sign the papers?"

For some inexplicable reason, directly after my father's death, my mother had begun leaving her apartment more often than usual. Perhaps all the havoc had caused her to temporarily overcome her phobias. Perhaps it was the sudden shock of loneliness, although I dropped by from time to time to keep her company.

At the moment we were sitting in a vinyl booth at a neighborhood coffee shop in Studio City, having just spent an interesting hour with my father's attorney, Jack Fellman. The reading of the Last Will and Testament of Victor J. Fussell was supposed to have been a fairly predictable task, no surprises, no bombshells. After all, my father had never been a particularly wealthy man. He had no stocks, no grand life insurance policies, no annuities. Just a small army pension, a monthly social security check, and a modest investment in U.S. savings bonds. But the moment we walked into Fellman's office I knew something was seriously amiss. There was a certain tension in the air. Jack was sweating and, for some reason, he was having some trouble making eye contact with my mother and me. But then Jack Fellman was a huge man with slits for eyes and every time I'd seen him in the past, he'd been perspiring. Merely walking the length of his office made him break out into a sweat. I wouldn't have wanted to be his cardiologist.

"Technically," Jack said as the three of us sat around a conference table, "I'm not supposed to even read the will unless all parties are present and accounted for."

I looked at my mother, she looked at me.

"The dog died five years ago," my mother informed him. "Who else is there?"

"I'm afraid there's another party," Jack said.

"Don't tell me he left something to that so-called cousin of his, that Lottie Neter," my mother fumed. "That gold digger! Once she came to visit! Once! In forty years! And after she left, I was missing flatware!"

"No," Jack said. "Not her."

"Who then?" I asked.

Jack cleared his throat. "Shall I read it now?"

"No, let's rearrange your office furniture first," my mother said sarcastically. "Yes, read the damn thing already, for God's sakes. The suspense is killing me."

Jack cleared his throat again, wiped the sweat from his forehead and began to read.

"I, Victor J. Fussell, being of sound mind and body, do hereby bequeath fifty percent of my estate to my wife of forty years, Gladys R. Fussell, and fifty percent of my estate to my wife of twenty-five years, Katrina F. Fussell."

There was a moment of absolute stillness as we both stared at Jack Fellman.

"I'm sorry," my mother said finally. "I must have missed something here, Mr. Fellman. What did you say?"

"Call me Jack," he said.

"Fine, whatever," my mother snapped. "What did you say? Please repeat it, if you would be so kind."

Jack was not eager to read it again, but he did and my mother was still confused. "To put it bluntly, Mrs. Fussell, it seems that Victor had another wife," he explained.

"Excuse me?" my mother cried, still unable to understand, not that I was faring any better. "When was this?"

"Now."

"Now? He has another wife now? Since when?"

"Since 1979."

"This is a joke, right?" I asked Fellman. "My father's playing a little prank on us from the grave. He had an odd sense of humor, my father, he could be quite amusing." I looked up at the ceiling. "Very funny, Dad. Ha ha ha. You got us good, Dad."

"I'm afraid it's no joke," Jack replied solemnly. "I wish it were, believe me. This is not easy for me."

"Then there must be some mistake," I said. "My father wouldn't do something as dishonest as that. He was a straight shooter, my father. It's impossible. Inconceivable."

"It's also illegal, am I right?" my mother asked. "It's—"

"Bigamy," I offered. "Unless you're from Utah."

"Technically you're right, but it would be difficult to prosecute him at this point," Jack informed us. "Being that he is deceased and all."

"I don't understand this." My mother sighed. "When did he see this other wife?"

"He was a traveling salesman for thirty-five years," I said. "He traveled all over the place. He was gone for weeks at a time when I was just a kid."

"Oh my God!" my mother cried.

"What is it?" I asked.

"I always wondered why his shirts came back so nicely laundered."

"And those trips back East twice a year to see old Uncle Socko," I added. "There obviously was no Uncle Socko."

"Did you know anything about this, Plato?" she asked, scrutinizing me with one eye closed. "You can tell me, I won't get angry at you, I promise."

"Of course not!" I cried, outraged. "How can you say such a thing? I'm just as flabbergasted as you are, Mother. I'm appalled! I'm aghast! I'm—"

"I'm afraid there's a bit more," Jack said.

"What? He has two more wives stashed away?" my mother

asked. "He robbed a bank? He was a Nazi sympathizer? He wore dresses and skirts? What?"

"No," Jack replied. "None of those."

"Then what?" I said testily. "Can we please cut to the chase?"

"Yes, by all means tell us," my mother agreed. "I can't wait. Already I've heard enough to have three heart attacks."

"Well, it seems that Victor also had another child," Fellman began, his voice tremulous. "*Has* another child, that is. A boy. Leopold. With this woman Katrina, the other wife."

My mouth was now agape and I almost fell off the edge of my chair. Then it hit me. "So *that's* what he meant!" I exclaimed.

"You *did* know about this!" my mother gasped.

"No, of course not, but in the hospital. The other day. Dad woke out of his coma for about five seconds. He squeezed my hand and said something to me. He said, 'Do not forsake Leopold.' I had no idea at the time what the hell he meant. I figured he was just delirious."

"I could use a glass of whiskey," my mother said, fanning her face with her hand. "I'm feeling a little bit faint. Do you have any whiskey, Mr. Fellman?"

"Of course," Jack said. He scrambled to his feet, an enterprise that, given his girth, was something of a struggle, and waddled over to a nearby cabinet, where he pulled out a bottle and a glass.

"Is Johnnie Walker okay?"

"Anything," my mother said. "But I usually prefer Dewars."

"Johnnie Walker is all I have."

"Fine."

"Ice?"

"Neat."

Jack poured a glass. Much to my amazement, my mother threw it back in one gulp and held the glass out for a refill.

"I think that's enough, Mother," I said.

She ignored me. "Fill it up, Fellman," she demanded.

Jack looked at me. I shrugged. He poured the glass full. My mother again downed it in one gulp. Who *was* this woman?

"I never knew you were such a big boozer," I remarked, somewhat shocked. "I thought you didn't like hard liquor."

"Only on special occasions," my mother assured me. "Like whenever I find out my recently deceased husband had another wife and various children stashed away all over the world."

"There's just one," Jack muttered helplessly. "That I know of."

"One is enough," my mother replied.

"It's absolutely appalling," I roared, turning to Fellman. "It's unbelievable. My father was not that sort of man. Did you know about all this, Jack?"

Jack looked away, cleared his throat, then it dawned on me.

"You must have known!" I cried. "You drew up the will!"

This was apparently the issue he had been dreading, for he suddenly began to shrink right in front of us. I thought he was going to slide out of his chair and crouch below the table.

"You did, didn't you?" my mother scolded, shaking her finger at him. "You miserable parasite!"

"I couldn't say anything," Fellman said. "Lawyer-client confidentiality. My hands were tied! But I did advise him any number of times that I thought it was a terrible thing he was doing and that he should end the other relationship."

"And what did he say?" my mother asked. "What did Mr. Big Shot Casanova say?"

"He said he couldn't. He said . . ."

"Yes?"

"He said . . ."

"Spit it out, Fellman," I insisted.

"He said he loved them. He loved you both, but he loved them too."

"That bastard!" my mother exclaimed. "That miserable son of a—"

"Where do they live, this Katrina and Leopold?" I interrupted.

"I'm not at liberty to say."

"At least give us a hint, Jack," I said angrily.

Jack sighed. "In New Jersey," he replied. "But that's absolutely all I can tell you."

"I can't believe he had the gall to use the name Fussell twice!" my mother said.

"Have you contacted them yet?" I asked Jack.

"Yes. She'll be here sometime next month. The law says I have to read the will to her too. There are papers she needs to sign."

"When?"

"I'm afraid I'm not at liberty to say," Jack said. "Apparently, the other Mrs. Fussell would prefer not to have any contact with either of you."

"Why?" I asked.

"I really don't know, but I must respect her wishes."

"It's fine with me," my mother said. "May she rot, the lousy home wrecker!"

"But this Leopold, he's my half brother," I said, suddenly realizing that I had a sibling. "And my father told me not to forsake him. 'Do not forsake Leopold,' he told me. These were his dying words."

"Don't you dare meet with them!" my mother warned. "I'm your only mother. You have no other mother. And you have no siblings."

"How old is he?" I asked Fellman.

"I'm sorry," he said. "I'll inform the other Mrs. Fussell of your feelings, and communicate your questions to her, but that's the best I can do."

My mother and I stopped for coffee on the way home from Fellman's office. The liquor had made her somewhat tipsy and I wanted to be sure she would be able to get around without falling down and injuring herself. One death in the family was all I could handle at the moment. I insisted that she drink at least two cups of black coffee or we would not leave the restaurant. It was only after

I instructed the waitress to boil the water for a full forty minutes that my mother agreed to my demands. Later I took her home.

Shortly after my father's funeral, on the recommendation of a friend of the funeral director, I had hired a fifty-eight-year-old caregiver named Maurice Castelli who was not only a younger man and a retired registered nurse, but an excellent dancer as well, or so he claimed. Tall and quite thin, he wore his slick black hair in a pompadour, highlighted with a gray streak, and sported a goatee and a gold tooth in front. I hired him at $1,000 a week to look after my mother every day, from nine in the morning to eight o'clock at night, but since he was not to officially start until the next morning, I spent the night at my mother's apartment just to make sure she was all right. We ate an early dinner of overcooked halibut, garlic pickles and salad, and by five o'clock that afternoon, she had already fallen asleep on the living room couch. She snored like a plow horse.

There was, in spite of her protests, no way that I was going to refrain from trying to meet my half brother Leopold. Somehow, I would find him.

Chapter 27: Eager as I was to learn as

much as I could about Katrina and Leopold, I knew—thanks to Dr. Wang's advice—that if I did not see Emily again very soon I would surely lose her forever. One must have priorities in life. And so I set my mind to devising a strategy that would get me back into Emily's good graces.

At first, I tried the simple but thoroughly fruitless route of leaving her countless e-mail messages. She responded to none of these attempts. Left with no other tactic, I camped out in a diner across the street from the building that houses her office, also to no avail. Wang's home address and home phone number were closely guarded secrets, and when I received my socks from Emily, there was no return address to be found on the package. The postmark was Sherman Oaks, but several hundred thousand people reside there. Obviously, more drastic and creative means would be required. After giving it some reflection, I succumbed once again to the most expedient method—I would try to wheedle something out of my poor, ignorant shrink, the accommodating Dr. Wang.

Only this time, it wasn't going to be so easy.

"Have you met my wife before?" Wang asked at my next session, while I was still slipping out of my coat and overshoes.

"Not that I can recall," I muttered, trying not to face him, lest he see my obvious discomfort. "Why do you ask?"

"I don't know," Wang said. "I just got a certain feeling about it when I introduced you to each other at your father's funeral."

"No idea why." I shrugged, attempting an unsuspicious smile.

"Just a feeling," Wang explained.

Just a feeling? Good God! Fortunately, he hadn't caught us shamelessly smooching in the closet. Needless to say, after this it would be most difficult for me to wheedle his home address and phone number out of him. I would have to take a completely different approach . . .

"She was most charming, I thought."

"Thank you, Fussell," he said. "I'm afraid she hasn't been very happy the last few days."

"Oh. I'm sorry. Send her my west bishes." (*Oh no!*)

"Are you feeling anxiety now?" Wang had swiveled in his desk chair to face me. "You just said 'west bishes.'"

"Anxiety?" I cleared my throat. "No, not at all. Just tired. Tip of the slongue. Continue, please. You were speaking about your wife."

"Yes, well, I think she's going a bit stir crazy," Wang opined. "She's been home, hasn't been to her office in weeks."

"How so?" I asked innocently, although I knew this was true from having staked out the place during office hours.

"Well, the fact is, she hasn't had much work lately," Wang said. "Don't know why. She's really very good at what she does, though I think a woman of her intellect could have chosen a more demanding career."

"What does she do?" I asked innocently.

"Interior design. Funeral parlors and morgues mostly."

"What an odd specialty."

"Yes. A bit morbid, but she enjoys her work. Problem is, there are just so many funeral parlors and morgues in this area and not all of them need to be redesigned."

"Perhaps she should branch out," I suggested. "Black isn't the only color on the spectrum."

"That's what I keep telling her but she won't even consider it," Wang said. "And what with me working all day, I'm afraid she spends a lot of time on her own."

"Hmmm," I said, not knowing what else to say. Yet I suddenly felt an idea germinating in my brain.

Wang waved his hand. "But that's neither here nor there," he said, brightening. "You're the patient, Fussell. Not me, and certainly not my wife. So what's new with you, my friend?"

"Other than the fact that I recently discovered that my late father had been married to another woman since 1979 and has another child living somewhere in New Jersey, not terribly much."

Altogether, it would end up costing me $35,000, a small fortune to many, perhaps, but a mere bagatelle to me. After all, what purpose is there in having money if not for the betterment of humankind? I would have been more than willing to spend oodles more than that amount to get my beloved Emily back. I would have gladly given away my entire fortune! The difficult part was convincing Bob Hoover that his funeral home—the same one that I had recently employed for my father's last rites—desperately needed to be redesigned.

"Let me see if I'm getting this straight," Bob said, after I had approached him with my offer. "You want to give me thirty thousand dollars in cash to have the interior of my place of business completely redecorated, with an extra bonus of five thousand dollars to me for not saying where the money came from."

"Correct."

"And you want me to hire this Emily Thorndyke to do the redesign."

"Again correct. And I want you to notify me immediately whenever she's here, on the site."

"Right," Bob said. "No other strings attached?"

"Not so much as a microscopic thread," I assured him.

"No small print?"

"No small print," I repeated. "So? What do you say?"

Bob gave it some thought, took a look around the place, scratched his head. I liked Bob but I found it annoying that, when spelled backward, his first name remained unchanged. And Revooh wasn't very interesting either—it sounded like an Indian curry dish.

"To be honest, I kind of like the place the way it is," Bob remarked, sweeping a hand in the air. "It has a certain style."

"What style is that, Bob, Early American Decrepit?" I said. "The dead people are not the clients. The live people are."

"It has a certain . . . warm feeling."

"So does a stable."

"It feels . . . cozy."

"Perhaps you need new glasses," I suggested. "I could recommend a good optometrist."

"No, these are fine."

"When was the last time you redecorated this place?" I asked. "Or should I say what part of the eighteenth century?"

"Fact is, I haven't done a thing to it, other than basic maintenance. I bought it as is twenty-five years ago."

"No offense, Bob," said I. "But look at these curtains, they're falling apart. Pea green carpeting, practically threadbare in spots? And plastic flowers?"

"What's wrong with plastic flowers?" he asked. "Who wants to water real ones all day?"

"Nobody said anything about real ones," I answered, recalling some of the information I had read regarding interior design some weeks back. "They make very nice flower replicas out of more realistic materials than plastic—mums, roses, orchids and such."

"Is that right?"

"Look at it this way," I said. "If you make this place classier, you'll attract a classier clientele. Rich people. People from Toluca Lake, possibly even Encino! You can mark everything up another twenty or thirty percent. How can you possibly lose?"

Bob put on his somber face and again gave the proposition some reflection. He adjusted his black armband, which had slid down to his elbow. A tall, gangly man, perpetually in a dark suit, who looked a little like the youthful Abraham Lincoln without the beard, Bob could go from jovial to somber in the wink of an eye. A trick of the funeral trade, I surmised.

"I'll admit it would be nice to have new furniture," he conceded. "This stuff is a little banged up."

"New furniture would help."

"Maybe a nice oak credenza by the wall over there. I like oak."

"Oak is great," I agreed. "Very classy."

"Black lace curtains."

"An excellent idea."

"Dark brown carpeting."

"Brown is always an attractive choice," I said.

"Perhaps even dark stained hardwood floors."

"Can't beat hardwood floors."

"The thing is I can't afford to have my business interrupted for too long. I have to make a living. I have a pretty big mortgage on this place."

"No problem," I said. "If it takes more than a month, I will reimburse you for the time lost."

"That could be sizable," he said. "Ten grand, maybe."

"No problem."

"It's a pretty hectic month," Bob added. "Fact is, a lot of people die in November."

"Why?"

"Nobody knows. December is worse. Or, from my standpoint, better. For business, I mean."

"Christmas suicides?"

"As a matter of fact, yes. How did you know that?"

"It's kind of an avocation of mine," I admitted. "Do we have a deal?"

After another pause, Bob sighed and said: "Sure, what the hell? Can't look a gift horse in the mouth, can I?"

Offended as I was at being likened to a horse, Bob and I shook hands, and before he could change his mind, I immediately wrote him a personal check for $35,000. He stared at it in disbelief for about five seconds, shook his head in wonder, then slipped it into the front pocket of his black funeral coat.

Chapter 28: Using my computer, I per- formed a White Pages search of the eight largest cities in New Jersey, only to discover that there were no Fussells listed. There was a Fustell and a Fishnell and several Fessells, even a Fuskatell and a Fusterbert, as well as two Fustabinches and three Furrelios, a Fullbertian and four Furbishers, but no Fussells. In the event that Jack Fellman had been mistaken (or deliberately misleading), I attempted a search of several smaller New Jersey metropolitan areas, also to no avail. A series of telephone calls to directory assistance yielded no positive results as well. From this I opined that Katrina Fussell (assuming she even used that name) had an unlisted number.

I did, however, locate a few private investigation companies that were doing business in the Hoboken, Tenafly, Trenton and Newark areas and, although obtaining the services of a private detective had not occurred to me at first, I decided to try one, and chose the largest Yellow Pages advertisement—Acme Investigations of Newark. Though their title manifested a serious lack of imagination, I dialed their 800 number and was put in touch with a somewhat unctuous gentleman named Mickey Koro, with whom I spoke for a good twenty minutes or more. In a gruff Brooklyn accent, he explained the costs and procedures involved in locating someone in the state of New Jersey. He assured me that his company would be able to find anyone, "no sweat," and that their techniques were aboveboard and the epitome of discretion. For $500, he would locate the address and phone number of Katrina Fussell and her son, Leopold; for another $250, Acme's Deluxe Package, he would also provide me with an array of black-and-white photographs of both Katrina and Leopold; another $100 would get me the Super Deluxe Package, which featured color eight-by-ten photos of superior clarity. Expenses would be extra, but he did not anticipate many. He practically guaranteed success but there was a complicated money-back guarantee should Acme be unable to find them, an unlikely prospect, he assured me. He would fax me a contract. So, with more than a little apprehension, I read him the digits of my credit card number over the telephone.

"What's your expiration date?" he asked.

"I don't know," I said, unable to resist a little jollity. "I was hoping to live another forty more years at least, which would put my expiration date at about 2044, give or take."

There was silence on his end. Perhaps he did not grasp the drollery, such as it was, or perhaps he was not a man interested in humor, so I quickly rattled off the expiration numbers on my American Express card, plus my address and telephone number, and he promised results within the following week or two.

In the meantime, I received a call from Bob Hoover the following Friday in which he informed me that he had, per our arrangement, engaged Emily's services for the interior overhaul of his place of business. They were to meet at the funeral parlor the following Monday morning to discuss the particulars and perhaps sign a preliminary contract.

I was so elated at the prospect of seeing my darling Emily again that I was barely able to get any sleep all weekend. By Monday morning, I had dark circles under my eyes and could hardly sit down without dozing off. Although I usually eschew coffee, I made a pot of strong decaf and drank so much of it that my hands began to tremble uncontrollably and an odd twitch developed under my right eye. I paced up and down my apartment corridor for several hours until I began to feel more relaxed and then stopped to decide on an appropriate wardrobe. Should I dress in sporty garb or don formal attire? As this was to be an "accidental encounter" I decided it would be best to wear casual apparel—I did not want Emily to suspect that there was any subterfuge involved in our "chance" meeting. So I wore a pair of blue jeans, a polo shirt, a wool sweater and a pair of comfortable brown tasseled loafers.

When I arrived at Bob's funeral home, I spotted Emily's old BMW parked out front. Suddenly, I was gripped by the most unpleasant feelings of anxiety—would Emily be cold and distant toward me, or warm and affable? Would Wang's hard-to-get strategy actually work? Could I even pull it off successfully or would I stammer and make a complete and utter fool of myself?

Nevertheless, I pressed forward. If the alternative was never to see Emily again, I had no choice. I simply had to proceed, damn the torpedoes. A life without her was unimaginable. Besides, had she not pulled me into a closet and covered my face with kisses at this very funeral home no more than a few days ago? Did that not clearly indicate how she still felt about me? So I parked my car next to hers and approached the front door. Before ringing the doorbell, I peeked through one of the small front windows and caught sight of my Emily walking around the front room, making notes on a clipboard, pointing to various things—furniture, potted plants and such. She was wearing a conservative dark business suit, but her blouse was somewhat low cut, revealing the pale upper spheres of her marvelous breasts. My heart fluttered, my stomach churned and something suddenly stirred in the general vicinity of my groin. With some hesitation, I rang Bob's doorbell.

He appeared right away.

"Ah, Mr. Fussell!" he said a bit too loudly. "Mr. Plato Fussell, how nice to see you again! Come right in, my good friend."

"Tone it down a decibel or two, Bob," I whispered as I stepped into the parlor. It suddenly occurred to me that perhaps Bob and I should have rehearsed this part of the scheme once or twice.

"Right this way, Mr. Fussell!" he said stiffly, dragging me over to where Emily was standing with her clipboard. Evidently Bob had decided that he was going to play the role of matchmaker.

"May I present Ms. Emily Thorndyke? Emily, this is my good friend and one of the nicest, most generous people I have ever met, Mr. Plato Fussell."

"We've met," Emily informed him.

"Isn't that a coincidence?" Bob exclaimed. I winced. "By golly, isn't it a small world?"

"Nice to see you again, Emily," I muttered, a bit tremulously. "I just came by to pay my father's buneral fill."

"Say what?" Bob asked.

"Funeral bill," I corrected. Hoover's absurd overacting was making me nervous.

"You could have sent me a check," Bob said. "I accept personal checks, you know. Always have."

"What?" I cleared my throat, which was suddenly very dry. "Yes, well," I stammered. "There are a few things I wanted to go over with you, some dinor metals."

"What things?" Bob asked. "I thought we went over everything already the other day."

Was this man a complete nincompoop? I winked at him a few times, but all he did was wink back. He probably mistook the wink to mean I thought he was doing well. I should have known better than to put my fate in the hands of a man whose first name did not change when spelled backward.

Emily was watching all this with a growing amount of amusement, impatience or confusion, I wasn't sure which, and I worried that, left unchecked, Bob would spill the beans.

"Excuse me for a moment," I said, trying to disguise my annoyance. "I have to make a very private phone call."

"You can use my cordless," Bob offered. I could have strangled the cretinous nitwit right then and there.

"Very kind of you," I said, giving him a fairly transparent look of disapproval, which he ignored. "But I've got my cell phone and the number I need to call is in its memory bank."

"Are you sure?"

"*Quite sure*," I replied firmly. "I'll just step outside. Better reception out there probably."

"I never have a problem with mine in here," Bob claimed. "I get crystal-clear reception all the way to San Luis Obispo."

"We probably have phifferent dones," I said.

Before Bob could protest, as I knew he would, I strode toward the door, opened it and let myself out. The moment I was out of earshot, I called Directory Assistance and asked for the number of the funeral home beside which I was currently standing. The operator connected me and the phone rang inside his office four times before Bob finally picked up.

"What in God's name are you doing?" I asked.

"Who is this?"

"It's Plato Fussell, of course," I said angrily.

"Why are you calling me?" he asked. "You were just in here."

"Why? WHY?" I said, trying to control my distress. "Because you're messing this whole thing up, that's why."

"What do you mean? I thought things were going quite nicely. You two were developing a real rapport."

"We already have a goddamn rapport," I cried.

"Oh."

"Look." I sighed patiently. "Here's the plan: I'm going to hang up my cell phone and come back inside momentarily. But I want you to remain on the line for fifteen more minutes and stay out of the parlor. Okay?"

"Who will I be talking to on the phone?" Bob asked.

"NOBODY!" I exclaimed. "Just stay in your office and don't come back into the parlor for fifteen minutes so I CAN BE ALONE WITH HER!"

"So you want me to *pretend* to be talking to someone on the phone," he said.

"Yes."

"Right," Bob said. "Got it."

"Good man."

"Fifteen minutes."

"Fifteen minutes.

"Starting now?"

"Yes, starting now."

I folded up my cell phone, took a few deep breaths and reentered the funeral parlor. This time, thankfully, Bob was not in the room, although I could hear him feigning a somewhat stilted phone conversation in the background. Emily was busy fondling a few scratches in Bob's antiquated leather upholstery as I shut the door behind me.

"He's still on the phone," she told me.

"Right," I muttered. "He must be pretty busy. I hear lots of people die in November."

"December's worse," she pointed out.

"Christmas suicides," I said.

She nodded solemnly. I followed suit.

"So how've you been, Fussell?" she asked.

"Bot nad," I said, silently cursing myself. "And you?"

"Well, it looks like I've got this incredible job," she announced happily. "Bob called me out of the blue."

"That's terrific!" I said. "I'm very happy for you."

"Really, Fussell?" she asked me. "Are you truly happy for me?"

"Sure. Why wouldn't I be?"

"I don't know." Emily shrugged. "My husband thinks I should be doing something more intellectual. He thinks I'm wasting my talents."

"Whatever makes you happy," I reflected. "That's the most important thing in life. Just an opinion, of course."

"Yes, I suppose you're right."

I paused. Had I struck the perfect note of mild indifference? Was I being annoyingly nonchalant and dispassionate? Yes, I believe I was. If not, at least I wasn't whining. As much as I was enjoying this new coy attitude of mine, I knew it was time for me to depart.

"Listen," I said. "Can you do me a little rovaf?"

"Am I making you nervous?"

"No, not at all, why?"

"You just said 'rovaf' instead of 'favor.'"

"Slip of the tongue," I replied. "So can you? Do me a favor?"

"Sure."

"Give this envelope to Bob when he gets off the phone," I said, handing her an empty business envelope with the name "Bob Hoover" written on the front in ink.

"Sure," Emily replied. "Are you leaving?"

Did I detect a minute degree of regret in her tone? A morsel of disappointment? By George, I believe I did!

"I'm afraid so. Busy day. Lots to do."

"I've missed you, Fussell," she said, taking a step toward me.

"I've missed you too," I said, taking a step in the opposite direction. "But I really must go."

"How about lunch? I'll be done here soon."

"Can't make it today," I said, feigning indifference. "My schedule is pretty full. Sorry. I'll call you."

"That's all you have to say to me?" she asked. "Your schedule is pretty full?"

"What more do you want me to say?" I responded mysteriously.

"Are you seeing someone else, Fussell?"

"Who, me?" This was going even better than I had anticipated. Could I make her jealous of an imaginary woman?

"Yes, you. Of course you. Who else? Is there someone else in the room I could be addressing? I don't see anybody."

"Well, umm . . ."

"Who is she?"

"What's the ecnereffid? You have your husband," I pointed out. "You didn't expect me to remain celibate for the rest of my life, did you?"

"Actually, yes," she conceded. "Is she as pretty as I am?"

"Who?"

"Your new girlfriend?"

"I really must be off."

"Is she better than me in bed?"

"I'm sorry," I said. "Duty calls."

"Is she more neurotic than I am?" she demanded. "Is that it? That's it, isn't it? She's more obsessive-compulsive than I am. Or more paranoid. Or bipolar? Am I right?"

"*Au revoir*, Emily," I said breezily. "Lovely to see you again."

Then I smiled and gave her a perfunctory salute, the sort of benign gesture one might use to bid adieu to a talkative taxi driver. Very irritating under these circumstances. Then I went for the door. I opened the door. I stepped outside into the harsh California sunlight. I slapped on my sunglasses. I shut the door. I waited two seconds and breathed in the noxious odor of a nearby vine of flowering jasmine. I walked to my car. I opened my car door. I got in. I turned on the ignition. I made a U turn and drove away.

How long, I wondered, would it take for Wang's devious, hard-to-get strategy to work? A day? A week? Or would it work at all?

Chapter 29: Who better to consult on

this matter than Dr. Wang himself? Repugnant, wicked and corrupt as it was, I simply could not resist using my own psychiatrist as a mole. I felt truly, truly horrible about it, but I was unable to help myself—I was a desperate man. When I next saw him several days later at his office, he appeared somewhat demoralized, not his usual chipper, effervescent self. Not only was he unshaven, I also noticed that he was wearing socks that did not match—a brown one on the left foot and a green one on the right. He was usually quite the dapper fellow, an impeccable dresser, a man of careful grooming and first-rate personal hygiene. He was, in point of fact, somewhat anal in this department. Something must have been wrong. I had a pretty good hunch what it was.

After the amenities, he jumped right in.

"I've tried," he said. "I really have, Fussell. I've given it all I have. I have nothing left to give. Nothing!"

"What's that?" I asked.

"I'm sensitive, I'm thoughtful. I don't snore."

"Everybody snores," I said.

"I put the toilet seat down when I'm through urinating. I take out the garbage. I hang up my towels. I make no demands."

"And all this is relevant to what exactly?" I inquired, although by now I had more than an inkling.

"My relationship with my wife. I'm patient. I'm loving. I'm affectionate. I'm doting. I'm caring. I'm even romantic. And I really do try not to analyze everything if I can help it."

"I'm sure you do," I said consolingly.

"And even if I do analyze things, so what?" he groaned. "She's an interior designer—do I ask her to stop moving our living room furniture around whenever she feels the urge, which is usually about once a month?"

"Do you?"

"No, of course not."

"Is there a problem again?" I asked.

Wang sighed. "Yes, no, I don't really know. She won't tell me what's wrong. And if I ask too many questions, she accuses me of trying to analyze her."

"Explain your feelings," I said.

"She's cold and distant again, Fussell. Detached. Doesn't want to have intercourse with me. Mopes around the house. When she does talk to me, she barks."

"Barks?"

"Speaks sharply."

Aha! Wang's plan *was* working! The hard-to-get approach had been effective! If only he knew. What excellent advice! But of course I couldn't tell him, tempting as it was for me to share my success with its creator.

If truth be told, I was actually beginning to feel sorry for him, the poor fellow. I certainly knew exactly what he was going through, having been through the exact same trauma with the exact same woman during the exact same time period myself. But giving up Emily forever, philanthropic and magnanimous as that might have been, would be entirely impossible for me. I had already tried it a number of times and I had failed miserably. I simply could not live without her. Both Wang and I were powerless, frustrated and miserable for exactly the same reasons.

"And how's it going with you, Fussell?" he asked after a while. "Have you met someone new yet?"

"Alas, no," I said. "I'm afraid I'm still pining away for Ahab. My darling sweet Ahab."

"You've still had no contact with her at all?"

"Actually, I bumped into her by accident the other day," I said. "I attempted to be coy, as you recommended, but to no affect, I'm sorry to report."

"A shame." Wang shook his head. "It usually works quite well for me. But then playing games is a bit puerile, I suppose."

"I'm afraid I'm not much good at it."

"Perhaps you weren't being coy enough," he suggested.

"Oh, I was plenty coy," I assured him. "I couldn't have been any coyer."

"In what way?"

"A general tone of indifference. I also implied that there was another woman. Actually she came up with that part all by herself."

"And this didn't work?"

"Afraid not," I said. "At least not yet. I suppose the jury is still out, but I'm not holding my breath."

Wang stood up and began pacing by the window. He had donned his thinking cap, I could tell. There was some serious cogitating going on in that cerebellum.

"I have an idea, Fussell!" he volunteered suddenly. "Why didn't I think of this before?"

"What is it?" I asked eagerly.

"It's genius!"

"What?"

He sat down and enthusiastically rubbed his hands together. He was beaming, his eyes were lit up.

"Why don't you and Ahab come into my office for a session to-gether?" he proposed, clapping his hands. "Perhaps I will be able to discern what the difficulty is."

"A joint session, you mean?" I asked.

"That sounds a bit . . . congressional. Call it premarital therapy."

"Pretherital merapy?"

"That gives you anxiety?"

"No," I stammered. "Um, not at all."

"So what do you say?"

"It's impossible."

"Why?"

"Well," I said, "for one thing, I can't even get her to return my phone calls."

"Perhaps if I called her myself?" he offered.

"You?"

"Yes, me. I do it all the time for patients in this sort of predica-ment. I'm a disinterested third party. Perhaps she'll return my call. You never know."

Disinterested third party? That was rich.

"I don't think so," I said. "She has caller ID."

"Yes, but she won't be able to ID my number, now will she?" Wang observed cleverly.

"She'll probably think it's a telemarketing call."

"Then I'll wait for her voice mail and leave a mysterious mes-sage," Wang said, his excitement rising. "I'll just say it's Dr. Wang and that I need to speak to her as soon as possible. I won't say why, you see!"

"She won't go for it," I said with growing trepidation.

"Sure, she will!" Wang exclaimed. "What's her phone number? I'll call her right now."

"Her none phumber?" I said, mortified. "I don't know. I forgot it. I may have even erased it from my electronic address koob, not to mention my own mailing femory." I clamped my mouth shut. Would the gibberish give me away?

He gave me a skeptical look. "Nonsense, Fussell," he said. "You certainly did not erase it. You're still in love with her, man! Besides, you're much too compulsive to misplace a phone number. Give me a break."

I suddenly realized that I had broken into a sweat. Perspiration was forming a small delta on my forehead. My armpits were getting moist. I even felt my back sticking to the chair. I needed a shower. Wang was not giving up on this inane idea of his. Was I about to be hoisted by my own petard?

"I'll bet it's in your wallet," Wang said. "Give me your wallet."

"What?"

"Your wallet, Fussell. Hand it over. Right now."

"But—"

"Don't worry, I won't steal anything. We're going to get to the bottom of this once and for all. Hand it over."

Having no choice, I dug my wallet out of my pocket and handed it to him. I was finished, done for, a dead man. Some time ago, I had copied Emily's cell phone number on the back of one of my business cards in ink, as her pencil scrawl on the original shred of paper had begun to smear and fade. He would find it, then he would get livid and promptly remove me from his patient roster.

Wang sat down and went through my wallet, first pulling out the cash, then the credit cards, then my health insurance cards, then the pictures of Isabella.

"Cute dog," he noted as I cringed. "My Emily has a little dog too. A mutt. Drools a lot. Very intelligent, though."

"Is that so?" I said. "There's nothing like a mittle lutt. They make excellent pets."

I cringed, but Wang did not appear to notice the word scramble.

"Hers can catch a Frisbee in the air," he told me. "Quite amazing to watch."

"I'll bet it is," I said.

He nodded and continued to rifle through the various receipts, the membership cards, my library card, doctor's addresses and grocery coupons, the usual wallet detritus. Then suddenly he stopped. He was holding one of my business cards. I closed my eyes, waiting for the guillotine blade to fall.

"Who's Ylime?" he asked.

"My cleaning lady," I blubbered, winging it. "She's from Nigeria. That's her Nigerian name. It's pronounced *Why-lee-me*."

"Oh."

"She comes wice a tweek," I added for no particular reason.

"Really?"

"I'm a stickler for cleanliness, as you well know. She's very good. Loves to use Lysol. I think she might even have stock in the company that makes it."

"Perhaps I should call her," Wang mused. "My housekeeper recently quit on me and I've been looking high and low for a new one."

"NO!" I shrieked. "I mean, no. She's all booked up, I'm afraid. Huge waiting list."

"Too bad." He sighed, staring directly at the back of the card. Surely he would recognize it as Emily's cell phone number. I checked the exits for a quick getaway, then realized I'd have to get my wallet back first.

Then, to my extreme incredulity, he put the incriminating business card back into its slot and returned the rest of the inhabitants of my wallet to their original places, albeit somewhat haphazardly.

"No sign of Ahab in here, Fussell," he said, tossing me the wallet. "I'm truly surprised at you. The woman of your dreams comes along and you don't even carry her phone number on you?"

I exhaled a furtive sigh of relief. Of course, he had been looking for the name Ahab, not the name Emily and certainly not Ylime, although he obviously knew all about my wordplay compulsion, and the Nigeria deception was not especially clever. Even though he was looking directly at it, Emily's cell phone digits did not register for some odd reason, but then perhaps he had not committed hers to memory (I don't even remember my own). Or perhaps he didn't call her cell phone number very often. Or he just wasn't paying close attention. Fortunately for me, I had once again escaped by the skin of my teeth. How much longer could this chicanery continue?

Naturally, I would have to rearrange everything in my wallet again. I cannot abide wallet disorder.

"Drat, I must have misplaced her number," I said, dabbing my forehead with a large wad of tissue paper. "Is it hot in here?"

Chapter 30: Three days later Emily

called. In keeping with my hard-to-get approach, I let the message machine pick up three times and waited two days to return her call. She was not all perturbed by this (perhaps because she had done it to me herself not too long ago) and told me that she had once again severed all ties with her husband (whom we could now both safely refer to as Dr. Wang) and had moved back into her studio apartment with her dog, perhaps implying that she was once again available for dating. She could no longer endure Wang and his incessant need to analyze her, to pick apart her every emotion. He was too affectionate, Emily complained. Too doting. He was too considerate, too selfless, too generous, too munificent and too kind—it was driving her crazy! Even when they argued, he refused to get angry, she said, and wore the beatific smile of the saintly that made her want to "strangle him with a piano wire." Ironically, it seemed that everything he considered a plus was, to her, a minus. Delighted as I was to hear this, I made an effort to appear somewhat indifferent to the news, keeping up the strategy of apathy that had worked so well thus far. Eventually, Emily would have to choose between us. This emotional roller coaster was driving me to distraction, though I had never actually been on a roller coaster due to a severe case of vertigo.

"Can we see each other soon?" Emily asked over the phone.

"Sure, why not?" said I with no particular enthusiasm.

"What about the other woman?"

"What other woman?"

"You said you were seeing someone else," Emily continued. "I must confess to being a bit jealous."

I'd forgotten about the nonexistent other woman I was supposedly seeing, a figment of Emily's paranoid imagination, which I had not entirely denied for tactical reasons. Should I continue this deception? Would it work in my favor or ultimately undermine my relationship with Emily? Would it make her want me more, knowing that there was someone else in the picture? I really needed time to think about all this, and not make a hasty reply.

"She's a very dear friend," I admitted finally, making it up and keeping it vague. "Someone I knew many years ago. We met again by chance on the Internet."

"How romantic," Emily said. "Not your ex-wife, I hope?"

"No," I said. "I may be a lot of things, but I'm not a masochist."

"Does she live nearby?"

"Yes, she does, actually," I lied. "Brentwood. She's an actress. Also a model. She's in all the magazines."

"Are you dating?"

"We've been to the . . . circus together," I said, winging it.

"You took a date to the circus?"

"It was her idea," I continued. "The whole time I was terrified that one of the elephants would break loose from his tether and trample me to death. Or that a lion or a tiger would—"

"Do you still love me?" Emily asked. "And don't give me ditto."

"The stench of elephant excrement was overwhelming," I added mischievously. "And enormous, as you can well imagine."

"Do you still love me, Fussell?" she repeated. "Answer the goddamn question!"

"A small family of mice could live very comfortably in a pile of elephant excrement," I noted. "It doesn't really smell that much."

"DO YOU LOVE ME OR NOT!"

I paused. She had caught me by surprise and I could think of no more interesting facts about the fecal matter of the pachyderm. What could I say? I decided to be completely honest.

"Do I feel warm and affectionate when I'm around you?" I asked. "Yes. Do I long for you when you're not with me? Yes. Am I happy when I'm with you? Yes. Is that love? Or is that merely a series of sharp chemical impulses in my gray matter? Hormones, pheromones and so forth."

"What difference does it make?" she asked. "You feel a chemical impulse in your stomach and that's called hunger."

"True," I conceded.

"You feel a chemical impulse in your large intestine and we call that having to go make doody. Am I right?"

"Actually, in point of fact, I think it's a feeling that originates in the rectal area," I said.

"Don't be an asshole."

"Excellent pun," I said.

"I'm not trying to be funny, Fussell."

"Sorry."

"Other chemical reactions a normal person might experience are anger, jealousy, fear, happiness."

"Yes, I suppose."

"Have you experienced any of those feelings, Fussell?"

"Yes, I have. Most of them within the last few weeks."

"All of our human feelings are chemical reactions," she said. "We give them different names, that's all. The warm, affectionate feeling you just described is called love. Simple as that."

"But I felt those same feelings for my first wife, Daisy Crane,"

I said. "I couldn't possibly have loved such a horrible gargoyle of a woman."

"Why not?" Emily said. "You were duped, that's all. You thought she was something she really wasn't. You fooled yourself. It happens to people all the time. It happened to me and my husband."

"Well, I suppose it's possible."

"Once you realized you'd been deceived, you simply denied the existence of love," she went on. "You'd been badly disillusioned with love so you decided it did not exist. You relegated it to a random series of normal chemical reactions. You dehumanized it."

"You sound like your husband," I observed. "Smarter, actually."

"Maybe a little rubs off," she conceded.

I didn't know why, but I suddenly felt awakened, as if someone had smacked me across the face with a soaking-wet bath towel. Was Emily right? Had my painful relationship with Daisy Crane caused me to deny the whole concept of love? Had I repressed my feelings by negating them, by believing that they did not really exist? Could it really have been that simple? All those years of therapy with Wang, and his wife turned out to be a better therapist. And it wasn't costing me ninety dollars an hour.

"Yes," I said.

"Yes, what?"

"Yes, I love you Emily Thorndyke. I love you with all my heart and soul."

"Ditto," she said.

Having finally declared my love for Emily, having actually used the word "love" in the declaration, having reached a certain higher plane in our relationship that could soon hopefully lead to cohabitation, engagement and ultimately to marriage, I decided that it would be prudent if she knew about all the skeletons in my closet, a closet that was rapidly beginning to resemble a storeroom in a shop that sells Halloween accessories. I had, of course, already told her in some detail about my catastrophic affair with and subsequent marriage to that Gila monster known as Daisy Crane, and how I had squandered eight million dollars to support her. Emily was most consoling on this topic and reacted quite maturely.

But of course there were other areas that needed explaining.

First, I told her as much as I knew about my father's dalliance with his other wife, Katrina Fussell, and about their son, Leopold. This shocked her almost as much as it had shocked me, even though she had never actually met my father. But she thought my mother was a sweet lady (apparently they had conversed at the funeral reception) and her heart went out to her. I was very grateful for Emily's kindness and understanding. I myself was trying to make sense out of these shenanigans and come to terms with my father's character.

As it happened, much to my surprise, Mickey Koro of Acme Investigations had already located Katrina Fussell and her son, my half brother, Leopold. They resided in a simple tract house on a pleasant, tree-lined street called Bellaire Avenue in Moorpark, New Jersey, a suburb ten miles from Hackensack. Mickey also sent an envelope full of pictures and I shared these with Emily. Katrina appeared to be in her late forties, a short, somewhat stocky woman with a long nose who wore her blonde wavy hair in the sultry style of Veronica Lake. She was, in other words, not particularly attractive in the conventional sense and I had to wonder why my father would risk his legitimate family and most of his estate, such as it was, for someone as unremarkable-looking as Katrina, not that outward appearances really meant anything. How had they met? What secrets did they share? What had caused him to fall in love with her? Of course, when you consider my mother's agoraphobia and her numerous other odd obsessions and compulsions, practically anybody who was halfway normal would suffice as a substitute, no matter what she looked like. From the photos, I gathered that Leopold was about ten years old. He resembled my father (and

me) at that age, a gangly youth with thick glasses and dark eyebrows. For some reason, I had expected him to be older. As he was
only ten, it meant my father had to have been virile enough to produce an offspring at the age of fifty-nine. I told Emily that when
the time was right, I expected to travel to Moorpark and meet
them. Mickey Koro informed me that for a small fee, he would
have one of his employees drive me to Katrina's domicile.

Next, there was the matter of Aunt Sophie, my mother's unmarried sister, the family murderer and most impressive of the Fussell
closet skeletons. As I told Emily, Sophie Russo was my mother's
younger sibling, a diminutive spinster who was considerably more
sociable and outgoing than my mother, but quite mercurial in demeanor. Unlike the other members of the family, Aunt Sophie possessed something of a belligerent temper and during infrequent
family gatherings I was always instructed to behave like an adult in
her presence. Even when I already *was* an adult, I was still lectured by
my mother to refrain from backtalk, excessive crying and tantrums,
and to wait on Aunt Sophie hand and foot. There was no telling
what would upset her. If the food lacked salt, she erupted. If her mattress was lumpy, she blew a fuse. If a dog barked while she tried to
sleep, she flew into a rage. My father, in particular, was terrified of
her and gave her a fairly wide berth whenever she came to visit,
which was, fortunately, not very often. When I was a kid, I remember that my father once warned me she might be "packing heat."

Abusive as Aunt Sophie might have been, no one in our family
actually thought she was capable of a homicide. And so we were all
slightly taken aback when, in August 1996, we got word from a detective in the San Francisco Police Department that Aunt Sophie
had been arrested for murder. Even before we knew any of the circumstances, it was clear to all of us that someone, some poor ignorant sap had gone a step too far with Aunt Sophie and had paid the
ultimate price. Aunt Sophie had always been a bomb waiting to go
off, and her victim, a poor street mime, had inadvertently lit her
fuse.

The trial dragged on for weeks and made all the local papers practically every day, as there appeared to be more than a few San Franciscans who, at various times in their lives, had wanted to seriously maim a mime. A small movement called PAM (People Against Mimes) grew out of the trial and soon there were picketers at the courthouse every day, ordinary people who would shout words of encouragement to Aunt Sophie as she entered and later departed the courthouse. The logo on their hand-lettered signs featured a picture of a white-faced mime enclosed within a red circle, with a thick red slash drawn across his face. Shortly thereafter, another movement, called the San Francisco Mime Anti-Defamation League, sprouted up, although I read in the paper that there were no more than three members and they were all mimes.

Nevertheless, Aunt Sophie was convicted by a jury of her peers and sentenced to fifty years in the big house.

After her trial and conviction, I had written to the court requesting a copy of the trial transcript, in the event that she might have been innocent, an unlikely possibility. The fact that about a hundred people had actually witnessed the crime did not bode well for Aunt Sophie's chances of a successful appeal. I gave a copy of the following trial transcript pages to Emily because they explained the situation much more accurately than I ever could.

PROSECUTOR: Ms. Russo, you realize that anything you say in court may be held against you?
DEFENDANT: Brad Pitt.
PROSECUTOR: What?
DEFENDANT: Brad Pitt. Are you deaf?
PROSECUTOR: I don't understand.
DEFENDANT: I want Brad Pitt held against me.
(Laughter in the courtroom)
JUDGE: Order!

PROSECUTOR: Ms. Russo, you say that on August 5, 1996, you had been having a bad day?

DEFENDANT: Yes. I bought a new pair of shoes that morning—a nice pair of brown low heels, quite an expensive item, and the right heel broke off an hour after I left the store! I almost broke my leg from the fall. I was thinking of suing. Then, the same day, I locked myself out of my car. Can you believe it?

PROSECUTOR: So is it fair to say you were angry?

DEFENDANT: You bet your ass I was angry. By the way, is that thing on your head a toupee or did a bird's nest fall on your head on the way to court?

PROSECUTOR: Why? Is that important to you?

DEFENDANT: No, but if you're going to invest in a toupee you should spend a few extra bucks and get one that at least matches your natural hair color.

PROSECUTOR: I'll take that under advisement.

JUDGE: (pounding gavel) Ms. Russo, please limit your comments to the questions at hand.

DEFENDANT: Your Honor, did you know that bald men such as yourself and this guy with the rug are very virile in bed? That's always been my experience anyway.

PROSECUTOR: Ms. Russo, please!

JUDGE: Last warning, Ms. Russo!

DEFENDANT: I bet you'd look pretty good without the rug, baldy. Can I see?

PROSECUTOR: No. It's glued on. May we get back to the questions, please?

DEFENDANT: Fine.

PROSECUTOR: How did the victim, Mr. Claude L. Daedelus, approach you?

DEFENDANT: He was wearing black and white makeup on his face, a striped shirt and black leotards, white gloves and a black beret. I was walking along the street, minding my business, and all of a sudden, he jumps right in front of me.

PROSECUTOR: And what was he doing?

DEFENDANT: Jumping around like a crazy lunatic. Doing weird things with his hands, like he was climbing an invisible ladder. Making funny faces, like he was taking a dump. Dancing around. Stuff like that. I told him in my sternest voice to buzz off but he wouldn't listen. I think maybe he was deaf.

PROSECUTOR: A deaf mime?

DEFENDANT: Right. This is America—anything is possible.

PROSECUTOR: Had Mr. Daedelus bothered you previously?

DEFENDANT: I'm not sure. All mimes look the same to me. But was I bothered by mimes before in that area? Yes.

PROSECUTOR: All right. On the day of the alleged murder, what did you do when Mr. Daedelus approached you?

DEFENDANT: I told him to back off again or I was going to kick him in the nuts.

PROSECUTOR: What happened then?

DEFENDANT: He went away.

PROSECUTOR: And then?

DEFENDANT: Then I walked a few more yards and suddenly he was in my face again. He scared the living shit out of me.

PROSECUTOR: Define "in my face."

DEFENDANT: In my face is what you're doing right now in relation to me.

PROSECUTOR: Does that bother you?

DEFENDANT: I'd rather be home soaking in a nice hot bubble bath, if you really want to know. There's room for two, honeybunch.

JUDGE: Ms. Russo, you are trying my patience.

DEFENDANT: Patients? You're a doctor *and* a judge? Wow. Your mother must be so proud. Is she here in the courtroom?

JUDGE: Of course not. Please continue, Mr. Eicher.

PROSECUTOR: So the mime was back "in your face" all of a sudden. What did you do?

DEFENDANT: I smacked him over the head with my purse.

PROSECUTOR: And what was in your purse?

DEFENDANT: Lipstick, rouge, unpaid parking tickets, a wallet, some hard candy, car keys, breath freshener, a roll of toilet paper, a pen, one of those mace thingies in case you get attacked . . .

PROSECUTOR: And what else?

DEFENDANT: Thirty or so pounds of rocks.

PROSECUTOR: Forty-six point five pounds of rocks, to be exact, Ms. Russo, according to the homicide detective's testimony. Do you always carry rocks in your purse?

DEFENDANT: No. But I happen to be an avid rock collector. In fact, I had just that very afternoon been to a rock and mineral fair near the Embarcadero and I bought some quite rare new rocks for my collection. Is there a law against collecting rocks?

PROSECUTOR: No, but three forensic geologists have testified that none of the rocks in your purse had any commercial value whatsoever. They were ordinary rocks that you could find on the ground anywhere.

DEFENDANT: Looks like I got cheated, don't it? You'd be surprised how many scam artists are out there selling phony rocks to unsuspecting collectors like myself. It's a damn shame! If you ask me, that's who you should arrest—the jerk-off who sold me those phony rocks.

PROSECUTOR: Isn't it true, Ms. Russo, that you had put these rocks in your bag for the express reason of assaulting Mr. Daedelus? Was this not a premeditated murder?

DEFENDANT: Like I said, I'm a rock collector.

JUDGE: Are there any more questions, Counselor?

PROSECUTOR: The State rests, Your Honor.

Except for a few suppressed giggles, Emily had no particular adverse reaction to the transcript or the fact that my aunt was a cold-blooded killer of mimes. She even recalled having read about the case in the newspapers when it was being tried.

"There's a black sheep in every family," was her quite sensible response. "Besides, nobody likes a street mime."

Chapter 31: As I had not heard a single

word from my mother for a full week following my employment of Maurice Castelli as her caregiver and dance instructor, I decided to look in on her one evening. Naturally, prior to hiring Castelli, I had requested and received several written references from various past employers, and they were all glowing reports. "Maurice is so trustworthy." "Maurice was a godsend." "Maurice has become part of our family." "Maurice has such patience, such poise, such grooming!"

Maurice, it would seem, was perfect. Perhaps too perfect. I would have felt somewhat more secure if Maurice had demonstrated a few minor quirks or peccadilloes. Nothing major, mind you. "Maurice snores," or "Maurice doesn't use enough deodorant," or "Maurice likes to wear ladies' hats" would have made him slightly more credible. The sad fact is, written references can be easily forged—anyone with stationery and a photocopier can counterfeit practically anything these days.

Nevertheless, his nursing credentials were legitimate (I

checked them out myself) and he seemed to possess an amiable personality, so I hired him after a three-hour interview.

Knowing my mother, she had probably thrown Maurice Castelli out on his keester after the first half hour of caregiving. Or, even more likely, Maurice, in spite of his legendary patience and the hefty salary I was paying him, had departed in disgust over any number of my mother's odd toilet obsessions or absurd demands.

Since my parents had given me a key to their apartment some years ago with instructions to "just come over anytime," I did just that. Much to my surprise, no one was home. I went from room to room calling out "Mother," to no avail. This was interesting to say the least—an agoraphobe who was not at home. Immediately, but for no particular reason other than my usual paranoid anxiety, I concluded that Maurice Castelli had abducted my mother and was holding her, gagged, blindfolded and tied to a chair with duct tape, in a dark, rat-infested basement somewhere. Perhaps he was even doing unspeakable things to her!

So I looked around for a ransom note and, once that search proved unsuccessful, I called my own voice mail to see if Castelli and his gang of thugs had left a ransom message there. After all, what good is an abduction for ransom if there is no ransom note? All the while I was berating myself for having been so careless and lackadaisical in my choice of this murderous felon as a guardian for my poor defenseless mother. What had I been thinking? What kind of a son was I? How could I have gotten my poor dear mother into this ghastly predicament?

It then occurred to me that if there had been an actual abduction, perhaps the local news station would have the story. I picked up one of the six or seven remote controls from the sofa in my mother's apartment and hit the On button. It must have been the wrong remote, because what came on the screen was not the nightly news or any semblance of it. What came on was an obscene shot of two naked young people engaging in sexual commerce, with intermittent extreme close-ups of their interacting genitalia and the accompanying moaning, groaning and annoying background music. I was aghast! I could hardly believe my eyes! Pornography? Hardcore pornography? In my mother's apartment?

Appalled and disgusted, I stopped watching the video when, about ten minutes later, I heard footsteps in the corridor, footsteps accompanied by laughter. No, not even laughter—more like childish giggling.

The key was suddenly thrust in the lock and in walked my mother with that blackguard, that cad, that fiend Maurice Castelli. They appeared to be somewhat intoxicated. It was four or five seconds before they noticed me sitting quietly in my father's old easy chair, impatiently drumming my fingers on the doily-covered arms.

"All right, Castelli," I said. "I know all about you and your little scam. I wasn't born yesterday."

"Pardon me?" Castelli said.

"What are you doing here?" my mother asked me as Castelli removed her evening coat and went to the closet to hang it up.

"Where were you, may I ask?"

"We ate at a restaurant and saw a movie," my mother said.

"Since when do you go out?" I asked. "You hardly ever go out."

"I went to your father's funeral, didn't I?" she said. "I went to the hospital twice. And I went to a diner with you."

"True enough," I conceded.

"And I went to the reading of the will," she added. "If I could survive that, I can survive anything."

"What restaurant did you just go to?" I inquired.

"Salome's in North Hollywood, if you must know," she said. "By the used bookstore. Then we went next door to a movie."

"You ate at an Indian restaurant?"

"Yes. I had the vindaloo, extra spicy."

"I'm not so brave," Castelli confessed. "I had a Tandoori chicken."

"With your bowels you had vindaloo?" I asked my mother, shocked.

"Yes."

"And then you went to the theater next door?" I asked. "The theater next door is a porno theater!"

"So that's why everybody was naked!" my mother said facetiously.

This had them in hysterics. Castelli threw his head back and guffawed with laughter while my mother, impressed by her own joke, doubled up with amusement. I tapped my foot angrily, waiting for their mirth to subside.

"That was a good one, Gladys!" Castelli said. Then he turned to me: "Your mother's quite the comedienne."

"My mother, for your information, has never in her entire life said anything that was even remotely funny," I assured him.

"I find that very difficult to believe," Castelli said, still chuckling. "Are you sure?"

"Quite sure."

"Maybe when you weren't here," Castelli suggested. "Maybe she was funny then."

"I strongly doubt it."

"We're going dancing," my mother announced. "The only reason we came home was to change into our dancing shoes. The night is young!"

"May I speak to you in private for a moment?" I asked my mother.

Before she could even answer, I dragged her by the elbow across the room to her bedroom and closed the door.

"What are you doing?" I whispered. "Dad hasn't been dead more than two weeks and already you're going out dancing and carrying on like a teenager?"

"If you'll recall, Plato," she asserted, "your father had the nerve to start another *family* on the other side of the country. Another wife *and a son*! I'm entitled to a little fun too."

"Yes," I conceded. "That's a valid point."

"Besides, your father, may he rest in peace, never took me dancing," she said. "He hated dancing. I happen to love dancing."

"Since when?"

"All my life. When I was much younger I wanted to be a dancer in a Broadway show."

"Why didn't you?"

My mother shrugged. "I met your father and we got married." She sighed. "I probably wasn't good enough anyway."

My mother sat on the edge of the bed and changed her shoes. The old dreary black shoes were replaced by a pair of low-heeled dancing shoes covered with red rhinestones. I wondered idly if she was going to break into a rendition of "Somewhere Over the Rainbow."

"These are brand-new," she said proudly. "Maurice helped me pick them out. I had some old dancing shoes from years ago, but my bunions hurt when I put them on."

"What about your agoraphobia?" I asked. "Suddenly you're cured?"

"Good question," she said. "I really don't know. It's quite a mystery. I guess Maurice has helped to cure me."

"In a week?"

"Amazing, isn't he? Such a lovely, patient man. A real find."

"May I ask how he managed this amazing feat?" I said. "In fact, the entire psychiatric community of the world might be interested."

"I really don't know," she answered.

"For the last five years you can't leave the apartment, except for emergencies and funerals . . ."

". . . and the hairdresser."

". . . and now all of a sudden you're painting the town red?"

"Maybe there was no place I really wanted to go that badly," she said reflectively. "Your father was content to sit in his chair and read his stupid yachting magazines all day long."

"So now you eat vindaloo and watch pornography every night?"

"Of course not. We had veal Parmesan yesterday."

"Have you had sex with that gigolo?" I demanded.

"What gigolo?"

"Castelli, of course. Is there someone else?"

"That's none of your business," she snapped. "And he's not a gigolo. I resent the implication. Maurice happens to be a very nice man. And he likes me. He's the first person who's liked me in a long time."

"He's ten years younger than you!"

"Nine. And I never said we've had sex. You're making absurd assumptions."

"What will the neighbors say?"

"Who gives a damn?" she said. "You're turning into an old curmudgeon, Plato. And you're only in your thirties. Don't let life pass you by. You'll regret it. If only I had known what I was missing all these years."

"Don't worry about me, Mother," I said. "I'm doing just fine."

"Since when is seeing a shrink twice a week for ten years considered doing just fine?" she asked pointedly.

"I have issues. It's nothing serious, I assure you. And it's only been nine years, eight months, three weeks and two days if you don't count Thanksgiving, summer vacation and Christmas when Dr. Wang takes time off."

"And your love life?"

"Admittedly sporadic."

"Close friends?"

"Teppelman."

"Just one?"

"Isn't that enough? How many friends does one need?"

"I don't know," she mused. "The more the merrier, I would suppose."

"Since when are you so interested in my social life?"

"Since I started having one myself again," she replied. "When I was a young woman, I used to have lot of friends."

"It's not easy for me," I admitted. "I'm a little eccentric. People tend to think I'm a little on the odd side, I suppose."

"Everybody is a little on the odd side," my mother counseled. "You're a very nice boy, Plato. You're handsome, resourceful, compassionate . . . a good son."

"Why, thank you, Mother," I sputtered, truly touched.

"A little maternal advice—don't take everything so seriously, Plato. Go out there and live life to the fullest. Embrace people. Have fun. Look at all the time I wasted staying in this apartment, a lonesome, pathetic old hermit."

I blinked several times in wonder. How was my mother's radical personality change possible in such a short period of time? Housebound for years and now she was suddenly dating Fred Astaire? Eating vindaloo with a digestive tract that had once experienced difficulty coping with plain toast? Pornography? Ballroom dancing? I stared at her for a few seconds hoping her face would provide me some answers. Had my father been at fault? Had he neglected her over the years in favor of his other family? Had his neglect caused her to lose an old zest for life that she was now rediscovering?

"I don't mean to be rude, Plato," she told me. "But would you please leave my bedroom now? I need to dress. My prince and his carriage awaiteth me."

"Now you're suddenly Cinderella?" I huffed.

"If the shoe fits." She smiled. "Pardon the pun."

Then she stood up in those ridiculous red shoes. I stayed right where I was, blocking the door. She put her hands on her hips and tapped her foot impatiently, a gesture she had used often in my youth. I obediently stepped aside, then left the room shaking my head. Castelli, the slick little fop, resplendent in his white ducks and blue blazer, was waiting in the foyer, holding the door open. With a weary sigh, I breezed by him and left the apartment, catching in my nostrils a whiff of his thoroughly revolting men's cologne.

Chapter 32: Predictably, Wang was

desolate the next time I saw him. Emily had moved out again, she despised him, they would never reconcile. Their marriage was over. Finished! Kaput! Although I already knew about all of this, I did my best to appear stunned.

"I'm absolutely stunned!" I cried. "Stunned!"

"I can't tell you what this has done to my self-esteem," he lamented at the beginning of the session. "I'm crushed. Devastated. Forlorn."

I truly felt sorry for him, but what could I say? I had been there myself. Recently.

"You'll meet someone else," I assured him.

"How? Where? When?"

"I don't know," I said. "At the grocery store?"

"What are you suggesting?" Wang asked. "That I pick up some tootsie in the produce section? I'm a little too old for that."

"Perhaps someone will set you up with a blind date and you'll hit it off," I ventured.

"Doubtful."

"Don't be so pessimistic," I scolded. "Look at the bright side."

"There is no bright side, Fussell," he moaned. "I can't go on."

"You shouldn't measure your self-esteem solely on the opinion of one person."

"Who told you that nonsense?"

"Actually, it was you."

"Don't listen to me," he said. "I'm obviously an idiot."

"Now you're telling me this?" I cried. "After ten years of therapy?"

"Nine and a half, to be exact," he said. "If you don't count Thanksgiving, Christmas and summer vacations."

"Whatever," I said. "We're still talking about $88,920, give or take, in psychiatric fees."

"You figured that out in your head just now?"

"No, last night," I confessed. "I had a similar discussion with my mother. It's a long story."

"And how is that fine lady?" he asked.

"My mother? You don't want to know," I said. "Suffice it to say she seems to have gotten a second wind."

We sat silently for a moment, so silently that you could hear Wang's alarm clock humming. I confess to being more than a little upset by his sad eyes, cheerless voice and overall despondent appearance. But what could I do? It was his very advice to me, advice I had gladly taken, that had led to his own present dejection. What was I supposed to do now? Ignore him? Confess? Blurt out the whole terrible secret about Emily and me? Tell him it was me all along, that I alone was the reason for his despair? Damn it, I loved her too! Had Emily decided to stay with Wang, my dejection and sorrow would no doubt have been of a similar intensity. The only thing that played in Wang's favor was the fact that he would most likely be able to fall in love with someone new much faster than I. He was outgoing and jovial; I was neither. He had patients that came to see him regularly and many of these were females. Females rarely came to see me for any reason. Except for a few minor oddities, he was not nearly as neurotic as I. Not yet anyway.

"I'm convinced it's the other man," he stated suddenly, making my pulse increase. "He's playing her like a yo-yo. I should have nipped this in the bud before, when I still had the chance."

"Probably," I agreed. We'd been through this before.

"I'm very angry about this, Fussell. Don't just blow me off with a 'probably.'"

"Sorry," I said. "Where do you feel this anger?"

"All over my body. My stomach, my hands, my legs."

"Perhaps you should work out," I suggested. "Relieve the tension. I hear Body World in Encino is having a half-price membership offer. Or perhaps you could purchase a bicycle or Rollerblades and—"

"This anger is much deeper. There's no easy way of working off this kind of anger."

"Pills?" I ventured.

"Not for this."

"So what in your opinion would be sufficient to placate this level of anger?"

"First-degree murder," he said.

I gulped. His eyes were on fire. His hands trembled on his desktop. You could almost hear his front teeth grinding. I had never seen this particular side of Wang. It was really quite horrifying.

"Calm yourself, man," I admonished. "You're scaring me."

"Sorry," Wang said, slumping. "I've had more than a few sleepless nights lately. It's taking its toll."

"Just curious, but upon whom exactly would this rurderous mage (oops) of yours be directed?" I asked, trying to hide the tremor in my voice. "Your wife or her paramour?"

"The lover, obviously," Wang answered impatiently, ignoring my tied tongue. "I still love Emily with all my heart. I would never raise a hand to hurt her."

"I see," said I. My salivary glands suddenly stopped functioning. I reached into my pocket and sprayed a few painful squirts of Binaca onto my tongue. After that, my mouth was still dry, but now it tasted like Glass Plus.

"But," I continued weakly, "you don't know who the lover is, correct?"

"That's right," Wang said. "But it would be pretty darn simple to find out."

"Oh really? How?"

"I could hire a private detective," he said. "I'd have the name and address of this asshole in less than a week."

"Yes, you certainly could do that," I concurrred, still trying to calm my voice lest he detect my involuntary vibrato. "But what if your wife found out? Wouldn't she be mad?"

"Who cares?"

"I hear they're extremely expensive," I said, grasping helplessly at straws. "Private detectives."

"No, they're not. I've already looked into it. Less than a thousand bucks would cover it."

"Oh really?" I mused, placing my trembling hands under my thighs. "So you've already hired a detective?"

Before he could answer, the alarm clock sounded, a rather shrill blast that could wake the dead and, this time, almost made me leap out of my argyle socks. My session was officially over. Wang abruptly dropped his pencil, stood up and walked me to the door. I was about to reask my last question regarding the status of the detective, when his damn phone rang.

"See you next week," he said to me before closing the door.

I hatched my desperate plan on the drive home from Wang's office that very afternoon. Fearing that Wang might actually hire a detective within the next few days, I decided to leave town immediately for a while. I would go to Buffalo, New York, to do some research regarding Fillmore and his relationship to the mysterious L.M. at the local historical society archive. Then, I would travel to picturesque Moorpark, New Jersey, and, with the aid of Mickey Koro, attempt to make contact with Katrina and Leopold, a venture I admit to having some misgivings about, but a venture I was equally determined to undertake.

The moment I arrived home I phoned my travel agent and instructed her to make the appropriate flight and hotel reservations. Then I made arrangements for Isabella to stay at the local canine Hilton. Following that, I began packing my suitcases, which, for someone of my slightly neurotic ilk, was a process that could take up to three months. There were so many choices and the annoyingly unpredictable weather on the eastern seaboard could go from hot to cold, humid to dry, calm to stormy in a matter of hours. We had no such fluctuations in this part of the world, other than drought, Santa Ana winds and the occasional monsoon. Would I require formal attire or just casual? How much rain gear should I pack? How much snow gear? Shaving cream and a new razor? A sweater or a heavy coat? All my medications or just enough to last me a week? But what if I had to stay longer, what if I was stranded there, then what?

Nevertheless, if Wang was going to hire a private detective—and for some reason I didn't believe he already had—it was essential for me to get out of town posthaste and not risk being seen with Emily. Staying home—even if I were to lock myself in my bedroom for a week—would make me a paranoid wreck.

But one question remained: Should I tell Emily about this detective business? Was it worth it to make her a paranoid basket case as well? Would she lash out at Wang if she found out? And if she did lash out, wouldn't Wang want to know exactly where she had gotten the information, thus jeopardizing my position as his patient?

Obviously, tempting as it was, I could not take her along on my journey—the whole idea was for the prospective detective to follow her and detect that she was *not* seeing anyone. If she came along with me, she might be followed, or the detective might simply wait until she (and I) came back from the trip, thus making the whole enterprise utterly pointless. No, I would have to go alone. And quickly. There was no other way.

"It's just a short business trip," I told Emily the next time we spoke.

"But you don't really have a business," she said. "Do you?"

"If you mean am I currently receiving money for services rendered, the answer is no," I said. "But I need to go to Buffalo to do some research at the archive and I thought I might stop in New Jersey and try to see Katrina and Leopold as well."

"I'll miss you terribly," she said.

"And I you."

"I'll be miserable."

"As will I."

"Perhaps I should come along," she suggested. "I love the East Coast. All those bizarre weather changes, filthy subways, mosquitoes, Lyme disease."

I already had an answer prepared for this possibility: "But what about your job?" I reminded her. "What if Bob Hoover needs you?"

"Yes, that would be a distinct problem," she responded. "We're at a fairly critical part of the process. Bob and I are hammering out the final details. And the contractors never do what you tell them, especially if you're a woman."

"I'd love for you to come, Emily," I said falsely. "It would be marvelous. Beyond marvelous! But the fact is, I would feel truly awful if it in any way jeopardized your work. I know how much you love it. I could never forgive myself."

"You're such a dear, thoughtful man, Fussell," she said, falling for my deception. "I do love you very much."

"And I do love you too," said I, amazed that I could so easily give voice to this controversial word.

"May I see you before you leave?" she asked. "For a drink?"

The temptation was overwhelming, but I needed the time to pack as I was expecting to depart quite early the next morning. Besides, I couldn't risk the possibility that Wang had already hired a shamus.

"You know me," I said humorously. "It'll take me half a century or more to pack. I'll have to call five cabs, just to make sure one of them comes to take me to the airport. Then I'll have to take three Xanax to even get through airport security, and another two to get on the plane. And then—"

"You'll call me?" she asked. "From New York?"

"Five times a day," I promised, heeding Wang's past words of wisdom about how much Emily detested being left alone for long periods of time. Leaving town was a risk I knew I had to take, but somehow I felt that our deep affection for each other had grown in the past few months, and that a week of loneliness would no longer be enough to seriously damage our relationship. Besides, now she had a job that would keep her thoughts occupied. Nonetheless, this time I would attempt to keep myself in her consciousness on a daily basis by making frequent telephone calls and by sending her the occasional box of Godiva chocolates and other mementos of my affection for her.

After several hours of utter confusion and indecision, after I was ready to tear my hair out, after I threw back two Xanax, I managed to fit the following essential items into three medium-size suitcases, plus a carry-on duffle and a briefcase, for a maximum of a one-week sojourn in Buffalo and Moorpark, New Jersey:

- 5 flannel shirts
- 5 dress shirts
- 5 short-sleeved knit shirts
- 3 wool sweaters
- 3 cotton sweaters
- 3 pair corduroy pants
- 3 pair dress pants
- 2 Fleet enemas
- 5 pair undershorts

- 2 pair long john underwear
- 5 pair undershirts
- 3 pair Bermuda shorts
- 10 pair socks
- 3 pair shoes
- 3 pair rain boots
- 3 collapsible umbrellas
- 1 raincoat, 1 rain hat
- 1 pair waders
- 5-day supply of K-rations
- 1 parka, 1 pair snow boots, 1 pair snowshoes, 1 pair snow pants
- 2 wool watch caps
- 4 belts
- 3 bottles of Xanax
- 2 bottles Tylenol, Motrin, Tums, Lipitor, Prilosec, Paxil, Kaopectate, Ex-Lax, assorted vitamins, Pepto-Bismol, Benadryl
- 1 tube extra-strength Preparation H
- 3 nasal decongestant sprays
- 1 bottle calamine lotion
- 1 large spray-on bottle insect repellent
- 3 tubes zinc oxide
- 2 spray bottles Lysol
- 6 rolls Charmin Ultra Soft toilet tissue
- 1 roll Brawny paper towels
- 2 bottles Visine
- Phone numbers of 3 board-certified MDs, dermatologists, psychiatrists, endocrinologists, gastroenterologists and neurologists in Buffalo, and 3 in Moorpark
- $2,000 in American Express traveler's checks
- 1 wallet belt
- 1 neck brace
- 3 hotel-size pillowcases and bedsheets

- 3 boxes Band-Aids, assorted sizes
- 1 large tube Neosporin
- 1 large tube 300 SPF sunscreen
- 1 paperback copy *Symptoms of Diseases: Deluxe Edition*
- 1 paperback copy *Physicians' Desk Reference*
- 15 assorted handkerchiefs
- 50 Q-Tips, 20 tongue depressors, 1 blood pressure kit
- 1 rectal thermometer
- Assorted Ace bandages
- 2 fluffy pillows
- My Millard Fillmore Association membership card
- An eight-by-ten framed photo of Emily

Chapter 33: I took a direct flight to

Buffalo, New York, from Los Angeles International Airport, which was, as usual, hopelessly crowded. Despite almost vomiting twice into an airline barf bag as soon as the aircraft became airborne (my stomach cannot abide takeoffs and landings), I found the flight happily uneventful, although the overweight gentleman sitting beside me, apparently disgusted by my retching, snickered derisively at me, called me a douche bag and moved himself to a permanent spot in the rear of the plane, never to return. Which was all the better for me—more room to stretch my limbs and no one to sneeze or cough in my food. Besides, this fellow was obviously something of a nitwit, for I had noted earlier that he had been clumsily lugging around a heavy suitcase at the airport check-in line, apparently unaware of one of mankind's greatest achievements—the merging of the concept of the wheel with the concept of the suitcase.

As usual, we experienced some turbulence at exactly the same moment the food arrived. How, I wondered, do they always manage to synchronize this so well? Not that it mattered. The food, if it can actually be given that definition, featured a slab of meat that resembled the foot of a deceased penguin, a limp salad with browning lettuce and soggy tomatoes, and for dessert, an odd, mysterious lump of something orange and sinister called "Orange Mouse" (sic). Fortunately, I had consumed an excellent self-made cream cheese and cucumber sandwich prior to entering the plane, so I covered the airline food tray with a paper napkin and told the flight attendant to give it a decent burial. She was not amused, although I had the distinct feeling that smiling was not part of her face's repertoire.

Five miserable hours later, I was in Buffalo, perhaps not the cultural abyss of the universe, but a close tie with Biloxi, Mississippi. My travel agent had rented me a roomy beige Lexus with eight airbags, which I picked up with no trouble whatsoever at the car rental office. Later, I received a detailed map from the Avis attendant and, after taking another Xanax in the event I became hopelessly lost, drove to my hotel, the Buffalo Palace, which, although considered to be the best hotel in Buffalo, would have received a huge laugh of derision from that segment of the world which was actually considered civilized. Indeed, it was once probably considered a veritable palace—perhaps in 1867.

I remade the double bed with my own sheets, pillows and pillowcases. After all, what if the room's previous inhabitants had had a communicable disease such as cholera, typhoid fever or plague, or even a bad case of the flu? And who knew whether the last residents of my room drooled during their sleep, thus contaminating the actual pillow itself as well as the pillowcase. Every surface, and especially the bed, could be a hotbed of insidious bacterial activity. A visit to the local hospital was not part of my itinerary.

I hung up my clothing and placed the rest of my attire in a slightly chipped bureau. Then I took a long, hot shower, swallowed another Xanax and went to bed. Naturally, since this was not my own bed in my own home, I spent most of the night tossing and turning and finally caught a few winks at about four o'clock in the morning after switching on a "Masterpiece Theatre" episode minus the sound.

The next morning, after a brief room service breakfast of undercooked bacon and a soggy yellowish thing that the hotel called "Les Egges," I drove at the steady rate of twenty-two miles per hour to the historical society on the other side of town. My Millard Fillmore Association membership card admitted me without cost and allowed me to peruse everything in their library, including a collection of old Buffalo newspapers and Fillmore letters, documents and memorabilia. I decided that my search for the mysterious L.M would commence with the correspondence, all of which was on microfilm.

As L.M.'s letter had been dated February 1854, I began with Fillmore's correspondence for that year, then traced it back to 1853 (the year his first wife perished), then forward to 1858 (the year he married his second wife). Alas, after an entire day of searching I came away with nothing of any use. There was no mention of anyone with the initials "L.M." I had a serviceable dinner of roast turkey at a local diner that was highly recommended by the librarian.

Later that night, I spoke to Emily by phone for over an hour. I detected absolutely no lessening of her affection for me; in fact she was downright jubilant that I had called after being gone for less than one day. But just to make sure everything was satisfactory, I arranged for a gargantuan box of Godiva chocolates to be sent to her apartment the following day. I even managed to instruct the clerk to write the words "I love you" on the little square greeting card.

The next day, I decided to tackle the local Buffalo newspapers, which were also on microfilm and dated back to 1830. I commenced by perusing the editions dating from mid-January through the entire month of February 1854, the time of Teppelman's inexplicable letter. I had only just begun my exploration when I hit pay dirt in the issue dated January 30, 1854.

. . .

"That's most peculiar," Teppelman reacted when I phoned him the next day with the electrifying news. "Most unsettling indeed."

"Most *unsettling?*" I practically shouted. "It's a downright historical bombshell is what it is! It could set the whole course of American History on its ear!"

"I wouldn't go quite that far, Fussell," he said. "Keep in mind we're talking about Millard Fillmore here, not Lincoln."

"Yes, but you must admit, it's quite an interesting bit of research," I insisted. "Quite interesting indeed. Historians will no longer think of my old Millard as a dullard, I can assure you of that!"

"You keep telling me you know everything there is to know about Millard Fillmore and now something as bizarre and unseemly as this just pops up out of nowhere," Teppelman observed.

"I'll admit it is quite unlike the Fillmore I know and love," I agreed. "I would never have expected something like this, true enough. It's quite out of character."

"It doesn't give me much faith in the art of biography, either," Teppelman said. "Not to mention history."

"Well, this sort of thing would have been very hush-hush in those days," I explained. "Most people just didn't talk about sexual matters in 1854."

"True," Teppelman conceded. "But don't forget, he married twice and had children."

"Yes, but they all did that," I maintained. "To cover up. To appear normal. The flowery handwriting suddenly makes sense. As do many other things."

I was as flabbergasted as Teppelman. Yet indisputably, there it was, in black and white, at the bottom of page 5 of the January 30, 1854 edition of the *Buffalo Union-Times*:

The acclaimd (sic) stage actor Leslie Montague of New York City and Boston, Massachussets (sic), star of the Broodway (sic) play "The Romanian Sled" will be giving his famous lecture on "Theartre (sic) and the Muse," on February 1st at 7:00 o'clock PM in the lecture roam (sic) of the Atheneum Librrary (sic), 612 York St. in Buffalo. Tickets are 50 cents. He will be staying at the home of Buffalo attornie (sic) and former President of the United States, Millard Fillmore.

"The six spelling errors don't bode well," Teppelman said. "Either the reporter or the typesetter was a class-A moron."

"Buffalo was not quite the cultural capital of the world in those days," I pointed out. "And, for your information, it is not now either."

"I have no particular desire to go there," Teppelman said. "Never have."

"If you do, don't stay at the Palace," I warned him. "The title is a fantastic misnomer."

"Perhaps you should do a little more research on this Leslie Montague person, before you come out with a scholarly paper saying Millard Fillmore was gay," Teppelman suggested.

"Of course!" I said, a bit perturbed that Teppelman thought I would be that slapdash in my work. "I wasn't born yesterday, Teppelman. I will corroborate this as many times as I can before writing a single word."

"Who knows? Maybe it's just a coincidence? Maybe there's another. L.M. who's a woman?" he speculated. "Maybe they both stayed at Fillmore's house on that night."

"It was a small house," I said. "I have a copy of the blueprint."

"Still . . ."

"Moreover," I continued, "it would have been unseemly for Fillmore, an unmarried man at the time and a pillar of the community, to allow a female to stay in his guest quarters. There would have been some substantial public displeasure with that, had it happened."

"Perhaps."

"Yet, having a man stay there for one or two nights would receive virtually no attention," I continued. "Who would suspect even the slightest malfeasance?"

"Have you looked through the papers for any other mention of this actor?" Teppelman asked. "Certainly his name would appear in the dramatis personae of this play 'The Romanian Sled'?"

"Yes, but I'm afraid I've found nothing thus far."

"I have some old books about the theater," Teppelman said. "I'll see if I can find anything about this Mr. Montague of yours."

"That would be splendid. Let me know if you find anything. I'll be in New Jersey tomorrow. I can always take a day and see what I can find at the New York Public Library if need be."

I gave Teppelman my cell phone number and began packing for my trip to points east. I had called my travel agent that morning and asked her to cancel my room at the Moorpark Inn and book me a suite at the Waldorf Astoria in New York. Two nights at the Buffalo Palace were as low as I wanted to sink in one lifetime. If one can afford to travel in high style with all the comforts, one should not hesitate. You may quote me.

Later that day, I called Emily's cell phone and informed her about my earth-shattering discovery. She was beside herself with joy at the likelihood of my imminent fame and fortune in the community of scholars. However, I was a bit perturbed that she had not once mentioned the chocolates.

"You sent me chocolates, Fussell?" she asked. "How awfully sweet of you, dear man."

"Did you not receive them?" I asked.

"I haven't been home since six o'clock this morning," she groaned. "They're about to start construction on Bob's place. I had to be up at the crack of dawn. Permits and all that."

"Where are you now?" I asked, suspicious. It was 7:00 P.M., Pacific time.

"In the car, on the way home after an exhausting day," she said. "I'll be home in about an hour, if traffic doesn't get snarled on the 405."

"Traffic is always snarled on the 405," I observed. "Hopefully they haven't melted on your doorstep."

"I'm sure they're fine," she said. "And thank you again, Fussell. That was such a romantic thing to do. I'm really very touched."

"I think about you all the time," I confessed. "Every minute. You are always in my thoughts."

"And I think about you too," she repeated. "Whenever I have a minute or two to myself."

"How often is that?"

"Not often enough, I'm sorry to say."

"So the work is going well?"

"Oh yes," she said. "Bob's a very easy-going guy. So far, anyway. It's as if he doesn't really care how much the whole thing will cost."

"Is that so?"

"I've never worked with someone like that," she said enthusiastically "So of course I'm going all out. The sky's the limit, right?"

Bob had evidently not taken seriously my admonition that he did not necessarily need to spend every last cent of the money I had given him. It had not occurred to me at the time that Emily, as his designer, might want to encourage him to spend as much as possible. She probably marked up all the furniture and accessories, on top of her fee.

"I'll see you soon," I said.

"I'm counting the minutes, Fussell," she replied.

I waited a few seconds for her to say she loved me, as she habitually did at the conclusion of our telephone conversations, but all she said, albeit in an affectionate tone, was "Sleep well."

Chapter 34:
My head swimming with

thoughts of Leslie Montague and Emily Thorndyke, not necessarily in that order, I arrived 12.5 minutes late by railway to New York's Grand Central Station and took a cab to the Waldorf Astoria. I chose for a taxi driver an elderly woman of Hungarian descent, assuming that her advanced age and gender would prevent her from driving as recklessly as most New York cab drivers, thus sparing both our lives on the traffic-clogged trek to the hotel. I was wrong. She nearly killed both of us. She had left her glasses at home.

Except for the fact that the toilet in my suite held in its bowl a small sliver of fecal matter the size and shape of a baby goldfish (for which I requested and was granted a room change) I spent a truly delightful night at the Waldorf indulging myself with a three-course repast via room service. I polished off a filet mignon (well done), a cup of applesauce with cinnamon, string beans, mashed potatoes and a lovely crème brûlée. One of the reasons I particularly prefer the Waldorf is that every person who works in its kitchen is required to wear hairnets and plastic gloves when handling the food. I had read this in a travel magazine in Wang's waiting room some years ago.

The next morning, after buying Leopold a large brown teddy bear at F.A.O. Schwarz on Fifth Avenue, I called Mickey Koro, the private investigator, and arranged for our trip to Katrina's house in Moorpark. The travel plan was for me to take a taxi to his office in Newark, and from there we would both travel to Moorpark in his car (which was to cost me a flat fee of $100). Having never actually met Mickey Koro, I had no idea what to expect. My only contact with those in the field of private investigation had come from the cinema—Sam Spade, Nick and Nora Charles, Charlie Chan and the like.

Mickey Koro turned out to be a somewhat rotund fellow who liked to pluck his suspenders with his thumbs and roll on the balls of his feet when speaking. An unlit cigar butt was permanently stationed in one corner of his mouth, his teeth were quite yellow and I haven't smelled breath that bad since, as a small impulsive child, I kissed a tame antelope on the mouth at a petting zoo. His tiny office, located in a red brick two-story in the downtown business district of Newark, smelled of bodily odor, as if someone had recently spent the night there. By the looks of things—the word "disarray" comes to mind—somebody probably had.

Nevertheless, he greeted me with good cheer and a hearty slap on the back, a gesture of friendship whose sincerity was somewhat compromised by his immediate request for the $100 transportation fee in cash up front. He probably owed the landlord, or some bookie, or maybe a racetrack tout or two. Apparently, he himself would be driving me out to Moorpark and not, as I had thought, an employee of Acme Investigations. Considering the size of the office, it appeared likely that the firm had but one employee. I peeled off a couple of fifties, then washed my hands thoroughly, and soon we were off to the wilds of the suburbs in Koro's vintage Chevy Impala, which reeked of tobacco smoke, old pizza and mustard. I made sure the seat belt was in good working order.

"So tell me, Mickey," I said, feeling the need to make conversation. "Are you packing heat?"

"Yeah, the gat's all tucked away in a shoulder holster," Mickey said. "And I always refer to women's legs as 'gams' too."

"I'm a little disappointed you're not wearing a tattered old fedora," I said.

"Can't wear them anymore," he told me. "I sweat right through the hatbands."

"You probably drink a lot of liquor, too," I ventured. "Scotch, neat, perhaps."

"That's right," Mickey replied. "And I hang around at the racetrack all day long with oily guys who look like Peter Lorre, betting on the nags."

"My mother drinks scotch neat," I informed him for no particular reason. "I've known her for over thirty years and I only just learned of it recently."

"Ah, the secrets of the human heart," Mickey mused. "I get a lot of that in my line of work."

"How so?" I asked.

"Typical case. A broad comes in, tells me she thinks hubbie's getting a little on the side. I follow the guy, take pictures of him in the act, show them to the wife and half the time she don't believe it. When it's right in front of her eyes! 'That can't be him,' she says. 'My husband wouldn't do that with a strange woman. I know him.'

"And it's not only normal sex," Mickey continued. "I find these guys dressing up in ladies' clothing, getting whipped by broads in black leather . . . you name it, I've seen it—judges, aldermen, cops . . ."

This was more than I cared to know. "An exciting line of work you're in," I said.

"It gets old after a while," Mickey replied. "Like everything else."

Then he switched on the radio, probably a subtle signal to me that he was uninterested in continuing this scintillating conversation. We listened silently to an agonizingly uneventful ball game.

Shortly thereafter, we passed a billboard welcoming us to Moorpark, New Jersey, and before I knew it we were driving through the downtown area, a motley row of old, forgotten stores, some of which were boarded up, a deserted park and a public library in the ancient Greek style, its walls and Doric columns covered with grafitti. Not surprising, when you consider that Moorpark spelled backward is Kraproom. We crossed some railroad tracks, drove past an old red brick leather factory that was shut down and a few vacant lots, then passed a more run-down park with an uninhabited basketball court.

"Almost there," Mickey said, and I suddenly became anxiety-ridden at the prospect of meeting my father's phantom family. Or at the prospect of *not* meeting them. What if Katrina was not interested in seeing me? What if she wouldn't let me see Leopold? What if nobody was home? My father's final words echoed in my head: "Do not forsake Leopold."

The neighborhood, as Mickey had described it, consisted of simple row houses that had been built in the late fifties when the leather factory was booming. Mickey pulled up in front of one of them, a light green, shake-shingled clapboard with a well-groomed front lawn shaded by an enormous chestnut tree and an old white Volvo in the driveway. This was no doubt the place my father came to when he visited his other family. Had he paid the rent and purchased the car? I wondered.

"Go ahead, Mr. Fussell," Mickey said, yawning. "I'll just catch forty winks."

"You're going to stay here?"

"Sure, why not?" he said. "Got nothing else going on today and I could use the shut-eye."

I was suddenly a bit nervous about this whole enterprise. I took a few cleansing breaths.

"Mind if I just sit here for a few minutes, Yekcim," I said.

"What?"

"Your name spelled backward," I told him. "Nervous habit. Sounds like something an Eskimo might say. Quite a pleasing sound, don't you think?"

"Actually I prefer it the other way."

"I wasn't suggesting you change it," I said.

But he wasn't paying attention anymore. He had lowered his seat back to a comfortable reclining position and was removing his sport jacket in preparation for his little nap. I sat there for a moment, trying to summon up enough nerve to complete my mission.

"That chrome doohickey over there will open the car door," he instructed me. "You just have to pull it towards you."

"I know how to get out of the car," I said testily. "I'm just a little nervous, that's all."

"Worst thing, she blows your head off with a shotgun," Mickey said. "If she does, you got a witness. Me."

"Most reassuring," I said.

Mickey shrugged, sighed, yawned, put his head back and closed his eyes. Before long, he was snoring. I opened the car door and stepped out, grabbing the teddy bear, which had been sitting in the backseat.

Suddenly, I was standing at the front door. After adjusting my tie, making sure my fly was closed and taking a few deep breaths to clear my head, I pressed the doorbell and heard the chime ring inside. At first, there was no reaction, but then I began to see something shadowy moving in the foyer. A moment later, Katrina (I recognized her from the photos) was peering at me through the door window's lace curtains. She was wearing a shower cap.

"Hello there!" I shouted. "I'm Flato Pussell! I've come to see you and Leopold!"

The lace curtain then fell back into place and Katrina disappeared. I waited. There was no sound or movement from inside the foyer. Had she decided not to let me in? Did she not want to see me, as I had feared? Should I leave or should I be steadfast and stay until she opened the door? Or should I go against my father's dying wishes and forsake young Leopold? No, leaving without seeing them was not an option, even if I had to sleep on the porch or in Mickey Koro's car until either or both of them emerged from the house. They couldn't stay in there forever. Eventually someone would have to come out for groceries.

I was about to ring the chime again when the door suddenly creaked open. Katrina stood in the foyer, tightening the belt of a white terry-cloth bathrobe. The shower cap was gone, but now her head was wrapped in a towel turban.

"Please accept my apologies if this is a bad time," I blubbered. "But I've come all the way from Ainrofilac to see you."

"Is fine," she said, slipping into a pair of tattered slippers. "Come in. Is all right. I have been expecting you for days."

"Oh?" I asked. "How so?"

She pointed to Mickey's car. "Your detective is perhaps not very good at keeping low profile."

"Ah."

I crossed the threshold. The first thing I saw, by the staircase wall, was a small picture of Jesus on the cross and next to it, a large photo of my father taken perhaps ten or fifteen years ago. He was wearing a tuxedo. I never even knew he owned one.

She led me into the living room, a comfortable space, where two large, overstuffed chairs faced a high brick fireplace. On the mantel were two more photos of my father, both portraits. One of them was draped in black lace.

"So," she said, gesturing for me to have a seat. "You are other son of my dear husband, Victor?"

"Yes."

"You do not look very much like him."

"No, I look more like my mother," I opined. "Did he ever speak of me?"

"Only to say that you were apple of his eyes," she said. I detected a distinct Eastern European accent. Hungarian, perhaps? Or Polish?

"Really?"

"Victor was very proud of you. Of success you achieved. He told me many times about your exploits."

This brought a tear to my eye. My father had never told me any such thing himself. How odd that I had to learn through his secret wife that he had been proud of me.

"Do you know what his last words to me were?" I asked.

"No."

"He said, 'Do not forsake Leopold,'" I told her.

"He loved very much his little boy Leopold also," Katrina said. "And now my poor son has no father."

"Perhaps I can help with that a little," I offered.

Then her eyes began to tear up. I stood up and handed her one of my handkerchiefs. She blew her nose in it and handed it right back. I motioned for her to keep it.

"Where *is* Leopold?" I asked.

"In school. He will be back in a few moments. Can I make you tea or something?"

"What kind of tea, if I may ask?"

"Lipton?"

"No thanks. Too much caffeine."

"A beer perhaps?"

"Have you got any bottled water?" I asked. "Preferably distilled?"

"Yes."

"That would be just fine, Anirtak."

"Pardon?"

"Nothing."

She rose and walked out of the room, shuffling a bit in a worn pair of slippers. As she stood in the kitchen and poured my drink, a bizarre thought suddenly occurred to me—could Katrina Fussell be considered my legal stepmother? I would have to ask my lawyer when I returned home, not that it really mattered, but the possibility of having two mothers was definitely intriguing. Would I be required to send two Mother's Day cards every May?

"Thank you," I said when she handed me a chipped highball glass clinking with ice cubes. I took a sip and placed the glass on a nearby end table.

"So tell me," I inquired. "Where are you from originally?"

"Latvia," she said.

"I hear it's a very beautiful country," I remarked, although I had never actually heard anything about Latvia one way or the other. "And how exactly did you meet my father?"

"In Moscow. It was winter 1978," she reflected nostalgically, dabbing her tears with a paper towel she had brought from the kitchen. "A park bench at Gorky Park, to be exact. February, I believe."

"My father was in Moscow? Victor Fussell was in Moscow?" I asked with some measure of disbelief.

"Oh yes, many times. Moscow, Berlin, Budapest, even Vladivostok once."

"Really? How so? For what purpose?"

She sighed and looked away. "I am not really supposed to speak to anyone of this," she whispered. "There is some secrecy involved."

"Secrecy?" I asked. "I'm his son, I have a right to know. Was he a criminal of some sort? On the lam? Did he embezzle money?"

"No, of course not," Katrina countered. "Victor was honest man."

"Then what?"

Katrina took a deep breath and studied me. "We were both with CCI Division," she admitted finally.

"CCI?"

"Counter-counterintelligence."

"For whom?"

"For the CIA, of course," she said. "Who else, K-Mart?"

"When you say CIA, you mean the Central Intelligence Agency, correct?" I asked. "The spies."

"Yes," she affirmed. "The one in Langley, Virginia. Is there another CIA which I am not aware of?"

"I thought perhaps it was a pharmaceutical company."

"No."

"So you're saying my father was a spy?"

"Yes," she said. "An excellent one too. One of best I ever had pleasure to work with."

"A spy?" I repeated. "My father. Victor Fussell."

"Da."

"Impossible!" I bellowed incredulously. "Victor J. Fussell of Van Nuys, California, was with the CIA? That's the most ridiculous thing I ever heard in my entire life! He was a pharmaceutical salesman who dreamed of owning a boat!"

"Yes, that was his cover," she informed me. "And as you see, it worked very well."

"This is absolutely incredible!" I said, awestruck.

"Not so incredible," she said blandly. "Men like Victor who are living—how you say?—ordinary lives in suburban cities are recruited often by CIA. Nobody suspects. Besides, counter-counterintelligence is mainly just paperwork. Deciphering codes and so on, but not much—how you say—cloak and dagger."

"Did my mother know anything about this?"

"No," she said. "Would she believe it?"

"Probably not."

"There, you see?"

"He never called you on the phone?" I asked. "You never called him? I found no letters in his personal effects."

"Victor and I communicated through a yachting magazine which was sent to him by CIA."

I was flabbergasted! My quiet, inconspicuous, daydreaming father was an agent with the CIA? It was absolutely preposterous! Absurd! Laughable! Ridiculous! Also fascinating. All those years, while I thought he was dreaming of owning a large, expensive schooner, my father was actually reading letters from his other wife and son, not to mention communiqués from the CIA. And I must admit, I was in many ways delighted to know that his life was not, as I had always thought, one of quiet desperation, but rather one of quiet undercover work.

"You perhaps still do not believe me?" Katrina asked. "Is understandable. He could tell you nothing. Here, I show you pictures."

She rose and scurried over to a short bookshelf from which she extracted a red photograph album. Red, I thought, how appropriate, communism's favorite hue, and the color of adultery as well. She placed it delicately on her lap and began silently leafing through its thick, yellowed pages. I came over and sat down beside her. She smelled slightly of peaches, the odor of her shampoo, perhaps.

She stopped at a page with a small snapshot of my father in front of the Kremlin. It was unmistakably the Kremlin, with its familiar onion-shaped domes in the background, and unmistakably my father, with his familiar big ears in the foreground. Then there was a color eight-by-ten of my father in the Oval Office shaking hands with Ronald Reagan, a man I knew he did not vote for. (Or did I really know anything?) Reagan had inscribed it *To Victor Fussell, With Thanks from a Grateful Nation, Best Wishes, Ronald Reagan*. A few pages farther along there was an official-looking Certificate of Merit, with my father's name emblazoned calligraphically as the recipient, and a signature below of the former director of the Central Intelligence Agency, William Casey.

"I'm utterly astounded," I said to Katrina. "I'm dumbfounded, I'm thunderstruck, I'm—"

Before I could finish, I heard the front door open and little Leopold suddenly appeared in the living room, a bulging school backpack on his shoulders. His dark hair was spiked after the fashion of the day, and his legs were so long and gangly I feared he would trip over them. He was quite pale, though his cheeks were red from the brisk wind. In person, his resemblance to my father was even more marked, and I felt my eyes well up slightly. I missed the old man.

"Come here, darling boy," Katrina said.

Leopold, who had stopped in the foyer, slung his cumbersome backpack over a chair and advanced shyly toward his mother, sneaking a furtive glance or two at me. She grabbed him by the arms and smothered his face with kisses until he had to push her away in embarrassment. As I recalled from my own youth, ten-year-old boys rarely enjoy demonstrations of affection from their mothers, especially the ones who have a tendency to slobber on or pinch their little cheeks.

"Leopold," Katrina said, "do you remember when I tell you about your big brother, Plato, who lives in California?"

"Is that you?" Leopold asked me.

"Yes, it is," I said. "That's me."

Frankly, I was a bit tense, having had very little experience with children. What was I to say? How was I to say it? How intellectually developed was a ten-year-old boy? I didn't want to appear condescending.

I extended my hand. He shook it. "Nice to meet you, Dlopoel," I said.

"Huh?"

"Leopold," I said. "I meant Leopold."

"Oh," was his reply. "I thought you were saying my name backward, Otalp."

I blinked. This was unbelievable! The boy was as adept as I at the fine art of saying words backward. Perhaps we both had the same compulsion in this area, a genetic legacy. Didn't Katrina say my father had deciphered codes? I looked into young Leo's eyes and again saw the image of Victor Fussell staring back at me. I was so moved, I did something very uncharacteristic.

"May I have a hug?" I asked him, extending my arms.

Leopold gave it some thought, looked at me skeptically, then shook his head.

"Give your big brother a little hug," Katrina urged. "He comes three thousand miles across whole country just to see you."

"Three thousand, five hundred and fifteen miles, to be exact," I said.

"Was it a 747 or a 727?" he inquired.

"I believe it was a 747 jumbo jet."

"Cool. Did you get to see the cockpit?"

"No, to be honest, I'm not that fond of flying."

"I love to go on planes," he declared. "Especially little ones."

"Really?"

"Someday I'm going to be a fighter pilot," he said proudly. "I'm going to the Air Force Academy."

"Is that so?"

"My dad said I'd make a great fighter pilot 'cause I have good hand-eye coordination."

It suddenly occurred to me that this "dad" he was talking about was my own father as well, Victor J. Fussell, and he had never said anything about my hand-eye coordination in thirty-seven years. Perhaps I wasn't gifted in that area, but an odd moment of jealousy swept over me. I ignored it.

"I brought you something, Leopold," I announced. I handed him the oversize stuffed bear from Schwarz's, fully expecting his eyes to light up with joy. No such thing happened—he looked at it blankly.

"What do you say?" his mother asked.

"Thank you very much."

"Thank you very much, what?" Katrina prodded.

"Thank you very much, brother Plato," Leopold said obediently.

"He is perhaps too old for stuffed bears," Katrina informed me. "He likes the Nintendo games."

"I'll send you a Nintendo game from California," I promised. "What kinds do you like?"

"I like the ones with fighter jets a lot," my little half brother said enthusiastically.

"Then fighter jets it is!" I exclaimed, although I had no idea what a Nintendo game actually was. I had seen the commercials, but they were still a mystery to me.

"Awesome."

"I just hope you don't spend all day playing Nintendo games," I lectured. "A boy has to get outdoors and play. Why, when I was a boy—"

"We limit the Nintendo games to two hours a day," Katrina said. "And only after homework and study are completed."

"Are you a surfer?" he asked me.

"Who, me? No, I'm afraid not. I've never been that crazy about the prospect of drowning."

"You have a funny name," Leopold observed. "It sounds just like Play-Doh, the sticky stuff, you know?"

Was I never to escape this infamy? Was I to become the laughingstock of yet another generation of ten-year-olds? Perhaps I should buy up the company that manufactures Play-Doh and change the name of that dreadful product once and for all or, better yet, yank it off the market forever.

"Most people call me Fussell," I said. "But it wouldn't make sense for you to call me Fussell because that's your last name as well. People might think you're talking to yourself."

"Can I call you Plato?" he asked.

"That would be fine," I replied. "May I have a hug now?"

He thought about it again, but by this time we were old friends, brothers in arms, comrades, Plato and Leopold, the Two Musketeers, and besides, I had promised to send him a Nintendo game with fighter jets. We spoke for a few more minutes, mostly about the enigma of how we could have different mothers and still be brothers, then he gave me a spontaneous but tentative hug and Katrina told him to go upstairs and start his homework. She then invited me to dinner, offering to make borscht and Chicken Kiev in my honor, but I politely declined, informing her that my driver was sleeping in his car and would probably awaken soon. When she invited him as well, I told her she probably didn't have sufficient liquor to sustain him for the evening. And so, I took my leave of them half an hour later, promising to keep in touch regularly via e-mail and by phone. Unbeknownst to Katrina, when I departed I surreptitiously left her a check for five thousand dollars under an ashtray on her coffee table.

When I stepped out into the chilly, overcast New Jersey afternoon, I was jubilant. My father had been a spy! A secret agent! A Cold Warrior! Possibly even a genuine American Hero! How quickly I had gone from disbelief to jubilation! And I, an only child for thirty-seven years, suddenly had a delightful little brother! And a stepmother to boot! I punched the air and took more than a little pleasure in waking up Mickey Koro by slamming his car door twice with all my might.

Chapter 35: I felt compelled to imme-

diately share this breathtaking news with my darling Emily and could barely wait to tell her all about it. Much to my chagrin, however, I was unable to reach her directly, and the best I could do was to leave long detailed messages on both her cell phone and private voice mail. I stayed in my hotel room for several hours waiting for her to return my calls, while indulging in another superb Waldorf room service meal (baked halibut, carrots, garlic potatoes, mixed green salad and tiramisu), but the phone only rang once and that was the hotel laundry service calling to tell me my dry cleaning was ready.

I must confess my inability to contact Emily troubled me. Perhaps it was just ordinary paranoia on my account, but I worried that once again my absence had driven her back to Wang. If this were true, I decided that I would have to seriously reconsider our relationship. After all, if we were ever to become husband and wife, as I fervently hoped, Emily would have to eventually make up her mind—this flitting back and forth between lovers was a recipe for disaster, not to mention extremely confusing. What if we were married and she continued this exasperating tendency? I was tempted to call Wang himself and somehow deceive him into revealing his current marital status, but his office hours were over for the day, and I must confess, these repeated acts of subterfuge were starting to have a deleterious effect on my very soul. So I wiled away the rest of the evening by standing at my window, which overlooked the hustle and bustle of Park Avenue, counting the Yellow Cabs that passed by the hotel. I did this for exactly one hour. I decided that if the frequency of passing Yellow Cabs added up to an even number, then that would portend good luck; an odd number would foretell trouble in the wind. I ended up with 266. My mind at ease, I went to bed.

I checked my messages the next morning and was more than a little disappointed to learn that there had been none from Emily. Zero. Zilch. Nada. My paranoia ran wild. Maybe she had not gone back to Wang—maybe something dastardly had happened to her. Had she perhaps succumbed to a horrible car accident? Had she fallen from a great height, choked on a chicken bone, fallen victim to a carjacking? Or had Wang murdered her in a jealous rage? There were simply too many possibilities, none of them particularly attractive. But then, I had been down this road before.

Heeding one of Dr. Wang's advisories, I called a florist and sent my Emily an enormous ficus plant, so huge that it would require two men to carry it to her apartment. Granted, three dozen long-stemmed red roses would have been far more romantic, but given poor Emily's allergies, roses would have amounted to a somewhat self-defeating gesture.

After a breakfast of dry rye toast, distilled water and prunes, I took a taxi to the New York Public Library and settled down with a notepad in the section featuring books devoted to Broadway theater. Before returning to California, I was determined to solve this bizarre ambiguity regarding the actor Leslie Montague and his unusual association with Millard Fillmore. I was in something of a quandary to say the least. Had historians, both past and present, completely misread Fillmore? After more than a few years of arduous, painstaking study, I had been convinced that I knew the true character of our thirteenth president, but suddenly the man was a complete mystery to me, and it made me wonder whether other more critical aspects of world history were suspect as well.

So I set to work in the library. My first clue was the play "The Romanian Sled," which the Buffalo newspaper had referred to as being Montague's Broadway claim to fame. I found no mention of him under the category "Actors" in any of the library's numerous biographical texts. After looking through five ancient tomes on "The Dramatic History of New York," books that were so filled with dust that I was compelled to wear two tied-together wet handkerchiefs over my nose and mouth while perusing them, I did manage to find a footnote regarding "The Romanian Sled." It had opened and closed during one week in January 1802. The reviews had apparently been scathing—one critic opined that "Leslie Montague has the stage presence of a somnolent squid and should be banned from acting by the New York City Chamber of Commerce." It went on to compare the play itself, which had been written by one Norbert Perlmutter of Clam Lake, Wisconsin, to "the screeching noise some types of carriage wheels make when they scrape against the curb."

From there on, the rest was simple. I located a library clerk who could help me find the proper microfilm, but unfortunately I had forgotten that I was wearing two wet handkerchiefs over my mouth and nose, and the poor clerk, a nervous young woman with a slight eye tic, thought I was attempting to rob the library and pleaded with me not to harm her. I laughed heartily, tore off the handkerchiefs immediately and told her why I was wearing them and that I had no intention of swiping anything from the library. After all, I said, all one needs to remove a book from the library is a library card, what point would there be in disguising oneself and blatantly stealing the books? This seemed to calm her, and after she caught her breath, she led me to the appropriate department, although she kept a good ten feet between us at all times.

I perused a microfilm of the *New York Herald's* infamous drama section for that particular week in 1802. After scouring every word, I finally came upon a quarter-page review of "The Romanian Sled." Leslie Montague was indeed part of the cast—he played the part of Fanny Mae Cutler, one of the top female roles. This stopped me dead in my tracks. *Female* roles? This was odd, indeed. Either Fanny Mae Cutler was a male with an odd name or Leslie Montague was a woman. On the other hand, it was not uncommon in those days for male actors to play female roles.

Reading further, I saw Leslie Montague consistently referred to as a "she" and a "her" and an "actress." ("*Actress* Leslie Montague turns every line into shamelessly maudlin syrup. *She* has the shrill, irritating voice of a drunken banshee—*she* should be encouraged to hang up *her* acting shoes posthaste, lest *she* do physical harm to an unsuspecting audience.")

Considering the number of typographical errors in the Buffalo paper's notice about Leslie Montague's visit to their fair city in 1854, I preferred to believe the *New York Herald,* which had not one typographical error or grammatical blunder. Leslie Montague was indeed a woman! Fillmore was not gay! And not only was Montague not a man, she had to have been, according to my rough estimate, at least seventy years old in 1854, possibly even eighty (I was unable to find an exact birth date for Montague but I deduced that she had to be at least twenty years old in 1802, when the play opened). Fillmore himself was, at the time, only fifty-four, which made the possibility of any sexual rapport between the two of them both unlikely and unappetizing to contemplate. As for the romantic language of the letter itself? The New York theater critic's reference to Leslie Montague's tendency to "turn every line into shamelessly maudlin syrup" would probably explain the mawkish language of her letter to Fillmore.

So much for my scholarly triumph. I was relieved to know that the historical record did not contain a serious omission, but I must also admit to feeling a trifle disappointed. What a coup it would have been! What an achievement! Oh well. The Pulitzer would go to someone else. Easy come, easy go.

Yet, what troubled me most was that, after having researched Millard Fillmore's life for nine years of my own, after having dredged up every blindingly dull, minuscule detail of his ancestors, his boyhood, his adolescence, his manhood, his early career, his marriages and his presidency, I had been more than willing to accept the remote possibility that he may have been a homosexual. Not that it would have made the slightest difference historically, unless he'd been caught in the act, which, to say the least, would certainly have dimmed his chances of winning the nation's highest elected office. Don't forget, this was a man who did not smoke, drink or gamble. Moreover, I don't think half the population of the United States even *knew* what a homosexual was in 1850, when Fillmore held the highest office in the land. He would have had to wear his wife's gowns and corsets to state dinners or put forth indiscreet advances toward Daniel Webster before anyone might have deduced that something about his sexual orientation was somewhat atypical.

But how could I have been so easily fooled? One hundred and twenty-six composition books filled with notes on Fillmore's life occupied the shelves of my office, not to mention the eight hundred pages of photocopies of his correspondence, yet one minor typographical error in a second-rate, backwater newspaper had me questioning everything I knew about the man. And what indeed *did* I know about him? I knew the places he had visited, dates, names of relatives, historic events, laws he had signed, laws he had not signed, causes he had advocated, his unfortunate involvement in the Know Nothing Party, but did I really *know* him? Were the newspaper reporters who wrote about Fillmore during his lifetime truly objective? Were his biographers biased? Did Fillmore's prolific correspondence actually reveal the true essence of the man? Was it even possible for me to understand a long-dead historical figure when I barely even understood my own family or, for that matter, myself?

Part
three

Chapter 36: "So," Wang said in a disturbing monotone, as I reclined on his Barcelona chair, "I trust you had a pleasant and productive journey?"

"Oh yes," I said. "Most pleasant, indeed. My little stepbrother is an absolute delight. And, believe it or not, it seems my father was actually a spy for the CIA. A secret agent! Can you beat that?"

"Isn't that nice," he said dully.

It did not take a genius to figure out that something was wrong here once again, something no doubt involving Emily. Wang's tone of voice held an odd undercurrent of indifference, possibly even a sub-undercurrent of belligerence. He did not look too well either. There were purplish circles beneath his eyes and his complexion was ashen. Had he discovered something about Emily and me during my absence? Had she confessed? Was he about to confront me? I felt a chill blast through my body like a hypodermic injection of cold saline solution.

He rose and began pacing, then stopped to gaze wistfully out his picture window, saying nothing for at least ninety seconds.

Wang rarely stood up during a session, preferring to be seated at his desk in front of his notes, lest he forget to which of his patients he was talking. In all my years as his patient, he had only once mistaken me for someone else, an apparently delusional patient named Harrison Fuchs. When I corrected him, he had apologized profusely, offering as an excuse that he had taken out the wrong file, as Harrison Fuchs's chart resided right before mine in his filing system. I had told him not to worry about it—mistakes happen to everyone, nobody's perfect and so forth—although I was a little perturbed that he had not discovered, until a good two minutes into the session (after inquiring whether I still believed my neighbor was an alien creature from Uranus), that the person he was addressing was not Harrison Fuchs. Even worse, he charged me the full price. Fuchs should have been charged for at least 10 percent of the session even though he wasn't present, but not being the confrontational type, I lodged no complaint with Wang.

"And how are things going for you, Doc?" I asked with more than a little apprehension.

"Do you really care, Fussell?" he responded despondently. "Does anybody really care?"

Oh God, what did this mean? "Of course I care. We've been friends for years."

"Friends?"

"Yes, friends," I repeated. "I consider us to be friends. You've used the word yourself on occasion."

"You don't really know who I am," Wang said. "How do you know I'm even a real psychiatrist and not a charlatan of some kind?"

"I suppose I don't," I replied "Are you a charlatan?"

"Of course not," he cried. "Can't you see all the diplomas and degrees on the walls?"

"Those could be fakes," I offered. "Kinko's can do practically anything with—"

"They're not fakes," Wang interrupted angrily. "How dare you even say such a horrible thing?"

"So sorry," I said. "But actually, it was you who originally pointed out the possibility."

"I'm disappointed in you, Fussell. How can you sit there and impugn my credibility like that?" Wang snapped. "We've been friends for years. Years!"

"Yes, I believe that was my original point," I recalled. "Now do you want to tell me what's troubling you, or do I need to pry it out of you?"

Wang slumped heavily into his chair, letting out a deep, anguished sigh. "I think I'd prefer the prying approach."

I had to be careful here and tread lightly. For all I knew, he had a revolver in his desk drawer and was currently loading it on his lap. Not his style, granted, but people can do odd things when they're in the grip of profound and unsettling rage.

"Okay," said I. "Does it by any chance have to do with the state of your marriage?"

"How the hell did you know that?" he asked, his eyes suddenly brimming with tears.

"Lucky guess," I said. "Plus, that's usually what we end up talking about at these sessions—your marriage difficulties."

Wang put his hands back on his desk. There was no revolver. I exhaled furtively, although I did notice something odd—his wedding ring was missing.

"She's seeing the other man again," Wang announced. "I tell you, Fussell, I can't endure it anymore."

"How do you even know there's another man?" I inquired, trying to sound as casual and benign as possible.

"I know. Believe me, I know," Wang clucked. "There's no question about it. None whatsoever. It is an immutable fact."

"Are we talking about shrink's intuition again?"

"No, we're talking about cold, hard reality, Fussell. For one, I haven't seen or talked to her in a week or more. She could be on Mars for all I know."

"I think we would have read about that in the papers," I noted.

"This is not a joke, Fussell!" he declared. "I'm a loose cannon today."

"Sorry," I said. "But perhaps she's just out of town on business or something. Why do you think there's another man?"

"I hired a detective."

Oh God! This was the bombshell I had dreaded. "When?" I sputtered. "When . . . did you hire him?"

"What's the difference?" he barked. "A week ago."

Oh no. I had only been gone five days! Had I seen Emily a week ago? Had we been in a public place together? Did a week mean seven days or five business days? My mind was in a dense fog.

But if he knew it was me, why hadn't he just accused me from the start? Shot me, strangled me, hit me with a blunt object the moment I stepped into his office? Perhaps he wanted to torture me first, then get me to admit it in his presence. Wheedle it out of me. *Then* clobber me with a blunt object.

I glanced around the room. Which blunt object would he choose? The base of his lamp? The signed Louisville Slugger on the wall? The enormous hard-bound *Physicians' Desk Reference* on his bookshelf? Whatever happened, I suppose I deserved it. I had behaved miserably. I was deeply ashamed of myself. I was ready to confess. I was prepared for the consequences. Then he picked up a manila envelope from his desk—hardly a threatening object—and pulled out a small stack of black-and-white photographs, then slid them across the desk toward me.

He sighed. "See for yourself."

"This is really none of my ssenisub," I stammered.

"Ssenisub?" Wang said, squinting at me suspiciously. "Are you nervous about something, Fussell?"

"No, no," I assured him. "Just tipped over my trongue."

"Go, look. What are you afraid of?" he asked. "As it happens, I am nothing more than a pathetic cuckold."

"You're being too hard on yourself," I said.

"Take a look, Fussell," he insisted. "Do me the favor. Please."

Reluctantly, I picked up the stack of photos and glanced at the top one. A trifle grainy, as if it had been taken through a mourning veil or a window, due probably to the long-distance lens, it showed Emily, apparently in a restaurant, smooching away with someone whose back was to the camera. It wasn't my back either. My back was not quite as wide and the hairstyle was not mine. It was another man's back! At first I was relieved, then I was angry. She was smooching *with another man*! How could she! I had only been gone a few days! The next photo, also grainy, caught most of the rotten interloper's ugly smiling face. Yes, my Emily was indeed having an affair! She was cheating on me! On *me!* Not just on Wang, but on me as well! I was crushed. I was distraught. I wanted to weep. But Wang was staring at me, so I tried to pull myself together.

"This is quite, um, incriminating," I said.

"Very perceptive, Fussell."

"Do you know who this man is?"

"What does it matter?"

"You're not even curious?"

"Not particularly."

"Does your detective know who it is?"

"Of course," Wang huffed. "But I told him to keep that information to himself."

"So what will you do about it?" I asked. "If anything?"

"Do you mean will I challenge the miserable rotten louse to a duel at twenty paces? Or arrange for a bout of fisticuffs?"

"Something like that," I remarked. "Although you would probably have to know his name and address for that."

"I'm not the violent type, as you know."

"Yes," I said. "And that's a very good quality. An excellent quality, a truly admirable—"

"If she prefers another man's company to mine, then so be it," Wang said. "I thought I knew Emily quite well—hell, I was her shrink for years—but apparently I don't know her at all. I doubt anybody does."

I could have said exactly the same thing, but for obvious reasons, refrained from doing so.

"You're not thinking of taking your revenge on your wife?" I asked with more than a little concern. "What's her name again?"

"Emily."

"Ah yes," I muttered, as if this were a revelation.

"Why bother with revenge?" Wang responded. "It accomplishes nothing. And frankly speaking, I doubt if her lover, whoever he may be, is the only stallion in her stable."

Once again I am compared to a horse, I thought to myself, though I much preferred Wang's "stallion" to Hoover's "gift horse."

"What are you going to do?" I asked.

"The court will be serving her divorce papers," Wang said. "In the meantime, I've put quite a lively personal ad in one of the local papers. Would you like to read it?"

Actually, I had absolutely no desire whatsoever to read it, but Wang had such an eager, needy look on his face, I didn't wish to disappoint him. So I nodded and he handed it over. With a sigh, I scanned the first line:

> Extremely handsome, well-educated doctor with vintage Porsche, active libido and first-rate personal hygiene seeks gorgeous female with Mensa IQ, gourmet tastes, analytical mind . . .

"Do you think it's maybe a little over-the-top?" Wang asked with a distinct touch of insecurity in his voice.

"No, no, not at all," I assured him. "It's perfect. Couldn't have said it better myself."

Chapter 37: Well, this was, as they say, yet another fine kettle of fish.

Emily, my Emily, my dearest Emily had, in my short absence, made yet another, new romantic affiliation! Had she forgotten me altogether? Had she forgotten the words of mutual affection we had exchanged over the phone no more than a few days ago? Was there to be no end to her incessant inability to make a commitment? Would she go through life picking up and dropping men every few weeks like so much spoiled haddock? Were we nothing but temporary amusements to her? No doubt by now she was already getting bored with her new boy toy and was scouting the territory for fresh meat. Whomever he turns out to be, God help him if he leaves town for a few days without her.

Yet, in spite of my anger, I still felt that Emily and I had had a special understanding, that our similar neuroses had given us a unique bond. Disappointed in her as I was, I was not as ready as Wang to throw in the towel, to say good-bye for good, although that would probably have been the sensible thing to do. But, as I had recently learned, there is no such thing as good sense where love is at stake. That is, if you actually believe in such a thing as love.

Did I really love Emily Thorndyke? Who knows? Certainly all the chemical bells and whistles responded whenever I was in her company. The endorphins kicked in, as did the rush of dopamine, the sparks snapped from the synapses like a mad family of fireflies and so forth. And for me, there was certainly no other woman on the horizon. I was hardly the type of person to inhabit singles bars and the very thought of blind dates made me gag, not that I even knew anyone who would set me up with one. (Teppelman had a younger sister, but she lived in Arkansas.) Admittedly, I was (and still am) somewhat eccentric and more than a little compulsive, not to mention anxiety-ridden, though my initial positive experiences with Emily and my numerous sessions with Dr. Wang had certainly relieved me of some of my more crippling symptoms.

Nevertheless, all the melodrama that Emily was causing in my life was quite difficult for me to contend with. I was, to put it succinctly, bewitched, bothered and bewildered, and I knew I was in deep trouble if I was describing the state of my life with song lyrics. Yet, there was something incredibly warm and tingly about wallowing in self-pity and I seldom passed up the opportunity.

I had to see Emily as soon as I could. I had to be with her in person to know if I still felt anything remotely resembling love for her. And I knew exactly where to find her.

But first, I had to see the other female in my life—my mother, whom I had not heard from since my departure for points east. I drove to her apartment the next morning, and when there was no answer after I pushed her doorbell several times, I feared the worst, as is my woeful tendency, and unlocked her door with my spare key.

Once inside, I realized that the loud, irritating salsa music I had heard in the hallway and attributed to the apartment next door was actually coming from my mother's ancient stereo system, which played only LPs. Walking from room to room, I finally located her in the bedroom or, more precisely, in bed, where, to my utter shock and amazement, she was engaged in sexual union or something closely resembling it with that insect Maurice Castelli. Both of them sat bolt upright when I cleared my throat a little more loudly and repetitively than would have been necessary merely to clear it of postnasal drip. My mother held a sheet over her chest. Castelli's face was instantly crimson, heading for purple.

Rendered instantaneously speechless, the three of us stared at one another for about ten seconds. Or rather, they stared at me and I at them.

"What in God's name is going on here?" I said, sounding a bit like a scolding mother who has just found her son playing doctor with the local neighborhood twelve-year-old.

"What do you think is going on here?" my mother said. "A game of Scrabble?"

"Mother, *really!*" was all I could think of to say.

"And since when do you not knock when you come into some-body's apartment?" she asked. "Did I bring you up to be rude?"

"I rang the doorbell," I claimed. "Nobody answered."

"I was busy."

"So I see."

"Maybe I should leave," Maurice offered.

"Stay put," my mother responded firmly. "You're not going anywhere, buster."

"I just came by to say hello," I said.

"Hello," she replied. "Now beat it."

"Mother, really, are you sure you're being . . . sensible? You hardly know this man."

"This is none of your business, Plato," she replied. "Maurice and I are adults. We're quite capable of making our own decisions without consulting you."

"Your first name is Play-Doh?" Maurice asked.

"Like the philosopher, not the kid's toy," I corrected. "Can't you find somebody your own age for this, Maurice?"

"We love each other very deeply and I don't care about the age difference." Maurice shrugged. "Right, Gladys?"

"Right, Maurice," she said, taking his hand and kissing it as if she needed to demonstrate it to me, as if the mere fact that she was in bed with him were not evidence enough.

"How do you know?" I asked, truly interested.

"How do we know what?"

"How do you know that you really love each other?" I said.

"Can we discuss this later?" my mother asked. "We're playing tennis in an hour."

"No, we can't discuss this later," I insisted. "I'm your son and I care for you and I need to know how you know you love each other. Is that too much to ask?"

Maurice and my mother looked at each other and shrugged.

"I guess it started as a sexual attraction," my mother opined. "We just clicked. You can't explain it. It just happens. Right, Maurice?"

"Oh yes," he said. "Definitely. Your mother's very attractive in that particular way."

"That particular way?" I repeated.

"Yeah," Maurice struggled. "You know."

"But over the last few weeks we've both developed a real fondness for each other as well," my mother added. "A mutual respect."

"That's right," Maurice said. "Your mother is a lovely lady and an amazing cook."

"My mother is an amazing cook?" I asked, flabbergasted. Perhaps Maurice enjoyed overboiled chicken and herring.

"Oh yes," Maurice continued. "She makes a coq au vin that's to die for. And her soufflés . . ."

"And Maurice has a terrific backhand," my mother said. "Among several other, more private talents."

This caused my mother to giggle and Maurice to blush an even darker crimson. It also caused me to blush, but for altogether dif-

ferent reasons. The very idea of one's parent having sexual intercourse is difficult to imagine—the actual sight of it is thoroughly
revolting. Besides, their declarations of mutual admiration were
making me nauseated.

It was then that I noticed the absence of my mother's enormous
collection of constipation nostrums, which had once littered her
night table like colorful little toy soldiers standing at attention.

"Constipation clear up too?" I asked. "Let me guess—Maurice
has a foolproof remedy."

"How did you know?" my mother said. "He's a miracle man! In
more ways than one."

"I know a guy who does Zen high colonics," Maurice explained. "That and the right health foods and vitamins have had an
incredible effect."

"I'm also happy now," my mother added. "I think that helps too."

Maurice smiled and they exchanged a light peck on the lips, the
sight of which I found somewhat unpleasant.

"Could you please do me a favor and *not* do that in my presence, Illetsac Eciruam?" I implored him.

"What?"

"It's your name spelled backward," my mother told him. "It's
one of Plato's little quirks, a nervous habit. He's been doing it since
childhood."

"Oh," Maurice noted, although he seemed a trifle confused. A
moment of uncomfortable silence ensued.

"So what's new with you, Plato?" she asked. "We haven't spoken in days."

"You don't want to know," I moaned wearily.

"I'm your mother, Plato. I love you dearly. Of course I want to
know. Now tell me, what's new?"

"What's new?" I began. "Well, my girlfriend is cheating on me
and her husband, my shrink is having a nervous breakdown, my father, as it turns out, was *not* really a pharmaceutical salesman but
rather an employee of the CIA for thirty years, I have a ten-year-

old stepbrother who likes fighter jets and I have spent approximately a week of my life in an attempt to prove something that everybody in the entire world already knows—that Millard Fillmore was indisputably heterosexual. I think that about covers it."

There was a long moment of quiet as this plethora of information slowly sank in.

"Did you say your father worked for the CIA?" my mother asked.

"That's right," I said. "For thirty years."

"Victor Fussell? My Victor Fussell? Are you certain of this?"

"I saw photographs of him in Moscow," I told her. "I saw letters of commendation from the federal government."

"Wow," Maurice exclaimed. "Was he a spy?"

"No," I retorted. "He was a busboy in the CIA cafeteria."

"There's no need to be sarcastic, Plato," my mother chided.

"Sorry," I said.

Now my mother was wagging a finger at me.

"I knew there was something fishy about your father's line of work," she decided. "I just knew it!"

"Why?"

"For forty years, every time I asked him for an aspirin or an Ex-Lax or some antibiotics, he never had any. Nothing. Not a bottle of anything. Not a bottle of iodine if you cut your finger! Always had to go to the store, in a blizzard even. Pretty strange if you're a pharmaceutical salesman, don't you think?"

"But you loved him, right?" I asked.

"Oh yes," she affirmed. "Victor Fussell was a complicated man, a dear man, a man with some excellent qualities. We had our ups and downs like every married couple. We bickered a lot, we slept in separate beds . . . but I miss him deeply. And I mourn his death."

"This is what you call mourning?" I pronounced bitterly, indicating, with a wave of my hand, their blatant cohabitation.

"I know it's a cliché," she said, "but when all is said and done, life is for the living, Plato. I haven't got that many years left to mourn."

"I can't believe you named him Play-Doh," Maurice said, shaking his head in inane wonderment.

"Victor had a thing for Greek philosophers," my mother explained. "Believe me, it could have been worse."

Then she turned back to me. "Now if you'll please excuse us, Plato, we have a tennis game to play. Let's have lunch one day soon. Ciao."

Ciao?

Dazed, I turned and left the apartment. When, I wondered on my way out, had my mother learned to play tennis?

Chapter 38: You might say I was in a somewhat surreal state of shock after catching my mother and Maurice Castelli in flagrante delicto, but in fact this embarrassing little revelation was just another in a series of roundhouse blows to the very solar plexus of my existence. Reality seemed to be shifting all around me; people I thought I knew were suddenly strangers, and I was quickly losing my bearings. My supposedly agoraphobic, constipated mother was now the lover of a gigolo, an aficionado of pornographic movies and a consumer of spicy Indian foods. My bland, unprepossessing father had been a bigamist and secret agent. And the woman who had proclaimed her undying love for me no more than a week before was, it appeared, an incorrigible liar and cheat. My brain felt as if it would explode; my memory cells suddenly held nothing but utterly useless misinformation, anachronistic tidbits of a counterfeit past. If I had been a computer, my hard drive would certainly have crashed. Frankly, I was amazed smoke was not coming out of my ears.

As a result of all these bizarre, mind-numbing factors, my memory of the events that followed is somewhat patchy at best. I walked numbly out of my mother's building, got into my car and headed out to Bob Hoover's funeral home, although I really had no idea what would happen once I arrived there. For the first time in my life, I actually felt that having a face-to-face confrontation with another human being might in fact be therapeutic. This was unbelievable! Had the old, crippling anxiety gradually given way to a new and unfamiliar state of aggression? Was the testosterone mixing it up with an onrush of adrenaline? Needless to say, this was a major sea change in my personality and I wondered if it was permanent or just a bout of temporary sanity.

I arrived at the funeral home twenty minutes later, but Emily's BMW was not in the gravel lot. No matter. I strode to the entrance and rang the bell. When no one answered I banged on the door with my fist. My heart was thumping against my chest and my body was quaking. After a rather long wait, Bob Hoover finally opened the door and smiled broadly at me.

"Why, Fussell!" he shouted jovially, offering me his hand. "I wasn't expecting you back in town so soon."

"Oh really?" I said, slamming the door shut and storming past him into the room.

"What brings you here?" he asked brightly. "Not another death in the family, I hope."

"I think you know exactly why I'm here," I bellowed with admirable firmness of tone and a facial expression that I was sure must have appeared appropriately stern and harsh.

"No, actually, I don't."

"Give it some deep thought," I suggested. "Take your time. My schedule for the remainder of the day is clear."

It was then that I noticed that the parlor was in a state of disarray, with new drywall up over half of the walls, two-by-fours, tools, nails, empty Styrofoam coffee cups, pizza cartons and buckets of paint everywhere. I believe the paint was a dark crimson. The odor was overwhelming and I prayed that I was not breathing in deadly lead or asbestos fumes in the bargain.

"I give up," Hoover said finally.

"Don't be coy with me, Revooh," I huffed. "You've been seeing Emily Thorndyke. Admit it."

"Did you just call me Revooh?"

"Of course not," I lied. "Now answer the question. Are you seeing Ylime Ekydnroht, yes or no?"

"Who?"

"Emily Thorndyke," I repeated. "Are you deaf?"

"Sure, I've seen her," he admitted. "She's my interior designer. I see her all the time, mostly on Fridays. We go over blueprints, fabric, upholstery, real exciting stuff like that."

"You're having an affair with her," I said, impressed with my own audacity. "Don't play dumb, Hoover, even if it does come naturally."

"That's ridiculous!" he responded. "An affair? With Emily Thorndyke? I'm a happily married man, Fussell."

"Oh, so you're married *and* you've been seeing my Emily," I said, even angrier now. "So you're a glutton as well."

"I am not having an affair with her," he said.

I took a few steps toward him, forcing Hoover to back into a stack of carpet samples. Was that fear in his eyes?

I was on a roll.

"I pay you thirty-five thousand dollars to have your place of business redesigned, specifically to keep my girlfriend busy so she won't go back to her husband, and what happens? *You* have an affair with her!"

"Nonsense," he stammered. "I swear it's not true."

"I'll bet you've even used some of that thirty-five thousand dollars to take her out to dinner and a show!"

"Where do you get this crazy idea?" Hoover asked. "I'm not that kind of person, Fussell."

"Don't give me that crap! I have photographs!" I shrieked. "Black-and-white eight-by-tens of the two of you smooching shamelessly in some restaurant. They're a little grainy, perhaps, but it's definitely you."

"What restaurant was it?"

"Why?"

"Just curious."

"I don't know," I said. "It makes no difference. Stop trying to evade the issue at hand."

"Are you sure it's me?"

"Positive."

That took some of the wind out of his sails. Actually, it took all the wind out of his sails. The expression on his face made the journey from defiance to guilt in a nanosecond.

"Oh," was all he said.

"Aha! So you admit it!" I pounced, triumphant.

I then approached him again by a few paces. He backed up the equivalent amount, then stumbled slightly over a box of tools. He probably thought I had a gun. I must admit I was enjoying this. It was downright liberating.

"Who took the photographs?" he wanted to know.

"Her husband hired a detective."

"And her husband showed the photos to you, her lover?" he asked. "Frankly, I'm not sure I'm getting this."

"He thought she was having an affair with someone," I explained. "So he hired a detective."

"How do you know her husband?"

"He's my psychiatrist."

"Ah," he noted sarcastically. "You're dating your shrink's wife. Is that wise?"

"That's neither here nor there," I said. "You were paid quite handsomely by me to keep her occupied!"

"I did keep her occupied," he said. "Dinners, shows, motel rooms . . ."

"That's not what I meant, you depraved womanizer!" I shouted. "You weren't supposed to have an affair with her, for God's sake!"

"She's a very attractive woman," he said. "And you didn't specify that she was off limits."

"And if I had?" I asked him. "Then you would have kept your hairy paws off her?"

"She came on to *me*, Fussell," he claimed, stepping back as I continued to stalk him. "It was completely her idea. I swear to God."

"Her idea? You had nothing to do with it? Next thing, you'll probably say she raped you!" I was quite inflamed at this stage, but letting it out felt marvelous.

"I tried to talk her out of it," Hoover said. "She was all over me, Fussell. I'm only human."

Then I did something that opened up a whole new vista in my life. I was acting purely on instinct. I could no longer bear the intensity of the fury I was feeling, so I hauled back, made a fist and punched Bob Hoover right in the nose.

He backpedaled a few paces and landed in the center of an enormous bouquet of wilted flowers with a sign that read: *Goodbye Forever Dear Poopsie.* His nose was bleeding and he touched it delicately with his index finger. I handed him a handkerchief and a large tube of Polysporin, which I always carry with me.

"Jesus F. Christ, Fussell!" he cried. "You may have broken my frigging nose. Are you a psychopath?"

"No, just your basic garden-variety neurotic."

"That's reassuring."

"Are you all right?"

"Not really," Bob Hoover said, as I took his hand and helped him to his feet. The possibility of retaliation occurred to me, so I kept a distance of about three feet between us.

"A word to the wise, Bob," I advised him. "Keep your hands off other people's women."

"Sure, fine, whatever," he croaked, still dabbing at his bloody nose with my handkerchief. "May I keep this?"

"Be my guest," I replied, though I suddenly realized that this was the second monogrammed hankie I had given away in less than a week, Katrina Fussell being the first recipient of my handkerchief largesse. I made a mental note to start carrying Kleenex tissues on my person from then on.

Having completed my mission, I was about to take my leave, but just then the front door opened. I looked over my shoulder, and there, standing in the doorway, bathed in yet another angelic halo of sunlight, was Emily. She looked positively gorgeous and I immediately felt those old stirrings in various parts of my anatomy. Those damned chemicals were at it again. I saw her look over at the bloodied Bob Hoover, and watched as she quickly determined what had transpired. Hoover offered her a sheepish shrug, but if she felt any sympathy toward him and his bloodied proboscis, it was not evident to me.

"Hello, Fussell," she purred demurely, in a low, throaty voice.

"Hello, Emily," I said curtly, walking toward the door. "And good-bye, Emily."

At that, I marched past her, out the door and into the blindingly sunlit afternoon.

Chapter 39: In spite of everything that

had happened between us, in spite of all the heartbreak and angry words, in spite of her shameless philandering and deceitfulness, we were married one year later, in late November. It was a lovely wedding. My tuxedo was splendidly cut, my cravat expertly tied, my black dress shoes professionally shined. Her bridal gown was exquisite, a veritable cascade of lace, silk and satin, featuring a train that actually had to be carried down the aisle by one of her younger nieces. The weather was excellent, a dry, sunny day with a light breeze but not quite enough to carry a chill. The weather forecast was most optimistic, so I threw caution to the wind (no pun intended) and left my rain gear at home, taking with me not even so much as a collapsible umbrella. For the ceremony and reception, I had booked the Bel Air Hotel, which has a delightfully lush garden for outdoor weddings, baby showers and bar mitzvah parties. It cost a small fortune but money was not an issue. Besides, how many times does a man get the opportunity to marry his one and only true love?

I had flown Katrina and Leopold in from New Jersey for the affair, two first-class seats, with a black stretch limo at LAX waiting to take them to a penthouse suite at the Beverly Hilton, all of which delighted young Leo. I had also purchased every new Nintendo game that featured fighter planes, and this time, Leopold was so overjoyed, he threw himself into my arms with total abandon. It was such a sudden, spontaneous gesture that it made my eyes fill up with tears. Eventually, he even taught me how to play one or two of these games and I became quite adept with the joystick, although I had not a clue what was actually transpiring on the screen or how to manipulate it.

Before the ceremony, Katrina and I had had a lengthy conversation. I offered to buy her a small house near my own residence in Sherman Oaks and to put Leopold through the best private schools in the area. I wanted them both to be geographically closer to me so that we could more easily succeed in becoming a true family. My goal was to get to know my little brother better and to be a significant part of his young life. She said she would give it some thought.

Maurice and my mother also attended the wedding, of course. My mother astounded me by being warm and courteous to Katrina and little Leopold from the moment they met, and I thanked her profusely for it. Apparently, by some miracle, she had recovered somewhat from my father's brazen infidelity and I think she even enjoyed telling others that she had been married for forty years to, as she liked to put it, "a real James Bond." By that time, she had moved out of her musty little apartment and she and Maurice had purchased a spacious two-bedroom condominium in Marina del Rey, which featured an excellent picture-window view of the entire harbor. Although they had not actually tied the knot, they behaved like a couple who had been married thirty years or more, complete with the occasional bout of senseless bickering. Most days, they either played tennis or golf, and went ballroom dancing at night. Over time, I had grown to appreciate Maurice, who, as it turned out, was greatly interested in American history and in particular presidential material. Whenever I saw him, he took a sincere interest in my Fillmore biography and would always inquire about my progress. At the time of the wedding, I was halfway through *The Early, Early Years* and was beginning to outline the opening chapters of *Volume Two: The Early Years.*

My mother also brought good wishes and a lovely handmade card from Aunt Sophie, who was up for parole in five years. In the meantime, People Against Mimes was apparently paying all of the legal expenses for her upcoming appeal. Their strategy was to unleash several real mimes inside the courtroom during the trial to demonstrate to the jury and the judge just how annoying mimes could be.

Since he was my only longtime friend, I had asked Teppelman to be my best man. Before agreeing to take on the position, he wanted to know exactly what it entailed, having never attended a wedding in his life, other than his own twenty years ago.

"You hold the ring, and give it to me when the minister asks me for it," I instructed him.

"Hold it where?"

"It doesn't matter," I said. "In your pocket."

"Front trouser pocket or front jacket pocket?"

"Didn't you have a best man at your wedding?"

"I forgot."

"Either pocket will do."

"That I can do," he replied. "What if I lose it?"

"Then I'll have to kill you," I said.

He nodded and took this in stride. "What else does the best man have to do?"

"You can make a champagne toast to the bride and groom if you want," I suggested.

"Is that optional?"

"Yes."

"What kind of a toast?"

"Entirely up to you," I replied. "Something inspirational about marriage is usually best. Or perhaps something humorous about the bride or bridegroom. Not that I've been to many weddings myself. In fact, the only wedding I've ever attended was my own, some years ago."

"I'm afraid I'm not much good at public speaking," Teppelman confessed.

"That's fine. No pressure."

"But come to think of it, I do have a copy of a letter in which Abraham Lincoln, writing to an old friend from his lawyer days, waxes positively rhapsodic about the splendid qualities of his wife, Mary Todd Lincoln."

"If you're going to steal, why not steal from the best?" I said.

"It's not really stealing," Teppelman pointed out. "Because I'm not getting paid for it, am I?"

"I'm sure the Lincoln letter will suffice," I assured him. "As long as you make sure to change the names. I don't really want people to think I just married Mary Todd Lincoln."

"She's dead, Fussell," he said. "She's been dead for over a century."

"I'm aware of that, Teppelman," I replied. Try as I might I could never seem to get Teppelman to laugh at any of my witticisms, such as they were.

"You know, she ended up in an asylum," Teppleman continued. "She was crazy with grief. Over Lincoln's death, of course. And the premature death of their little son years earlier."

"Yes, a sad story indeed."

"But that's a mere bagatelle compared to William McKinley and his wife," he went on. "She suffered from some form of epilepsy and sometimes, when she had a fit during a state dinner, she would go into epileptic convulsions right there on the dining room floor."

"Is that so?"

"You know what McKinley would do? He would cover her face

with a pocket handkerchief and continue eating. Can you imagine that?"

"Actually, yes," I said.

And so Daisy Crane and I were married once again, this time with a proper ceremony, one that involved a seven-layered wedding cake, a gaggle of bridesmaids in pink gowns, a best man, witnesses we actually knew by name, and a large, raucous audience of assorted friends and family members. The service itself was conducted by Daisy's father, the Reverend Donald Crane, with whom Daisy had reconciled several years before. I had met most of the members of Daisy's immediate family by that time and found them all to be decent, well-meaning people, although the Reverend himself tended to be a somewhat dour fellow who seldom cracked a smile.

Daisy and I had started dating again several months after I dissolved all romantic ties with Emily Thorndyke. Directly following my self-imposed separation from Emily, I reverted to style and became something of a confirmed, dedicated bachelor once again. Actually, it was closer to monkhood than bachelordom. It was a lonely time indeed, this self-imposed exile from the female of the species, but I was determined to avoid any future heartbreak. Once again, I became quite cynical and bitter about the very concept of *l'amour*, and resolved to live alone for the remainder of my life, dedicating all my time to my Fillmore biography and minor acts of philanthropy.

My relationship with Daisy reignited quite by accident when one day, I received in the mail an invitation regarding an animal rights fund-raiser that was to be held at UCLA. Having nothing better to do, and thinking it a worthy charity, I attended the event and was more than a little astounded to learn that Daisy Crane was to be the keynote speaker. I stayed long enough to hear her oration, which, to my further amazement, was articulate, persuasive and surprisingly moving. When she concluded her remarks to tumultuous applause, I stole inconspicuously out of the room and drove

myself home, too bashful, anxiety-ridden and emotionally confused to remain and speak to her.

The next day, however, I called the UCLA Alumni Office and,
pretending to be a potential employer, inquired about Daisy's ed-
ucational credentials. To my amazement, she had indeed graduated from UCLA as she had said, and summa cum laude to boot!
And she had indeed received a master's degree from Berkeley,
also summa cum laude, quite an admirable accomplishment. Her
academic credentials were, in fact, far superior to my own. I was
also able to verify her gargantuan contribution to the United
Way, a tax deduction I was unfortunately unable to claim retroac-
tively. And so, feeling slightly guilty about my rather spiteful response to her phone call following my father's death, I threw
caution to the wind and asked her, with more than a little mumbo
jumbo, to meet me at the park for a picnic lunch on a sunny afternoon in early March. It was truly quite astounding—when I
caught sight of her walking toward me that afternoon, backlit by
the sun as it sparkled through the leaves of a maple tree, she
looked exactly like the Daisy Crane I had fallen in love with on
our first day of kindergarten so many years ago, the Daisy Crane
of petticoats and little ballet flats, and I suddenly remembered
that indeed she had not laughed at me that first day of school
when the revelation of my odd first name had been such a source
of hilarity, that she had been the only sympathetic one in the
classroom.

Later, as I was to discover after several more dates, Daisy had
indeed changed her entire character and outlook on life. It was as if
she had had a reverse frontal lobotomy, which she assured me she
had not. She was not only educated and articulate, but kind and
generous to a fault and had long since given up smoking, drinking,
gambling and philandering. She dressed as conservatively as a business executive and her grooming, sense of style and personal hygiene were as impeccable as mine. This time around she was more
willing to tolerate my neuroses, compulsions, and obsessions,

which, thanks to several new drugs that had just come on the market, had become somewhat more manageable.

In any case, Daisy Crane and I dated again for about four months, whereupon we decided to live together (in secrecy lest her father find out) at my spacious home in Sherman Oaks. Despite a few minor wrinkles, our cohabitation proceeded well and we soon began to discuss marriage. Daisy desperately wanted to have four children, my children, two boys and two girls. Her maternal instincts were soon to find a living target in young Leopold, whom she smothered with kindness and lavished with gifts whenever he visited us in California. I had never seen such an amazing transformation in a person before and, at first, I must confess to having been somewhat skeptical about Daisy. How long would it last? Would I wake up one morning to find her packed and gone with my credit cards and Cartier watch? Would she abandon me again? Would another version of Slick Slocum take her from me? But Daisy proved herself to me many times over. And so, one starry evening, after several weeks of rehearsal, I got down on my knees and asked her to be my wife.

Much to my delight, the wedding ceremony was a grand success. In spite of my former disdain for anything resembling romantic love, Daisy and I read inane gushing poems to each other and meant them, and the audience broke into wild applause when it was time for me to kiss the bride, which I did rather handily, I must admit, considering my former crippling anxiety. Several of the female guests wept for joy, my mother included, and I confess to having been somewhat lachrymose myself.

The wedding cake, which Daisy and I cut together while the flashbulbs exploded around us, was a Mount Everest of cream and raspberries, with excellent likenesses of Daisy and me at the summit, surrounded by small groups of strawberry sherpas.

The only slight ruffle occurred when Teppelman's somewhat stilted and overlong toast, taken almost verbatim from the Lincoln missive, referred at one point to "the recent emancipation of our Negro brethren."

Nonetheless, the speech received great applause and shouts of good cheer and Teppelman was so overcome with emotion, he had to leave the room. I found him hiding in a hotel broom closet later that night and coaxed him to rejoin the party.

Bob Hoover and his wife drifted in during the formal cutting of the cake. In an effort to let bygones be bygones, I had invited Bob, who had been kind enough not to sue me for assault and battery, although he never did return any part of the $35,000 I had given him, not that I expected him to. His nose, as it turned out, had not been broken at all, only bruised slightly, and the only long-term effect was a slight case of snoring, which his wife solved by making him sleep in the downstairs guest room for a few weeks. Moreover, the redesign of the funeral home had increased his business by over 25 percent, so he was one of the happiest morticians I had ever met. In fact, he had taken to wearing a small yellow happy face button on the lapel of his funeral coat.

Unfortunately, I was unable to invite Dr. Wang to the ceremony as he had inexplicably vanished from the face of the earth. Shortly after divorcing Emily, he shut down his practice and moved to points unknown, leaving no forwarding address, although he was thoughtful enough to email me a note recommending another capable psychiatrist, a tall, soft-spoken woman by the name of Lydia Tyler, whom I began to see once a month. Nevertheless, at the time, Wang's sudden departure left me utterly devastated. As I've noted previously, he had been my anchor, my confidant and my friend for many years. How could he abandon me so blithely? I felt completely shipwrecked without him, a waterlogged hunk of flotsam marooned in dark, shark-infested waters.

Fortunately, I was dating Daisy at the time of Wang's unexpected exodus, and it was she who threw me a lifeline.

"Never mind Wang," she consoled me. "Let me be your an-

chor, your confidant and your friend." And so, I managed somehow to muddle through this challenging period.

Unlike Wang, my new psychiatrist, Dr. Tyler, never answers
phone calls during my sessions, has yet to mix me up with another
patient and rarely dwells on her own personal problems. Because of
doctor-patient confidentiality, I was also able to discuss with her my
past romance with Emily Thorndyke without fear of repercussion.

Though Emily was obviously not at the wedding, I felt her
presence everywhere. Directly following my pugilistic encounter
with Bob Hoover or possibly because of it, Emily had declared her
undying love for me for the umpteenth time and claimed that
Hoover was a boor, a womanizer and a sex maniac who had gotten
her repeatedly inebriated on vodka gimlets and seduced her. Moreover, she would have me believe that he had done this to her *six or
seven times* in a row. Once, maybe twice, but six times in a row? She
must have thought I was an imbecile! Who else would believe such
unmitigated malarkey? And as far as I could tell, poor Bob Hoover
was really more of a family man who had strayed rather than a
boor, a womanizer or much of a sex maniac, so I was inclined to believe his version of events.

Yes, I admit I was sorely tempted once or twice to start up again
with Emily, especially in those dreary days following our breakup,
just prior to my self-imposed quarantine from the weaker sex (a
misnomer, if you ask me). God knows, Emily can lay it on somewhat thick when she wants to, but I managed to hold my ground.
In spite of the onslaught of hormones, those little Wehrmacht
storm troopers goose-stepping through the Maginot Line of my
pitiful resistance onward toward the center of my libido, the sensible angel on my shoulder would have none of it (pardon the mixed
metaphors). I was through with Emily Thorndyke. Through, once
and for all! Not really aware of what he was doing, Wang had
helped me survive this thorny separation. Difficult as it was, I told
her flatly that although I understood her bouts of loneliness and
her constant and unrelenting need for affection, I could no longer

endure her philandering and her rank dishonesty, and that I never wanted to see or hear from her ever again. Period.

Which apparently did not exactly devastate her, far from it. Less than two weeks later, I heard that she had taken up with the contractor she had hired to redesign Bob Hoover's funeral home, a gruff grizzly bear of a man named Roger Gage, and that she and this Gage had moved north to Ventura and were living in a rented houseboat. Whether they remained together for long, I do not know, but if I were a gambling man, I would not put money on it.

Yet, in retrospect, I suppose I owe Emily Thorndyke a considerable debt of gratitude. Had she not bravely crossed my many psychological moats and minefields, had she not penetrated my solid and implacable cynicism regarding the very existence of love, had she not illustrated her point so effectively by comparing mankind's desire for love to peptic pangs of hunger and the urge to relieve one's bowels, I strongly doubt I would have ever had the mental or emotional fortitude to begin again with Daisy or, for that matter, any other woman. I might have lived and died a miserable, self-loathing, wretched old bachelor. If indeed romantic love is nothing more profound or complex than an arbitrary sequence of basic chemical reactions, the conclusion we must derive from this can be summed up easily in two little words:

So what?

As for Daisy, having witnessed both her good and evil incarnations, and having known her since childhood, I truly believe that I understand her as well as one human being can possibly hope to know another human being. As Dr. Wang pointed out some time ago, we hapless humans prance around in our insufferable arrogance as if we understand the world's countless anomalies, conundrums and enigmas, but when you get right down to it, we don't know excrement from shoe polish, if you'll pardon the paraphrase. All I know for sure is that I don't know anything for sure and I'm not even certain about that certainty. My own life is a perfect example—at one time I was convinced I would never be able to live without the lifelong love and companionship of Ms. Emily Thorndyke, but here I am, my dull hermit days behind me, and, all things considered, more than a little content in my own somewhat quirky, pseudo-insane manner.

Perhaps this whole gaudy carnival was simply intended to be mysterious, confounding and utterly exasperating just to keep us from killing ourselves out of abject boredom.

But of course, I don't really know that for sure.

A few months following my wedding ceremony, Dr. Wang suddenly appeared unannounced at my doorstep wearing a Stetson hat, a string tie and cowboy boots with metal tips. As it happened, he was visiting Los Angeles to attend a psychiatric convention and had decided beforehand to pay me a call. Apparently, he had been feeling quite guilty about his sudden, stealthy departure from the area, for he apologized profusely and was eager to know how I was holding up mentally. I was thoroughly delighted to see him in such fine spirits, though I could have lived without the odd fashion statement.

Over a glass of Cabernet, he explained that his divorce from Emily Thorndyke had plunged him into a depression so profound and so utterly incapacitating that it had made him psychologically unfit to be of any further use to his patients. On a whim, he had moved to Taos, New Mexico, where, after a long, tempestuous wallow in self-pity involving large quantities of whiskey and Zoloft, he had met a sculptress of Cherokee descent named Samantha White Horse, who had helped him suffer through this difficult time in his life. Coincidentally, they tied the knot exactly one week before my own wedding to Daisy. Shortly thereafter, Wang began to practice psychiatry again, nailing his shingle to a large flowering cactus plant in the front yard of his new adobe house in Taos.

When it was my turn, I told him all about Daisy, how she had altered her personality so radically and how we had gradually kindled a new and profound affection for each other. I also informed him of my mother's curious affiliation with Maurice and my own fondness for my little brother, Leo. Naturally, I refrained from mentioning anything about my passionate but ill-fated affair with Emily.

"And that new shrink?" Wang asked. "How's she workin' out?"

"Just fine," I declared. "I'm down to only two visits a month!"

"I'm darn glad to hear it, Fussell," he said in an accent slightly reminiscent of Gabby Hayes. At that, he slapped me on the back and pumped my hand. "You've made some darn good progress. More than most of my patients, that's for sure!"

"Thanks largely to you," I mused.

"I don't know 'bout that," he said. "Sometimes I wasn't sure which of us was the goldarn shrink."

"You were always a sherrific trink," I quipped, reverting back to my old neurotic gibberish, but this time entirely in jest.

"But not good enough to rid you of that carticular compulsion," Wang replied jokingly.

"Well spoken!" said I.

"I'll accept the compliment," he continued. "But even if I am a good shrink, we're just the mapmakers. You patients are the bonafide explorers, the Ponce de Leóns, the Ferdinand Magellans, the Lewis and Clarks, if you will, of the psychic wilderness. If anyone gets hurt on such a perilous journey, I'll tell you this—it usually ain't the mapmaker."

I'm not sure I had the slightest clue what he was driving at with that metaphor, but I offered him a polite chuckle anyway.